Praise for the Kate Burkholder series

"Swiftly paced . . . Castillo again captures Kate's empathic understanding of Amish culture and Deutsch, and adds atmosphere with falling-down, peeling-paint, rural settings. If they haven't already, readers looking for a fierce female-fronted procedural should check out Castillo's bestselling series from the get-go." —*Booklist* on *Shamed*

"The tension mounts [to] a gripping conclusion. . . . Another violent, fascinating story." —*Library Journal* on *Shamed*

"Electrifying . . . more than one twist propels the plot to its dramatic conclusion . . . a morally complex tale."
—*Publishers Weekly* on *Shamed*

"A captivating story by a gifted storyteller."
—*The Washington Book Review* on *A Gathering of Secrets*

"An atmospheric thriller about fear, revenge, and the dark side of Amish life. . . . Linda Castillo is a true master of suspenseful police procedurals." —**Bustle** on *A Gathering of Secrets*

"Magnetic." —*People* magazine on *A Gathering of Secrets*

"Exquisitely plotted . . . a standout in a stellar series."
—**Associated Press** on *A Gathering of Secrets*

"Castillo weaves the particularities of the Amish mindset into a complex mystery that will leave you crying with pity or seething with rage."
—*Kirkus Reviews* (starred review) on *Down a Dark Road*

"Thrilling . . . Castillo skillfully sets each scene, compelling readers to fear the raging stream, sense the tension in a room."

—*Publishers Weekly* on *Down a Dark Road*

"A first-rate and very unusual thriller; Castillo builds suspense brilliantly, using both the snowbound setting and the difficulty of working as an undercover Amish woman to great advantage."

—*Booklist* on *Among the Wicked*

"[An] incisive and affecting series. Castillo showcases her many talents: a harrowing plot in which she ratchets up the suspense to nearly unbearable levels; a heroic and fully human protagonist; an ability to engage heart and mind; a reminder that no place is immune from the intrusion of evil; and, in this novel in particular, the dangers of liars—and false prophets."

—*Richmond Times-Dispatch* on *Among the Wicked*

Murder in Amish country has a certain added frisson, and Castillo's the master of the genre."   —*People* magazine on *The Dead Will Tell*

"Castillo weaves a taut mystery in her sixth series title that will keep suspense fans glued to their books and e-readers."

—*Library Journal* (starred review) on *The Dead Will Tell*

SHAMED

A KATE BURKHOLDER NOVEL

Linda Castillo

MINOTAUR
BOOKS
NEW YORK

First published in the United States by Minotaur Books, an imprint of St. Martin's Publishing Group

www.minotaurbooks.com

Designed by Omar Chapa

The Library of Congress has cataloged the hardcover edition as follows:

Names: Castillo, Linda, author.
Title: Shamed: a Kate Burkholder novel / Linda Castillo.
Description: First Edition. | New York: Minotaur Books, 2019. |
　　Series: Kate Burkholder novel
Identifiers: LCCN 2019006908| ISBN 9781250142863 (hardcover) |
　　ISBN 9781250142887 (ebook)
Subjects: LCSH: Murder—Investigation—Fiction. | GSAFD: Mystery fiction.
Classification: LCC PS3603.A8758 S53 2019 | DDC 813/.6—dc23
LC record available at https://lccn.loc.gov/2019006908

ISBN 978-1-250-76320-4 (trade paperback)

Our books may be purchased in bulk for promotional, educational, or business use. Please contact your local bookseller or the Macmillan Corporate and Premium Sales Department at 1-800-221-7945, extension 5442, or by email at MacmillanSpecialMarkets@macmillan.com.

First Minotaur Books Edition: 2019
First Minotaur Books Paperback Edition: 2020

10　9　8　7　6　5　4　3　2　1

This book is dedicated to my readers. Thank you for your support and loyalty. I'm incredibly lucky—and thankful—for the opportunity to do what I love every day, creating characters and stories that will be read and loved by you.

ACKNOWLEDGMENTS

An incredible amount of passion, expertise, and experience goes into the process of transforming a manuscript into a novel. With the publication of *Shamed* I have many talented and dedicated individuals to thank. First and foremost, I wish to thank my editor, Charles Spicer, who always sees the magic and never fails to help me bring it to big, bold life. I'd also like to thank my agent, Nancy Yost, whose insights and ideas are always right on. I hope both of you know how much I appreciate those phone calls—and the smiles. I'd also like to thank my publicist, Sarah Melnyk, whose keen instincts, ceaseless energy, and warmth are always a bright spot. Thank you for always being there and for always being willing to go above and beyond. And of course, I wish to thank the rest of the Minotaur Books team: Jennifer Enderlin. Sally Richardson. Andrew Martin. Kerry Nordling. Paul Hochman. Allison Ziegler. Kelley Ragland. Sarah Grill. David Rotstein. Marta Ficke. Martin Quinn. Joseph Brosnan. Lisa Davis. You guys are the crème de la crème of the publishing world and I'm endlessly delighted to be part of it.

SHAMED

PROLOGUE

No one went to the old Schattenbaum place anymore. No one had lived there since the flood back in 1969 washed away the crops and swept the outhouse and one of the barns into Painters Creek. Rumor had it Mr. Schattenbaum's 1960 Chevy Corvair was still sitting in the gully where the water left it.

The place had never been grand. Even in its heyday, the house had been run down. The roof shingles were rusty and curled. Mr. Schattenbaum had talked about painting the house, but he'd never gotten around to it. Sometimes, he didn't even cut the grass. Despite its dilapidated state, once upon a time the Schattenbaum house had been the center of Mary Yoder's world, filled with laughter, love, and life.

The Schattenbaums had six kids, and even though they weren't Amish, Mary's *mamm* had let her visit—and Mary did just that every chance she got. The Schattenbaums had four spotted ponies, after all; they had baby pigs, a slew of donkeys, a big tom turkey, and too many goats to count. Mary had been ten years old that last summer, and she'd had the time of her life.

It was hard for her to believe fifty years had passed; she was a grandmother now, a widow, and had seen her sixtieth birthday just last week. Every time she drove the buggy past the old farm, the years melted away and she always thought: If a place could speak, the stories it would tell.

Mary still lived in her childhood home, with her daughter and son-in-law now, half a mile down the road. She made it a point to walk this way when the opportunity presented itself. In spring, she cut the irises that still bloomed in the flower bed at the back of the house. In summer, she came for the peonies. In fall, it was all about the walnuts. According to Mr. Schattenbaum, his grandfather had planted a dozen or so black walnut trees. They were a hundred years old now and flourished where the backyard had once been. Every fall, the trees dropped thousands of nuts that kept Mary baking throughout the year—and her eight grandchildren well supplied with walnut layer cake.

The house looked much the same as it did all those years ago. The barn where Mary had spent so many afternoons cooing over those ponies had collapsed in a windstorm a few years back. The rafters and siding were slowly being reclaimed by a jungle of vines, overgrowth, and waist-high grass.

"Grossmammi! Do you want me to open the gate?"

Mary looked over at the girl on the seat beside her, and her heart soared. She'd brought her granddaughters with her to help pick up walnuts. Annie was five and the picture of her *mamm* at that age: Blond hair that easily tangled. Blue eyes that cried a little too readily. A thoughtful child already talking about teaching in the two-room schoolhouse down the road.

At seven, Elsie was a sweet, effervescent girl. She was one of the special ones, curious and affectionate, with a plump little body and round eyeglasses with lenses as thick as a pop bottle. She was a true gift from God, and Mary loved her all the more because of her differences.

"Might be a good idea for me to stop the buggy first, don't you think?" Tugging the reins, Mary slowed the horse to a walk and made the turn into the weed-riddled gravel lane. "Whoa."

She could just make out the blazing orange canopies of the trees behind the house, and she felt that familiar tug of homecoming, of nostalgia.

"Hop on down now," she told the girls. "Open that gate. Watch out for that barbed wire, you hear?"

Both children clambered from the buggy. Their skirts swished around their legs as they ran to the rusted steel gate, their hands making short work of the chain.

Mary drove the horse through, then stopped to wait for the girls. "Come on, little ones! Leave the gate open. I hear all those pretty walnuts calling for us!"

Giggling, the girls climbed into the buggy.

"Get your bags ready," Mary told them as she drove past the house. "I think we're going to harvest enough this afternoon to fill all those baskets we brought."

She smiled as the two little ones gathered their bags. Mary had made them from burlap last year for just this occasion. The bags were large, with double handles easily looped over a small shoulder. She'd embroidered green walnut leaves on the front of Elsie's bag. On Annie's she'd stitched a brown walnut that had been cracked open, exposing all that deliciousness inside.

Mary drove the buggy around to the back of the house, where the yard had once been. A smile whispered across her mouth when she saw that the old tire swing was still there. She stopped the horse in the shade of a hackberry tree where the grass was tall enough for the mare to nibble, and she drew in the sight, felt that familiar swell in her chest.

Picking up their gloves and her own bag, Mary climbed down. For a moment, she stood there and listened to the place. The chirp of a cardinal from the tallest tree. The whisper of wind through the treetops.

"Girls, I think we've chosen the perfect day to harvest walnuts," she said.

Bag draped over her shoulder, Elsie followed suit. Annie was still a little thing, so Mary reached for her and set her on the ground. She handed the two girls their tiny leather gloves.

"I don't want to see any stained fingers," she told them.

"You, too, Grossmammi."

Chuckling, Mary walked with them to the stand of trees, where the sun dappled the ground at her feet.

"Look how big that tree is, Grossmammi!" Annie exclaimed.

"That's my favorite," Mary replied.

"Look at all the walnuts!" Elsie said with an exuberance only a seven-year-old could manage.

"God blessed us with a good crop this year," Mary replied.

"Are we going to make cakes, Grossmammi?"

"Of course we are," Mary assured her.

"Walnut layer cake!" Annie put in.

"And pumpkin bread!" Elsie added.

"If you girls picked as much as you talked, we'd be done by now." She tempered the admonition with a smile.

Stepping beneath the canopy of the tree, Mary knelt and scooped up a few walnuts, looking closely at the husks. They were green, mottled with black, but solid and mold free. It was best to gather them by October, but they were already into November. "Firm ones only, girls. They've been on the ground awhile. We're late to harvest this year."

Out of the corner of her eye, she saw little Annie squat and drop a walnut into her bag. Ten yards away, Elsie was already at the next tree, leather gloves on her little hands. Such a sweet, obedient child.

She worked in silence for half an hour. The girls chattered. Mary pretended not to notice when they tossed walnuts at each other. Before she knew it, her bag was full. Hefting it onto her shoulder, she walked to the buggy, and dumped her spoils into the bushel basket.

She was on her way to join the girls when something in the house snagged her attention. Movement in the window? She didn't think so; no one ever came here, after all. Probably just the branches swaying in the breeze and reflecting off the glass. But as Mary started toward the girls, she saw it again. She was sure of it this time. A shadow in the kitchen window.

Making sure the girls were embroiled in their work, she set her bag on the ground. A crow cawed from atop the roof as she made her way to the back of the house and stepped onto the rickety porch. The door stood open a few inches, so she called out. "Hello?"

"Who are you talking to, Grossmammi?"

She glanced over her shoulder to see Annie watching her from her place beneath the tree, hands on her hips. Behind her, Elsie was making a valiant effort to juggle walnuts and not having very much luck.

"You just mind those walnuts," she told them. "I'm taking a quick peek at Mrs. Schattenbaum's kitchen."

"Can we come?"

"I'll only be a minute. You girls get back to work or we'll be here till dark."

Mary waited until the girls resumed their task and then crossed the porch, set her hand against the door. The hinges groaned when she pushed it open. "Hello? Is someone there?"

Memories assailed her as she stepped inside. She recalled

peanut-butter-and-jelly sandwiches at the big kitchen table. Mrs. Schattenbaum stirring a pot of something that smelled heavenly on the stove. Sneaking chocolate-chip cookies from the jar in the cupboard. The old Formica counters were still intact. The pitted porcelain sink. The stove was gone; all that remained was a gas line and rust stains on the floor. Rat droppings everywhere. Some of the linoleum had been chewed away.

Mary was about to go to the cabinet, to see if that old cookie jar was still in its place, when a sound from the next room stopped her. Something—or someone—was definitely in there. Probably whatever had chewed up that flooring, she thought. A raccoon or possum. Or a rat. Mary wasn't squeamish about animals; she'd grown up on a farm, after all. But she'd never liked rats. . . .

She glanced out the window above the sink. Annie was pitching walnuts baseball style. Elsie was using a stick as a bat. Shaking her head, Mary chuckled. Probably best not to leave them alone too long. . . .

Turning, she went to the doorway that opened to the living room. It was a dimly lit space filled with shadows. The smells of mildew and rotting wood laced the air. The plank floors were badly warped. Water stains on the ceiling. Wallpaper hung off the walls like sunburned skin. Curtains going to rot.

"Who's there?" she said quietly.

A sound to her right startled a gasp from her. She saw movement from the shadows. Heard the shuffle of shoes against the floor. Someone rushing toward her . . .

The first blow landed against her chest, hard enough to take her breath. She reeled backward, arms flailing. A shock of pain registered behind her ribs, hot and deep. The knowledge that she was injured. All of it followed by an explosion of terror.

Something glinted in the periphery of her vision. A silhouette coming at her fast. She saw the pale oval of a face. She raised her hands. A scream ripped from her throat.

The second blow came from above. Slashed her right hand. Slammed into her shoulder and went deep. Pain zinged; then her arm went numb. It wasn't until she saw the shiny black of blood that she realized she'd been cut. That it was bad.

Mewling, she stumbled into the kitchen, trying to put some distance between her and her attacker. He followed, aggressive and intent. The light hit his face and recognition kicked. Another layer of fear swamped her and she thought: *This can't be happening.*

"You!" she cried.

The knife went up again, came down hard, hit her clavicle. Pain arced, like a lightning strike in her brain. The shocking red of blood, warm and wet on her arms, her hands, streaming down the front of her dress, splattering the floor.

And in that instant she knew. Why he'd come. What came next. The realization filled her with such horror that for an instant, she couldn't move, couldn't speak. Then she turned, flung herself toward the door, tried to run. But her shoe slipped in the blood; her foot went out from under her, and she fell to her knees.

She twisted to face him, looked up at her assailant. "Leave her alone!" she screamed. "In the name of God *leave her alone!*"

The knife went up. She lunged at him, grabbed his trousers, fisting the fabric, yanking and slapping. Hope leapt when he staggered sideways. The knife slammed into her back like a hammer blow. A starburst of pain as the blade careened off bone. Her vision dimmed. No breath left. No time.

Her attacker raised the knife. Lips peeled back. Teeth clenched and grinding.

She scrambled to her feet, threw herself toward the window above the sink, and smashed her hand through the glass. Caught a glimpse of the girls.

"Run!" she screamed. *"Da Deivel!"* The Devil. "Run! *Run!"*

Footfalls sounded behind her. She looked over her shoulder. A flash of silver as the knife came down, slammed into her back like an ax. White-hot pain streaked up her spine. Her knees buckled and she went down. Her face hit the floor. Above, her attacker bellowed like a beast. *Da Deivel.*

He knelt, muttering ungodly words in a voice like gravel. Another knife blow jolted her body, but she couldn't move. No pain this time. A rivulet of blood on the linoleum. More in her mouth. Breaths gurgling. Too weak to spit, so she opened her lips and let it run. Using the last of her strength, she looked up at her attacker.

Run, sweet child, she thought. *Run for your life.*

The knife arced, the impact as violent as a bare-fisted punch, hot as fire. The blow rocked her body. Once. Twice. No more fight left. She couldn't get away, couldn't move.

She was aware of the linoleum cold and gritty against her cheek. The sunlight streaming in through the window. The crow cawing somewhere outside. Finally, the sound of his footfalls as he walked to the door.

CHAPTER 1

You see a lot of things when you're the chief of police in a small town. Things most other people don't know about—don't want to know about—and are probably better off for it. I deal with minor incidents mostly—traffic accidents, domestic disputes, petty thefts, loose livestock. I see people in high-stress situations—friends, neighbors, folks I've known most of my life. Sometimes I see them at their worst. That reality is tempered by the knowledge that I see them at their best, too. I see courage and strong character and people who care, some willing to risk their lives for someone they don't even know. Those are the moments that lift me. The moments that keep me going when the sky is dark and the rain is pouring down.

My name is Kate Burkholder and I'm the police chief of Painters Mill. It's a pretty little town of about 5,300 souls—a third of whom are Amish—nestled in the heart of Ohio's Amish country. I was born here and raised Plain, but I left the fold when I was eighteen. I never thought I'd return. But after twelve years—and after I'd found my place in law enforcement—my roots called me back. Fate obliged when the town council offered me the position of chief. I like to think their interest was due to my law enforcement experience or because I'm good at what I do. But I know my being formerly Amish—my familiarity with the culture, the religion, and being fluent in *Deitsch*—played a role in their decision. Tourism, after all, is a big chunk of the economy and our city leaders knew my presence would go a long way toward bridging the gap that exists between the Amish and "English" communities.

It's a little after four P.M., and I'm riding shotgun in the passenger seat of my city-issue Explorer. My newest patrol officer, Mona Kurtz, is behind the wheel. She's all business this afternoon, wearing her full uniform, which still smells of fabric softener. Her usually unruly hair is pulled into a ponytail. Makeup toned down to reasonable hues of earthy brown and nude pink. She works dispatch most nights, but recognizing the importance of patrol experience, I've been spending a couple of hours with her every day when our schedules align. I want her to be ready once I get a new dispatcher hired and trained.

It's a brilliant and sunny afternoon; cool, but pleasant for November in this part of Ohio. The X Ambassadors are feeling a little "Unsteady" on the radio, which is turned down low enough so that we can hear my police radio. We've got to-go coffees in our cup holders, and the wrappers of our burger lunch in a bag on the console. We're cruising down County Road 19 when we spot the dozen or so bales of hay scattered across both lanes.

"Looks like someone lost their load," Mona says, slowing.

"Driver hits a bale of hay doing fifty and they're going to have a problem."

Hitting the switch for the light bar, Mona pulls over and parks. "Set up flares?"

I look ahead and sure enough, an Amish wagon piled high with hay wobbles on the horizon. "Looks like our culprit there. Let's toss the bales onto the shoulder and go get them."

We spend a few minutes lugging bales onto the gravel shoulder, and then we're back in the Explorer heading toward the wayward driver.

It's an old wooden hay wagon with slatted side rails, half of which are broken.

"At least he's got a slow-moving-vehicle sign displayed," I say as we approach. "That's good."

"Shall I pull him over, Chief?"

"Let's do it."

Looking a little too excited by the prospect of making a stop, she tracks the wagon, keeping slightly to the left. We can't see the driver because the bed is stacked ten feet high with hay. It's being drawn by a couple of equally old draft horses. Slowly, the wagon veers onto the shoulder and stops.

Taking a breath, Mona straightens her jacket, shoots me an I-got-this glance, and gets out. Trying not to smile, I follow suit and trail her to the left front side of the wagon.

The driver isn't what either of us expected. She's fourteen or fifteen years old. An even younger girl sits on the bench seat next to her. Between them, a little boy of about six or seven grins a nearly toothless smile. I can tell by their clothes that they're Swartzentruber Amish; the boy is wearing a black coat over blue jeans and high-top black sneakers. A flat-brimmed hat sits atop the typical "Dutch boy" haircut. The girls are wearing dark blue dresses with black coats and black winter bonnets.

The Swartzentruber Amish are Old Order and adhere to the long-standing traditions with an iron grip. They forgo many of the conveniences other Amish use in their daily lives. Things like running water and indoor plumbing. They don't use windshields in their buggies or rubber tires. The women wear long, dark dresses. Most wear winter bonnets year-round. The men don't trim their beards. Even their homes tend to be plain.

As a group, they get a bit of a bad rap, especially from non-Amish people who don't understand the culture. Most complaints have to do with their refusal to use slow-moving-vehicle signage, which they consider ornamental. I've also heard some non-Amish grumble about the personal hygiene of some Swartzentruber. Having been raised Amish, I appreciate the old ways. Even if I don't agree with them, I respect them. I know from experience how difficult it is to lug water when it's ten below zero outside. Such hardships make it impractical to bathe every day, especially in winter.

The kids are uneasy about being pulled over, so I move to set them at ease. "*Guder nochmiddawks,*" I say, using the Pennsylvania Dutch words for "good afternoon."

"Hi." The driver's gaze flicks from Mona to me. "Did I do something wrong?"

I nod at Mona, let her know this is her stop. "No, ma'am," she tells the girl. "I just wanted to let you know you lost a few bales of hay."

The girl's eyes widen. "Oh no." She glances behind her, but can't see past the stacked hay without getting down. "How many?"

"Ten or so." Mona motions toward the fallen hay. "About a quarter mile back."

Now that I've gotten a better look at them, I realize I've seen these children around town with their parents. I've stopped her *datt* on more than one occasion for refusing to display a slow-moving-vehicle sign on his buggy. It's gratifying to see he heeded my advice.

"You're Elam Shetler's kids?" I ask.

The driver shifts her gaze to me. "I'm Loretta." She jabs a thumb at the younger girl sitting beside her. "That's Lena. And Marvin."

I gauge the size of the wagon and the stability of the load. It's a big rig that's overloaded. The road is narrow, without much of a shoulder. I'm about to suggest she go home to unload and return with an adult when she gathers the reins and clucks to the horses.

"*Kumma druff!*" she snaps. "*Kumma druff!*" Come on there!

The horses come alive. Their heads go up. Ears pricked forward. Listening. *Old pros,* I think.

"Are you sure you can turn that thing around?" I ask her.

"I can turn it around just fine," the girl tells me. There's no petulance or juvenile showmanship. Just an easy confidence that stems from capability and experience.

I glance at Mona. "Let's back up the Explorer and get out of the girl's way."

"You got it, Chief."

I retreat a few feet and watch with a certain level of admiration as the girl skillfully sends both horses into a graceful side pass. The animal's heads are tucked, outside forelegs crossing over the inside legs in perfect unison. When the wagon runs out of room, she backs the horses a couple of feet and once again sends them into a side pass. Within minutes, the wagon faces the direction from which it came.

"I have a whole new respect for Amish girls," Mona whispers.

I cross to the wagon, look up at the girl. "Nicely done," I tell her.

She looks away, but not before I see a flash of pride in her eyes, the hint of a blush on her cheeks, and I think, *Good girl.*

I motion toward the fallen bales of hay. "Pull up to those bales, and Mona and I will toss them onto the wagon for you."

The children giggle at the thought of two *Englischer* women in police uniforms loading their fallen hay, but they don't argue.

I've just tossed the last bale onto the wagon when the radio strapped to my duty belt comes to life. "Chief?"

I hit my shoulder mike, recognizing the voice of my first-shift dispatcher. "Hey, Lois."

"I just took a call from Mike Rhodehammel. Says there's a horse and buggy loose on Township Road 14 right there by the old Schattenbaum place."

"On my way," I tell her. "ETA two minutes."

I slide back into the Explorer. "You hear that?" I ask Mona.

"Yep." She puts the vehicle in gear.

A few minutes later we make the turn onto the township road. It's a decaying stretch of crumbling asphalt that's long since surrendered to the encroaching grass shoulder and overgrown trees. There are two houses on this barely-there swath of road. Ivan and Miriam Helmuth own a decent-size farm, growing hay, soybeans, and corn. The other property is the old Schattenbaum place, which has been abandoned for as long as I can remember.

I spot the buggy and horse ahead. The animal is still hitched and standing in the ditch against a rusty, tumbling-down fence. The buggy sits at a cockeyed angle.

"No sign of the driver." Mona pulls up behind the buggy and hits the switch for the light bar. "What do you think happened?"

"The Helmuths have a lot of kids." I shrug. "Maybe someone didn't tether their horse or close a gate." I get out and start toward the buggy.

The horse raises its head and looks at me as I approach. The animal isn't sweaty or breathing hard, which tells me this isn't a runaway situation. I peer into the buggy, find it unoccupied, three old-fashioned bushel baskets in the back.

"Well, that's odd." I look around and spot a red F-150 rolling up to us.

"Hey, Chief." Local hardware store owner Mike Rhodehammel lowers his window. "Any sign of the driver?"

I shake my head. "Might belong to Mr. Helmuth down the road. I'm going to head that way now and check."

He nods. "I thought someone should know. Hate to see that horse get hit. I gotta get to the shop."

"Thanks for calling us, Mike."

"Anytime, Chief."

I watch him pull away and then start back toward the Explorer. "Let's go talk to the Helmuths."

I'm in the process of sliding in when I hear the scream. At first, I think it's the sound of children playing, but the Helmuth farm is half a mile away, too far for voices to carry. Something in that scream gives me pause. I go still, listening.

Another scream splits the air. It's high-pitched and goes on for too long. Not children playing. There's something visceral and primal in the voice that makes the hairs at the back of my neck prickle.

Mona's eyes meet mine. "What the hell, Chief?"

"Where is it coming from?" I say.

We listen. I step away from the Explorer, trying to determine the direction from which the voice came. This time, I discern words.

"Grossmammi! Grossmammi! Grossmammi!"

Panic and terror echo in the young voice. I glance at the Schatten-baum house, spot a little Amish girl running down the gravel lane as fast as her legs will carry her.

"Grossmammi! Grossmammi!"

Mona and I rush toward her. In the back of my mind, I wonder if her grandmother had an accident or suffered some kind of medical emergency.

I reach the mouth of the lane. The gate is open. The little girl is twenty yards away, running fast, darting looks over her shoulder as if she's seen a ghost—or a monster. She's about five years old. She looks right at me, but she doesn't see.

"Sweetheart. Hey, are you okay?" I ask in *Deitsch* as I start toward her. "Is everyone all right?"

When she's ten feet from me, I notice the blood on her hands. More on her face. On her dress. A lot of it. *Too much.* A hard rise of alarm in my chest. I glance at Mona. "I got blood. Keep your eyes open."

The girl's body slams into me with such force that I stumble back. She's vibrating all over. Mewling sounds tearing from a throat that's gone hoarse.

"Easy." I set my hands on her little shoulders. "It's okay. You're all right."

"Grossmammi!" Screaming, she claws at my clothes, looks over her shoulder toward the house. "*Da Deivel* got her!"

"What happened?" I run my hands over her. "Are you hurt?"

The girl tries to speak, but ends up choking and crying. I kneel and ease her to arm's length, hold her gaze, give her a gentle shake. "Calm down, honey. Tell me what happened."

"*Da Deivel* hurt Grossmammi!" the girl cries. "She's bleeding. He's coming to get me, too!"

"Where is she?" I ask firmly.

Choking, she lifts a shaking hand, points toward the old house. "In the kitchen. She won't wake up!"

I look at Mona. "Get an ambulance out here. Call County and tell them to send a deputy." I ease the little girl over to Mona. "Stay with her. I'm going to take a look."

Normally, I'd take Mona with me, but this child is too young and too panicked to be left alone. I don't expect anything in the way of foul play. Chances are, Grandma had an accident, a fall or heart attack or some other medical episode. Of course, that doesn't explain the blood. . . .

I hear Mona hail Dispatch as I jog toward the house. I notice the buggy-wheel marks in the dust as I run. A burlap tote someone must have dropped.

I reach the back of the house. No movement inside. No sign anyone has been here. I go to the porch, spot a single footprint in the dust. The door stands ajar. The hinges squeak when I push it open the rest of the way.

I smell blood an instant before I see it. An ocean of shocking red covers the floor. Spatter on the cabinets. The sink. The wall. Adrenaline burns a path across my gut. I slide my .38 from its holster. A female lies on the floor. She's Amish. Blue dress. White *kapp*. Older. Not moving. There's no weapon in sight. All I can think is that this was no accident or suicide, and I may not be alone.

"Shit. Shit." I hit my radio. "Ten-thirty-five-C. Ten-seven-eight." They are the codes for homicide and need assistance.

I train my weapon on the doorway that leads to the next room. "Painters Mill Police! Get your hands up and get out here! Right now!" I hear stress in my voice. My senses are jacked and overloaded. My adrenaline in the red zone. Hands shaking.

"Get out here! Now! Keep your fucking hands where I can see them! *Do it now!*"

Keeping my eyes on the door, I go to the woman, kneel, and I get my first good look at her face. I've met her at some point. My brain kicks out a name: Mary Yoder. She lives with her daughter and son-in-law, Miriam and Ivan Helmuth, at the farm down the road. I bought a cake from her last fall.

"Damn." Even before I press my index finger to her carotid, I know she's gone. Her skin is still warm to the touch, her eyes open and glazed. Mouth open and full of what looks like vomit.

I rise and sidle to the doorway, peer into the living room. It's dark; curtains drawn. Shadows ebb and flow. Lots of blind spots. I yank the mini Maglite from my belt. I listen, but my heart pounds a hard tattoo against my ribs. I shine the beam around the room. The front door is closed. No sign of anyone. No movement or sound.

"Chief?"

I spin, see a Holmes County deputy come through the back door. He does a double take upon spotting the victim. "Holy shit," he mutters.

"Place isn't cleared," I tell him. "Victim is deceased."

"Fuck me." Drawing his sidearm, he sidesteps the blood, moves past me, into the living room.

"Holmes County Sheriff's Department!" The voice comes from outside an instant before the front door flies open. A second deputy enters, shotgun at the ready.

"House isn't cleared," I tell him. "Deceased female in the kitchen."

Sunlight slants in through the door, allowing us to see. The men exchange looks. The first deputy strides to a casement doorway, peers into an adjoining room. "Clear!"

The other deputy calls for additional units. Together, they start up the stairs to the second level.

I go back to the kitchen, stop in the doorway, bank a swift rise of revulsion. I've seen a lot of bad scenes in the years I've been a cop. Traffic accidents. Knife fights. Serious beatings. Even murder. I can honestly say I've never seen so much blood from a single victim. What in the name of God happened?

"Chief?"

I look up to see Mona come through the back door. She spots the victim and freezes. After a moment she blinks, shakes her head as if waking from a bad dream. A tremor passes through her body.

My newest deputy is no shrinking violet, but she's not ready for this.

"Mona." I say her name firmly. "Get out. I got this."

Without making eye contact with me, she backs away onto the porch, bends at the hip, and throws up in the bushes.

That same queasy response bubbles in my own gut; no matter how many times you see it, there's something inherently repellent about blood. The sight of death, especially a violent one. I shove it back, refuse to acknowledge it.

"Where's the girl?" I ask Mona.

"She's with a deputy, in the backseat of his cruiser." Hands on her hips, she spits, and then looks at me. "Chief, kid says a man took her sister."

The words land a solid punch to my gut, adding yet another awful dimension to an already horrific situation. "Did you get names?"

"Helmuth."

"I know the family," I say. "They live down the road."

"What do you think happened?"

I shake my head. "Hard to tell. Looks like she was . . . stabbed."

Butchered, a little voice whispers.

We're both thinking it, but we don't utter the word.

I hit my lapel mike and hail Dispatch. "Possible ten-thirty-one-D," I say, using the ten code for kidnapping in progress.

I look at Mona. "We need to look around, talk to the parents," I tell her. "Confirm if the girl is missing."

If we were dealing solely with a likely homicide, my first priorities would be to protect the scene, limit access, set up a perimeter, canvass the area, and get started on developing a suspect. The possibility of a kidnapped minor child changes everything. The living always take precedence over the dead.

"Did the little girl say anything else?" I ask.

"Couldn't get much out of her, Chief. She's pretty shaken up."

I take a final look at the victim, suppress a shudder. "Let's go talk to her."

CHAPTER 2

I find the girl huddled in the backseat of a Holmes County Sheriff's Department cruiser. Someone has draped a Mylar blanket across her legs, given her a bottle of water, and a teddy bear to hold. Some cops, my small department included, carry a stuffed animal or two in the trunks of our official vehicles for situations exactly like this one, when we want to keep a child as calm and comforted as possible.

I make eye contact with the deputy as I approach. I've worked with him before; we had Fourth of July parade duty last summer. He's a good guy, a father himself, and a decent cop. We shake hands. "She say anything?"

"Been crying mostly, Chief. Said something in Dutch." He shrugs. "Wants her mom, I think."

I tell him about the possibility of a missing sister. "Best-case scenario she got scared and ran home."

The door to the backseat stands open. I go to it and kneel so that I'm eye level with the girl. "Hi there," I say. "My name's Katie, and I'm a policeman. Can you tell me what happened?"

She looks at me, her face ravaged and wet with tears. "I want my *mamm*."

She's a tiny thing. Blue dress. Blue eyes. Light hair. Blood on baby hands. Smeared on the bottle of water, which she isn't drinking. She's shaking violently beneath the blanket. I switch to *Deitsch,* try to kick-start her brain. "Who did that to your *grossmammi*?"

"*Da Deivel.*"

The devil.

The words put a chill between my shoulder blades. They're words no child should ever have to speak. A scenario no kid should ever have to witness or recount. "A *mann*?"

She nods.

"Do you know his name? Have you seen him before?"

She shakes her head.

"Is your sister with you?"

"Elsie." She whispers the name as if she's afraid to say it aloud. "He took her."

"Do you know where they went?"

She closes her eyes; her face crumples. "I want my *mamm.*"

I ignore the tears, all too aware of precious minutes ticking away, and I press for more. "Just one man?"

A nod.

"What did he look like?"

She stares at me.

"Was he English? Or Plain?"

"I want my *mamm.*"

"Sweetheart, do you know where he went?"

She shakes her head.

I keep going. "Was he in a buggy or an *Englischer* car?"

The child begins to cry. Huge, wrenching sobs. I consider pressing, but back off. For now.

I reach out and squeeze her little knee. "I'm going to go get your *mamm* and *datt.*"

Rising, I dig my keys from my pocket, turn to Mona and the deputy. "We need to look around for the girl. Set up a perimeter. Protect the scene. We've got a male subject who's possibly taken a little girl. I want all hands on deck." I address Mona. "Tell T.J. and Pickles to canvass the area," I say, referring to my officers by their nicknames. "Tell Glock and Skid to clear the barn and outbuildings, and fan out from there. Call the sheriff's department, see if they have someone with dogs. I want the property searched and I want everyone on scene mindful of evidence. Everything gets marked and preserved."

"Got it."

Yanking out my phone, I hit the speed dial for John Tomasetti and start toward the Explorer. He's an agent with the Ohio Bureau of Criminal Investigation. He's also my significant other and the love of my life. Painters Mill falls within his region. We've worked together on several cases. In fact, that's how we met. He's aggressive and thorough and good at what he does. At the moment, I'm glad I have someone like him to count on.

He picks up on the second ring. "I hear you've got a body and a missing juvenile on your hands," he says without preamble.

"Word travels fast." Some of the tension building in my chest eases at the sound of his voice. I lay out what little I know. "I think the five-year-old saw the killer, and I think she may have seen him take her sister."

"One man?"

"I think so. This kid is traumatized, so I need someone good to come down and talk to her. I need to know what she saw and I need it five minutes ago."

"I'm on it," he says.

"Tomasetti, this woman wasn't just stabbed. She was . . ." The image of Mary Yoder's butchered body flashes in my mind's eye. "She was cut to pieces."

"Sounds personal."

"And now he may have a little girl. I'm going to check with the parents, confirm it before we pull out all the stops." I hit the fob to unlock the Explorer.

"I'll be there in twenty minutes," he says.

I hit END and drop the cell into my pocket. I've just opened the door when I spot the Amish man running toward me, a boy of about nine or ten hot on his heels. I recognize him immediately as Ivan Helmuth. More than likely he heard the sirens or saw the police vehicles pulling in, and came down to see what happened. His expression tells me he's worried as hell.

"Chief Burkholder!" he calls out.

I go to him. "Mr. Helmuth—"

"What happened?" he says. "Why are all of these police here? Where are my children? My mother-in-law?"

"I've got one girl in the car, sir. She's okay."

"One? But . . ." Leaving the sentence unfinished, he rushes to the vehicle, pushes past Mona and the deputy, and looks into the car. "*Annie.*" He pulls the girl into his arms.

"Datt!" Sobbing, the little girl clings to him.

"Where is your *shveshtah?*" he asks. Sister. "Your *grossmammi?*"

"*Da Deivel* got Grossmammi!" the little girl cries. "He took Elsie!"

"*What?*" The Amish man is so startled by the assertion that he presses his hand against his chest and stumbles back. "Took her? *Da Deivel?*" His eyes find mine. "Where are they, Chief Burkholder? What's happened here?"

"Mr. Helmuth." I set my hand on his arm, let my eyes slide to the little girl. "I need to speak with you privately."

His eyes connect with mine; then he looks down at the boy who'd followed him over. "*Bleiva mitt die shveshtah.*" Stay with your sister.

Looking shell-shocked, he lets me lead him a few feet away. When we're out of earshot of the children, I stop and turn to him. There's no easy way to tell him what needs to be said. There's no way to cushion the blow or ease the deluge of terror that will follow.

"Mr. Helmuth, Mary Yoder is dead. She's inside the house." I motion toward the structure a hundred yards away where half a dozen deputies mill about.

"*What?*" He blinks, disbelieving, staring at me as if I've played some cruel joke on him and he's expecting me to slap him on the back and admit all of this is a hoax.

"But . . . *dead?* How—" He bites off the word, his eyes zeroing in on mine. "It's not possible. Mary was fine when she left earlier."

I struggle to find the right words. Pose them in some way or put them in some order that won't send him into a panic, but the only thing that comes are facts that will be excruciating for him to hear. "All I know at this point is that Mary Yoder is dead and we haven't been able to locate the other girl."

"Elsie?" He struggles for calm. "We need to find her," he snaps. "She's got to be around here somewhere."

"She's not in the house. We're searching the property now. Is it possible she's at home?"

"No, she was with her sister and grandmother."

"Mr. Helmuth, there was foul play involved—"

"You mean someone did this thing?"

I nod. "Annie told me a man took Elsie. We have reason to believe it was the same man who attacked your mother-in-law."

"Took her? *Mein Gott.*" Comprehension suffuses his face. His mouth opens, but he doesn't speak. He stares at me; the brim of his hat begins to shake. "Who?"

"I don't know."

"We must find Elsie," he says. "She's just a child."

His entire body is vibrating with a terror he can't contain. Raising his hand, he presses his thumb and forefinger to his eyes. "Chief Burkholder, what happened to my mother-in-law? How did she . . ."

Not wanting to upset him further when I don't yet have all the facts, I fudge. "I'm not sure, but it's bad."

He nods, but he looks bewildered and blindsided. Most of all he looks terrified. "Miriam will want to know."

I don't suspect this man of anything, but as we talk, I find myself looking for blood on his clothes, on his hands. Any wounds. There's nothing there. "Mr. Helmuth, is it possible a neighbor or family member picked up Elsie? Took her home?"

"No," he snaps, growing increasingly anxious. "My children were here with their *grossmuder*. Gathering walnuts. That is all."

"Is it possible Elsie got scared and ran home?"

"I didn't see her, but . . ."

"We need to check." I motion toward the Explorer and we start toward it. "Do you have a phone at your house?"

"No."

"I know this is a lot to take in. But time is of the essence. We need to hurry. Grab Annie and come with me."

Snapping out of his fugue, the Amish man looks at the boy. "*Bringa da waegli haymet*," he tells him. Bring the buggy home.

"Take the horse," I tell him. "Leave the buggy. I need to check it for evidence."

The man nods at the boy and then we're off.

A minute later, I pull into the gravel lane of the Helmuth farm, driving too fast, and park in the driveway behind the house. Helmuth opens the passenger door before I've even brought the Explorer to a complete stop and scrambles from the vehicle.

"Miriam!" he calls out as he rushes toward the back porch. "*Finna Elsie! Finna Elsie!*" Find Elsie.

The screen door squeaks open. A heavyset Amish woman with hips as wide as the doorway and a kind, tired face looks out at the man running toward her. "*Was der schinner is letz?*" What in the world is wrong?

"Elsie is missing," he says as he reaches her. "Did she come home?"

"No," the woman says, looking startled. "She went with—"

He cuts her off. "Search the house. I'll look in the barn."

He trots toward the barn. The woman shoots a worried, questioning look my way, then disappears inside.

I get out of the Explorer and open the door for the girl in the backseat. She's not making a sound, but her cheeks are shiny with tears. I notice the dried blood on her hands again, and a quiver of sympathy moves through me. "Let's go inside, sweetheart."

Taking her hand, I walk with her to the back door. We enter a mudroom with dirty plywood floors and a wall of windows to my right. An old wringer washing machine squats in the corner. A dry sink against the wall. A clothesline bisects the room at its center, half a dozen pairs of trousers hanging to dry.

Annie and I have just stepped into the kitchen when the screen door slams. Footsteps pound and then Ivan Helmuth enters the room. "She's not in the barn," he says breathlessly.

I hear shoes in the hallway and then Miriam enters the kitchen. "Elsie's not upstairs. She's not in the cellar. Why are you looking for her? What's happened? Where's Mamm?"

"Elsie's missing." Ivan's voice breaks. "Mary is . . . gone."

"Gone? But . . . what do you mean? You don't know where she is? Ivan, Mamm is with the children. They were—" The Amish woman's gaze lands on Annie; her eyes go wide when she spots the blood. "*Mein*

Gott." She rushes to the child, falls to her knees, and takes the girl into her arms. "Are you hurt? How did you get that blood on you?" she asks in *Deitsch.*

"*Da Deivel,*" the little girl whispers.

Miriam pales; even her lips go white. "What is she saying?" She pushes her daughter to arm's length to get a better look at her. "Whose blood is this? Where did it come from?"

As she clutches the little girl, the Amish woman's eyes dart to her husband, then me, her voice rising with each word she utters. "Chief Burkholder? What's happened?"

"Mrs. Helmuth, I need to speak to you and your husband privately." I let my eyes slide to the little girl.

Taking the girl by her hand, the Amish woman rushes from the kitchen, goes to the base of the stairs, and calls out. "Irma!"

A girl of ten or eleven clatters down the steps, but slows upon spotting us, her eyes flicking from her mother to me and back. "What's wrong?"

"Take Annie. Get her cleaned up."

The girl's eyes widen when she sees the blood. "Oh!"

"Go on now. Get her washed up. Quick."

When the children are gone and we're seated, I tell them everything.

"*Mamm* passed? But . . ." Miriam leans forward, covers her face with her hands, and begins to rock. "*Elsie.* Gone? *Mein Gott.* It's too much. I can't believe it."

Ivan looks at me. "Who would do this terrible thing?"

"Did your mother-in-law have any enemies?" I ask. "Any disagreements or arguments with anyone?"

The couple exchange looks, as if the answer lies in the other person's face. "No," Ivan says after a moment.

"Maybe it was something that didn't seem important at the time?"

27

I press, trying to get them to work through the shock of grief and fear for their daughter and *think*.

"No." The Amish man shrugs. "Nothing."

"Has anything unusual happened to Annie or Elsie recently? Any strange incidents? Maybe while you were in town? Shopping? Running errands? Maybe someone said something that struck you as odd?"

He shakes his head adamantly. "No."

"Any problems with family members? Or neighbors? Any arguments or bad blood? Money disputes?"

"No," he tells me. "Nothing like that."

"Have you had any workers here at the farm? Day laborers? Repairmen?"

"I do everything myself," Ivan says.

I give the questions a moment to settle, and shift gears. "How many children do you have?"

Miriam raises her head, fear and misery boiling in her expression. "Eight."

"Any problems with any of them?"

"Of course not," Miriam snaps. "We are *Amisch*." As if that explains everything. In a way, it does.

"Have you noticed any strangers in the area? Any cars or buggies you didn't recognize? Anyone on the road? On your property?"

Ivan gives another head shake. "No."

"I just want my baby." Miriam begins to cry. "She must be so frightened." She raises her gaze, her eyes beseeching. "Please, Chief Burkholder. Elsie is . . . special. Sweet and innocent. She won't understand what's happening."

The word "special" gives me pause. "Elsie is special needs?" I ask.

"She's a slow learner. We took her to the clinic and she was diagnosed with Cohen syndrome when she was four. Please, we've got to find her. She's so sweet. So innocent."

Cohen syndrome is a rare gene disorder that's slightly more common among the Amish owing to marriage patterns and a smaller gene pool. It carries with it a host of problems, including delayed physical development and intellectual disability.

I set my hand on the Amish woman's arm. "Do you have a photo of Elsie?"

"We do not take photos of the children."

"Can you tell me what she looks like? What was she wearing?"

She describes the girl—seven years old, blue dress, brown hair and eyes. Slightly overweight. Thick, round eyeglasses. I jot everything in my notebook. All the while I feel as if I'm being pulled in a dozen different directions. The urge to get back to the scene is powerful. The need to work the case eats at me. I need to look at the evidence. Find it. Churn it. Answer the questions pounding my brain. No one does something like what was done to Mary Yoder without some perceived reason, without leaving something behind. It's my job to find it—and fast.

More than anything, I want to find the girl. That need is tempered by the knowledge that the information-gathering phase of the investigation—speaking with family and friends and possible witnesses—is critical. The majority of homicide victims know their killers. Most kidnappings are committed by family members. If either of those statistics is true in this instance, the most vital information I receive will come from the people closest to Elsie: her family, right here and now.

"Mr. and Mrs. Helmuth, you mentioned Mary and your two daughters went to the house to pick up walnuts. Has Mary ever had any problems there? Any strangers hanging around? Or signs of vandalism? Graffiti? Tire tracks? Anything unusual?"

Miriam shakes her head. "She never mentioned anything. I just can't believe . . ." Looking as if she's going to be sick, she presses her hand to her mouth. "Oh, dear Lord."

Ivan nods. When his gaze meets mine, his expression is grim. "She had words with the Graber boy once. He lives over to Rockridge Road."

"Big Eddie," Miriam says in a small voice.

The mention of "Big Eddie" garners my attention. The Graber farm abuts the Helmuth property; they share the back fence. The family is Amish. Eddie is a teenager; I've seen him around town or walking along the road. He's a troubled kid with a tragic story. A near drowning a decade ago left him with brain damage.

The one and only time I ever had reason to interact with him was an incident at the Butterhorn Bakery. According to owner Tom Skanks, Big Eddie bought six apple fritters, and proceeded to eat all of them before leaving the bakery. Some non-Amish teenagers made fun of Eddie and a fight broke out. By the time I got there, Eddie had two of the kids on the ground, and they were bloodied and bruised. It was a nasty scene with an ugly origin: the bullying of a mentally challenged teenage boy. No charges were pressed, but the incident put Eddie on my cop's radar.

"What happened with Big Eddie?" I ask.

"We caught him spying on the girls when they were swimming down to the creek," the Amish woman blurts. "He tried to get our oldest to . . . take off her underwear and go into the woods with him." She looks away, shakes her head. "Asked her to 'show him her thing.'"

"Did he touch her?" I ask.

The Amish woman shakes her head. "No."

"Did you talk to Eddie's father?"

Ivan raises his gaze to mine. "I told him about it. He said he'd keep an eye on him."

"Anything since?" I ask.

"Last year. Eddie was walking by the old Schattenbaum place. Our boys were there, gathering walnuts. There was a fight. I found out later our boys threw some walnuts at Eddie while he was walking by." The Amish man looks down, ashamed.

"We're not proud of what our boys did," Miriam says.

"Anyone get hurt?" I ask.

Ivan shakes his head.

"Elam had a black eye," Miriam puts in.

"Figured he deserved it," the Amish man mutters.

"How old were your boys at the time?" I ask.

"Elam was seven."

Too young to get punched in the face by a teenager twice his age and three times his size—even if he did deserve it. "Is there bad blood between your family and Big Eddie?" I ask. "His family?"

"Lord, no." Miriam shakes her head. "We see them every couple of weeks at worship. Eddie's a sweet thing usually, but he's got a temper, gets mean when he's mad."

Ivan looks down at his hands, grimaces. "We try to look the other way. But . . ."

"I'll talk to them." I pause. "Look, I know Annie has been through a lot. But I need to ask her some questions."

The couple exchange another look. After a moment, Ivan tips his head at his wife.

Miriam rises. "I'll fetch her."

A few minutes later, the four of us are seated at the kitchen table. Annie is sitting in her mother's lap. Miriam has her arms wrapped around her daughter, and she can't seem to stop kissing the top of her head. The woman is doing her utmost to remain calm and maintain her composure, if only for the child's sake, but she's not quite managing.

Annie's hands and face are clean, and she's wearing a fresh dress. Miriam supplied me with the soiled one, which I tucked into a gallon freezer bag I keep in my vehicle. I'll send it to the BCI lab to have the blood tested. Chances are it belongs to Mary Yoder, but you never know when you might get lucky. Oftentimes, an attacker with a knife will cut himself in the frenzy, which would supply us with DNA.

"Hi, sweetheart," I begin.

The little girl's eyes slide away from mine. Lifting her hand, she puts her thumb in her mouth and starts to suck. Miriam gently takes the child's hand and lowers it. "Chief Katie has a few questions for you, my little peach."

Again, I feel the minutes ticking by and I struggle for patience, with the need to be gentle, to not frighten this child who has already been so traumatized. All of those things are in direct conflict with my need for facts.

"My *grossmuder* used to call me little peach." I tilt my head, and make eye contact with Annie. "Your cheeks kind of look like peaches."

A ghost of a smile floats across the child's expression.

"Makes me want to pinch them."

This time, a full-blown grin.

I jump on it. "Can you tell me what happened when you and Elsie and your *grossmammi* were gathering walnuts?"

The little girl shakes her head, then turns, wraps her arms around her mother, buries her face against her *mamm*'s bosom. "I'm scared," she whispers.

I try again. "Was there someone else there?"

"*Da Deivel,*" she mumbles.

"Can you tell me what he looked like, sweetie?"

"I can't remember," she whispers, not looking at me. "Just a man."

I pull a lollipop from my pocket. Hearing the wrapper crinkle, she turns her head and eyes the candy.

"It's strawberry." I offer it to her.

An almost-smile, and then the girl reaches for the lollipop.

"What was the man wearing?" I ask matter-of-factly.

The process is excruciatingly slow, and again, I feel precious time slipping away. Minutes I can't get back. Minutes in which a little girl is in grave and immediate danger. I feel the tension coming off these parents. My own tension wrapped tight around my chest. And I remind myself: This has to be done. No other way to move forward.

When Annie doesn't respond, I try another tactic. "How about if we play a game?"

The little girl turns, looks at me with one eye, the other obscured by the fabric of her *mamm*'s apron.

"I'll guess what he looks like and you tell me if I'm right or wrong."

Nodding, she slides the lollipop into her mouth.

"Was his hair blond, like yours? Or brown, like mine?"

"Like yours," she says in a small voice.

"Okay." I pretend to think for a moment. "Was his skin the color of mine? Or was it the color of chocolate pudding?"

The mention of pudding elicits the whisper of a smile. "Yours."

I pull out my notebook and write. *White male. Brn.* "Did he have a beard like your *datt*?"

"I didn't see."

"Was he Plain or English?"

"Plain."

It isn't the answer I expected. In the back of my mind I wonder how

33

reliable she is as a witness. Usually by the time a child is five years old, they are considered relatively dependable. That said, I'm no expert on the child interview process. There are techniques and procedures and protections in place. In light of a missing sibling, I don't have time to wait.

"Good job." I say the words with a little too much enthusiasm. "Were his eyes blue like your *mamm*'s or brown like your *datt*'s?"

The child looks up at her mother, lets her eyes slide to her father's face. In the end her brows knit and she shakes her head.

"Was he old? Like Bishop Troyer? Or young, like your *mamm*?"

"Kind of in the middle."

"Was he tall or short?"

"Tall. *Grohs*." Big.

"Fat or skinny?"

The girl shakes her head. "Just big."

"So you and Elsie and Grossmammi were gathering walnuts." I switch to *Deitsch* to keep her mind moving, so she doesn't clam up. "What happened next?"

"Grossmammi went in the house to look at Mrs. Schattenbaum's kitchen. We heard something break and then yelling so me and Elsie went in to find her."

"What did you see when you went inside?"

"Grossmammi was on the floor. She was all bloody. Like when Datt takes the cows to make meat. She was making noises. Elsie tried to help her. Then the man came."

"He came into the kitchen?"

"*Ja*." Her nose is running now, her upper lip covered with snot. She doesn't seem to notice. Lower, her foot begins to jiggle. "I thought he was going to help Grossmammi. But he grabbed Elsie. Real rough like. And she got scared."

"Did he say anything?"

"I . . ." She takes the lollipop out of her mouth. Her eyes fill with tears. "I got scared and ran."

"What about Elsie?" I ask. "Did she say anything?"

"All she did was scream."

CHAPTER 3

One hour missing

The Schattenbaum place is teeming with activity when I pull into the driveway. I see a Holmes County Sheriff's Department vehicle. An Ohio State Highway Patrol Dodge Charger. Two Painters Mill cruisers tell me my own department has arrived on scene. While I want all available law enforcement looking for the little girl, I'm cognizant that any evidence left behind needs to be protected and preserved. Not an easy feat when there are a dozen cops tromping all over it.

An hour has passed since Mary Yoder was killed and Elsie Helmuth disappeared, and already the hounds of desperation are nipping at my heels. I park behind Tomasetti's Tahoe and call my dispatcher.

"I need you to get me the names and addresses of all registered sex offenders in Painters Mill and all of Holmes County," I say. "If the offender has an Amish-sounding name, flag it. Let me know if any of them live in close proximity to the Schattenbaum place. Start with a five-mile radius and expand from there."

I hear her typing in the background, noting everything. "Got it."

"Run Ivan and Miriam Helmuth through LEADS. Run Mary Yoder as well as her deceased husband. Check Edward Graber, too. See if anything comes back." LEADS is the acronym for the Law Enforcement Automated Data System, which is operated by the Ohio State Highway Patrol and stores information such as criminal records and outstanding warrants.

"Okay."

"Did you call Doc Coblentz?" I ask, referring to the Holmes County coroner.

"He's on his way."

"Any media inquiries?"

"Steve Ressler called ten minutes ago."

Not for the first time, I'm astounded by how quickly word travels in a small town. Ressler is the publisher of Painters Mill's weekly newspaper, *The Advocate*. "Do not confirm anything at this point. Nothing is for public consumption."

"Sure."

"Lois, I need an aerial map with topography of the Schattenbaum property and the surrounding area. Call the Holmes County auditor. Ask them to fax it to you. Tell them it's an emergency and I need it yesterday."

I end the call and hit my shoulder mike as I slide out of the Explorer. "Mona, what's your twenty?"

"Glock and Skid and I just cleared the barn and the smaller outbuilding."

"Anything?"

"Negative."

"I need you to ten-fifty-eight," I tell her, using the ten code for direct traffic. "I want the road in front of the Schattenbaum place blocked off at both Ts, flares and cones. No one comes in or goes out. I'll get County out there to help you."

"Roger that."

"Tell Glock and Skid to search the back of the property. It's a big spread. Grab some deputies, set up a grid, and get it done."

"Ten-four."

"Pickles? What's your twenty?"

"T.J. and I are talking to neighbors, Chief. We split up to cover more ground. He's south. I'm north."

"Anything?"

"No one saw shit."

I blow out a breath of frustration. "Keep at it."

As I near the house, I spot a Holmes County deputy standing just off the back porch. He looks my way and I recognize him. He was the first deputy to arrive on scene.

"Chief." He crosses to me, looking relieved to be away from the carnage inside. "Damn this is bad."

"Anyone else in the house?" I ask as we shake hands.

"BCI guy ordered everyone out. Their crime scene truck is on the way."

Tomasetti, I think, and I'm thankful he got here so quickly. "House is clear?"

"Yep."

"Outbuildings are clear." I look past him toward the barn and field. "Look, I just sent two officers to search the back of the property. Maps of topography and plat are on the way. If you can spare a couple of deputies to help us with the search, I'd appreciate it."

"You got it." He reaches for his shoulder mike.

"Chief Burkholder."

I turn to see Tomasetti come out of the house. I go to him and we shake hands, a ridiculously formal greeting considering we're living together. Since it's not common knowledge among our peers, we're ever cognizant of appearances.

He holds on to my hand an instant too long. "Any word on the kid?" he asks.

I shake my head. "I talked to the parents. She's not there. I need to put out an Amber alert."

"We meet the criteria." He pulls out his phone, thumbs something into it. "I need a physical description. Photo, too."

"Seven-year-old white female. Brown eyes. Brown hair. Three feet nine inches. About sixty pounds. Tomasetti, she's special needs."

"Shit."

"No photo." I describe her clothing—a white *kapp* and light blue dress—and he types all of it into his phone.

"You have anything on the suspect?" he asks.

I recite the particulars from memory. It isn't much. It isn't enough. But it's all I have, so we've no choice but to run with it.

He doesn't look away from the screen or question me about any of it as he sends the information. Both of us are too aware that a stranger kidnapping of a child is the most dangerous kind. Every minute she's gone raises the possibility of a negative outcome. For me, the passage of time is like the pound of a tine against a broken bone.

"Vehicle?" he asks.

"I don't know. The sister said he was Amish."

"Still, he could be driving a vehicle. He could be disguised as an Amish person. But we'll go with it for now." He sighs. "I'll get this put into NCIC," he tells me, referring to the National Crime Information Center system. "I'll call the coordinator over at DPS." The Department of Public Safety. "Amber alert broadcast will go out within the hour.

I'll send what I have and we'll fill in the rest of the blanks as we figure things out."

The crunch of tires on gravel draws our notice. Relief eases some of the tension at the back of my neck when I see the BCI crime scene truck pull into the driveway. Tomasetti and I start toward it. Normally, I'd stick around for the collection of evidence. I'd wait for the coroner to arrive. But with a child missing, my efforts are best used looking for her or developing a suspect.

I look at Tomasetti. "You got this?"

"Got it covered, Chief. Go."

I leave him with the crime scene unit. I'm on my way to locate the fence line to the east when I run into Glock and Skid along with two Holmes County deputies.

"You been to the back of the property?" I ask.

"Heading that way now," Glock tells me.

I look around. Another Holmes County cruiser has arrived on scene. I think about the missing girl again, feel that incessant beat of time. . . .

"I think the Schattenbaums owned about sixty acres," I tell them. "Ran cows for a while, so it's fenced. Probably cross-fenced."

Skid motions right. "Woods are pretty thick along that creek on the east side."

"Whole damn place is overgrown," one of the deputies pipes up. "Nooks and fuckin' crannies."

"Got some deep pools in that creek," Glock adds. "Water runs swift in a couple of areas."

"All right." I bring my hands together and relay a description of the girl. "Name is Elsie. Seven years old. Amish. Special needs." I motion toward the rear of the property. "Set up a loose grid. Glock, you take the east woods. Keep your eyes on the brush and water, especially any deep pools. Skid, you got the fence line. Keep your eyes west." I look at the two deputies. "Can you guys handle the pasture?"

Both men nod.

"Keep your eyes open for blood," I tell them. "Stay cognizant of evidence. Mark anything suspect. We'll do a more thorough grid search when we get more guys." I motion toward the greenbelt. "I'll take the creek in front. Eyes open. Let's go."

The four men head toward the back of the property. I cut between the house and barn, head toward the woods. The grass is hip high as I pass through a microforest of saplings, most of which are taller than me. It's a huge, overgrown area. I try not to think about how easy it would be to miss something important. Midway to the fence line, I rap my shin on a solid object, realize it's the remains of a doghouse. From the look of things, no one has been this way for a long time. No broken branches. None of the grass is laid over.

I find a stick, use it to poke around, hopefully avoid running into something hidden. Fifty yards and I reach the fence that runs front to back along the east side of the property. Rusty barbed wire is propped up on a combination of cedar posts and steel T-posts. The fence is falling down where the wood has rotted through. I make the turn, head south toward the road.

The house is now behind me and to my right. I stick to the fence line, ducking beneath branches, glad it's too late in the year for snakes. I hear the rush of water over rocks to my left, telling me I'm not far from the creek.

I'm thirty yards from the road when I spot a patch of disturbed grass. I stop, my pulse kicking, eyes tracking. The grass is laid over. A path, I realize. It starts at the house, weaves through a dozen trees, and leads to the fence. From there, it follows the fence line toward the road.

I hesitate, taking it in, aware that if someone left the house in a hurry and didn't want to be seen, this would be the perfect route.

That said, there are a lot of deer in the area. My *datt* was a hunter and I went with him often enough to know the animals are creatures of habit and use trails. Still . . . I move right, as to not disturb the path. When I'm close enough, I squat and lean over to check for cloven hoofprints, but there are none. This is not a deer path. Upon closer inspection, I see that the tall blades of grass are broken in places. I'm no tracker, but it looks fresh.

I've gone another dozen yards when I spot the shoe. It's a girl's sneaker. The laces are still tied. Canvas. Cheap. The kind of footwear a growing Amish girl might wear. Avoiding the path, I travel another ten feet, and a glint of red on the grass stops me cold. I know even before I move closer for a better look that it's blood.

"Shit," I whisper. "*Shit.*"

I check my duty belt for something with which to mark the location. The only thing I can come up with is a yellow sticky note. I skewer it on my stick and poke the length of wood into the ground. I move on.

I find more blood. A footprint. Adult size with visible tread. No more sticky notes; I'm going to have to rely on my initial marker and my memory. In the back of my mind, a little voice chants: *Please don't find that little girl dead. . . .*

There's no way to tell whose blood it is. There was a copious amount inside the house; it's likely the killer carried it out on his clothes or shoes or both, and it transferred to the grass. It's also possible he cut himself during the attack. Knives get bloody; they get slippery. The good news is I now have evidence to collect and send to the lab. Worst-case scenario, the blood belongs to the girl. . . .

I snap several photos and then traverse the ditch that parallels the road in front of the house. I step onto the asphalt. A quarter mile away, police lights flicker where the sheriff's department has closed the road. Somewhere in the distance an ambulance sings. I walk through the ditch again and go back to the mouth of the path. Keeping my eyes on the ground, I walk slowly alongside the trail, watching. Another smear of blood on the trampled blades. I bend, study the ground, spot the heel mark. Not a child's, but an adult's. Large, probably male.

Tugging out my cell, I call Tomasetti. "I got blood. And a decent footprint."

"Where are you?" he asks.

I look around. I can just make out the roof of the house through the trees. "A couple hundred yards southeast of the house, near the fence line."

"I'll get another agent out here. We're running out of light."

He's right; dusk is fast approaching. If the clouds to the west are any indication, we've probably got rain on the way, too. Neither of those things bodes well for evidence collection, some of which is out-of-doors.

"You have a generator?" he asks.

"At the station." I'm walking toward the road, looking down at the ground, when I spot tire marks in the moist soil. Not from a buggy, but a car or truck. "I got tire imprints, too."

A thoughtful moment and then, "Tread?"

I pull the mini Maglite from my duty belt and kneel. "Yup."

The rumble of thunder in the distance reminds me that we don't have much time. "Tomasetti, if these marks get rained on, we'll lose this."

"I'm on my way."

A few minutes later, his Tahoe rolls up on the road and stops. Leaving the engine running, the headlights shining in my direction, he gets out and starts my way. "An agent with some plaster should be here in twenty minutes."

"Rain isn't going to wait," I tell him.

"That's why they invented garbage bags." He snaps open a large trash bag. "Might work if it doesn't pour."

Flipping on my flashlight, I take him to the tire-tread marks, shine my beam on the ground. He squats, careful not to get too close.

"Looks like he came down the road, heading east," I say. "Pulled over here. Left that imprint." I shift the beam to the falling-down fence at the edge of the property. "From there he went to the fence, used the trees for cover. Walked to the house, sticking to the fence line, and then cut over, keeping out of sight in case someone drove by."

His gaze jerks to mine. "You got guys out canvassing?"

I nod, but we both know that in light of the tire tracks, the man we're looking for is probably gone.

"Dogs?" he asks.

"County is working on it."

"If this guy knew Mary Yoder and those kids were coming, if he knew their routine, he may have gone inside and waited for them," he says.

"If they were already here," I say, "all he had to do was sneak up to the house along this fence line and make entry."

"If he knew the victim, he's likely local." Tomasetti looks around as if trying to imagine the scenario. "Were they targets or did they surprise him?"

"If he targeted them, who was he after?" I murmur. "Mary Yoder? Or the girl? Both?"

Kneeling, he spreads the bag over the tire-tread imprints.

"How's it coming along inside?" I ask.

"It's a damn mess, Kate." He anchors the plastic with a couple of stones, rises, and sighs. "Mary Yoder wasn't just stabbed," he tells me.

"She was butchered. Slashed. Defensive wounds. She put up a hell of a fight."

"You think this is personal? That he knew her?"

"Or he's a fucking psycho or both."

"You guys get anything?"

"Footwear imprints. Large. Definitely male. A shitload of blood. Probably hers, but if he cut himself and they can isolate a second set of DNA, it could be helpful."

He reaches into the side pocket of his jacket. "Crime scene agent found this on the victim." He pulls out a clear plastic bag containing a single sheet of notebook paper. "We've still got to log it, but I wanted you to take a look to see if it means something that might help us find the kid."

I shine my flashlight on the bag. White notebook paper. Lined. From a spiral binding. Printed in pencil by an inept hand.

Food gained by fraud tastes sweet, but one ends up with a mouth full of gravel.

"Mean anything to you?" he asks.

"It's from the Bible," I say. "A proverb, I think." I look at him. "Something to do with deception."

"Any idea how this might fit with any of this?"

I shake my head. "No clue."

We fall silent, look around, trying not to notice that it's nearly dark. "Tomasetti, this woman . . . she was a grandmother. Amish. Who does something like that? And why take the child?"

He shakes his head. "The first thing that comes to mind is that he's a sexual predator." He shrugs. "Maybe he wanted the kid, the woman got in the way, and it's no more complicated than that."

The words are a physical pain. My mind whirrs with what I know—and all I don't. "That level of violence. It seems like . . . overkill. Like he wanted her dead, not just out of the way."

"Or he was afraid she'd identify him."

Neither of us put into words what we're thinking. That the same could be true for the girl.

I tell him the story about Eddie Graber.

"You think he's capable of something like that?" he asks.

"He's got the physical strength. A temper. Self-control issues." I shake my head. "I don't know him very well. I'm going to talk to them."

I look around the property, the dilapidated house, the isolated and overgrown nature of the land.

"How did he know they'd be here?" I say, thinking aloud.

"Could be a crime of opportunity. He was in the area. Saw them." He shrugs. "Or maybe he's a stalker. Had his eyes on the kid for some time. Followed them. Figured this was his chance."

"You think he lives in the area?"

"I think that's the most likely scenario." But he sighs. "Tough to figure what's in the mind of someone capable of hacking an Amish grandmother to death." His expression darkens. "We need to find that kid."

The sense of dread I'd been feeling since I laid eyes on the body of Mary Yoder augments into a knot in my gut that's being drawn inexorably tighter. All children are innocent, but for this to happen to a child with special needs heaps on another cruel layer of urgency.

I watch as Tomasetti sets a branch over the garbage bag to keep the wind from blowing it away. "I'm going to talk to the sheriff, check on the status of getting dogs out here."

My cell vibrates against my hip. I check the display. My dispatcher. "Hey, Lois."

"I got two registered sex offenders within a ten-mile radius of the Schattenbaum address, Chief. One of them is Amish."

I pull out the small notebook I keep in the back pocket of my trousers. "Give me the Amish guy first."

"Lester Nisley." Computer keys click on the other end, and then she reads. "Twenty-two years old. Convicted of rape of a thirteen-year-old girl in 2015. Got out on parole last September. Current address 5819 Township Road 4."

Less than five miles away. . . .

"What about the other guy?"

"Gene Fitch. Fifty-seven years old. Convicted of rape of a nine-year-old girl in 1992. On parole since 2016. Home address 9345 County Highway 83, Painters Mill."

. . . *rape of a nine-year-old girl* . . .

"Anything on Eddie Graber?" I ask.

"Nothing."

"Thanks, Lois."

"Only thanks I need, Chief, is for that little girl to get home safe and sound."

"Amen to that."

CHAPTER 4

Two hours missing

A few minutes later I'm in the Explorer with Glock in the passenger seat, and we're northbound on Ohio 83. I left Tomasetti with the tire and footwear marks and relinquished the collection of evidence to the capable hands of BCI. Both of those things freed me up to do exactly what I need to be doing: looking for Elsie Helmuth.

"So what's the story on Eddie Graber?" Glock asks.

I tell him about the near drowning. "It left him with some emotional issues. Impulse control. A temper."

"Bad combination."

"Yeah."

The Graber farm is just two minutes from the Helmuth place. I take the long gravel lane up a rise, past a couple of derelict barns and a good-size garden. The house is brick and set behind three evenly spaced maple trees. I see Big Eddie's father standing in front of yet another barn, running a currycomb over a nice-looking Standardbred gelding, so I pull up to him and shut down the engine.

Glock and I exit the vehicle and start toward him.

"Guder Ohvet." Good evening. I hold out my badge as I approach.

Edward Graber is a large man. Six-three. Two fifty. I guess him to be about forty years of age. He's a widower, having lost his wife a couple of years ago to pancreatic cancer. They have one son, Eddie, and the two live alone here on the farm.

The Amish man nods, his eyes moving from me to Glock. "Been hearing lots of police sirens," he says. "What's going on over there? Are Miriam and Ivan okay?"

"Is your son home, Mr. Graber?"

"What do you want with Eddie?" he asks.

"There was an incident over at the Schattenbaum place earlier. I need to ask him some questions. Is he here?"

A brief hesitation and then he brings two fingers to his mouth and whistles. It's an odd way to summon a young man, but it works. A few seconds later, Big Eddie appears at the barn door.

"Big Eddie" Graber is just sixteen years old, but he's already as large as his father. Not exactly overweight, but . . . meaty. Strong-looking. He's wearing a straw hat. A black coat. Work trousers with suspenders. Greasy brown hair brushes the collar of his coat. Leather gloves cover hands the size of dinner plates.

"Hi, Eddie," I say by way of greeting.

"Hey," the boy mutters, and then slogs over to us, looking at the ground, at the barn, anywhere except at me. Like many teenagers his age, he's got acne on both cheeks. He looks uncomfortable. Probably because I was there the day he got in a fight at the Butterhorn Bakery. Or else he has something to hide. . . .

"Can you tell me where you've been all day today?" I ask.

The boy's eyes slide from me to his *datt* and then back to me. "Here."

"All day?"

"*Ja.*"

The elder Graber narrows his gaze on me. "What's this all about, Chief Burkholder? Why are you asking about my son's whereabouts?"

49

I don't answer, wait, let the pressure build to see how they handle it.

"I been here," Big Eddie says defensively. "Helping Datt shore up the loft there in the barn. We're going to pick up hay tomorrow."

"Did you leave this property at any time?" I ask.

"I took a walk down to the pond to see the ducks."

"Alone?"

"*Ja.*"

"Did you see any of the Helmuth family today?"

"No."

I look from man to boy. "Do either of you have access to a vehicle?"

"We are *Amisch,*" the elder Graber tells me. "No."

I look at his son. "When's the last time you were at the Schattenbaum place?"

"I dunno." His brows go together, as if he's struggling to remember. "A couple months maybe."

"When's the last time you saw Mary Yoder?"

"The old lady?" He looks at his *datt,* then back at me. "I don't remember. A few months?"

"When did you last see Elsie Helmuth?"

"The little retarded kid?"

I grit my teeth. "The seven-year-old little girl," I say.

The elder Graber steps in. "Why are you asking my son these things?"

I don't look away from Big Eddie. "Answer the question."

For the first time he looks upset, a combination of confusion and frustration. A drop of sweat rolls down the side of his face, just in front of his ear. I think about his temper; I think about the missing little girl, and I push harder. "You wouldn't lie to me, would you, Eddie?"

The boy's face reddens. "I . . . I don't lie!"

"Why are you sweating?" I ask.

"My son has no reason to lie to you or anyone else," Edward says. "He's a good boy."

"Was he here all day?" I ask the elder Graber.

"Just like he said."

I look at the boy. "Would you mind taking off your gloves?"

"Huh? My gloves?" But he's already tugging at the fingertip of his glove, pulling it off.

"Show me your hands," I say. "Both sides."

He does as he's told. His hands are large and strong, with dirty, chewed-off nails and a plethora of calluses. A two-inch-long half-moon-shaped slice mars the heel of his hand.

Next to me, Glock shifts.

"How'd you cut yourself?" I ask.

Eddie lets his hand drop, shoves it into his pocket. "I caught it on barbed wire."

"Weren't you wearing your gloves?" I ask.

"I took them off," he mumbles.

"When did you do it?"

"This morning."

"Looks like you might need stitches," Glock says. "Any reason you didn't get it taken care of?"

"I didn't do anything wrong!" The boy casts an uneasy look at his father. "Why is she looking at my hands, Datt? What did I do?"

"Chief Burkholder, my son . . . he's *engshtlich*." Upset. "I saw him cut his hand. He was handling a big coil of wire and it slipped. He's telling the truth."

I turn my attention to the boy. He stares back, sputtering now. His hands clenched into fists. Temper, I think, so I press on.

"You get along with the Helmuths?" I ask him.

"I like them just fine."

I look at the elder man. "Do you mind if we take a quick look in the house, Mr. Graber?" I do not have the right to search the home of any individual without a search warrant issued by a judge. But if he gives me permission, I can have a look free and clear. Better yet, anything I find can be used to build a case against him.

"I don't understand," Edward says. "What are you looking for?"

"There was an incident at the Schattenbaum place this afternoon, Mr. Graber. Mary Yoder was killed. Elsie Helmuth is missing. As you can imagine, everyone is extremely concerned. I need to take a look in your house. Just to eliminate you and your son from the equation. Are you okay with that?"

A hard silence falls, thick and echoing. Edward Graber stares at me as if the news has rendered him speechless. His mouth opens, lips trembling, but he doesn't make a sound.

Standing next to him, the younger man begins to shake. He's clutching the gloves, slapping them against his thigh as if he wants to hit something. I think about his temper. His lack of self-control.

"You think my son did that?" Edward asks, his voice shaking.

"I think I'd like to get back out there and look for that little girl." I look from father to son and back to the elder man. "It would be a big help if I could just have a look-see in your house and then I'll get out of your hair."

"Go ahead," Graber says. "But I don't like these questions."

"Neither do I."

I send Glock to the barn. I head toward the house. I hear father and son behind me, but I don't wait for them. I go through the back door, enter a narrow porch that's been enclosed and is being used as a mudroom. Boots lined up on the floor to my right. I pick up a rubber boot, check it for blood, check the tread. The size, which is thirteen. I look at the coats hung on wood dowels. Dry and clean. No blood.

The kitchen is a mess, but it's the kind of mess that's the result of two men living in close quarters without a woman. I tug open a couple of drawers. The only knives I see are cheap steak knives. I go to the living room. No sign of anything out of place. No footprints. Nothing that looks as if it would belong to a little girl.

There's a single bedroom at the rear of the house. Large. A full-size bed. Faded Amish quilt. No closet. I look under the bed. Nothing. I check the bathroom. It's filthy, but again, it's normal wear and tear. I check the hamper. No bloody clothes or towels. I make eye contact with Edward and then take the steps to the second level.

There are two bedrooms upstairs. The first has a twin-size bed. A ratty blanket. A horse saddle on the floor. Another pair of boots. No closet. Nothing under the bed. The second room is littered with boxes. A woman's dress hangs from a dowel on the wall. A *kapp*, strings hanging down. Mrs. Graber's things, I think, and I take the steps back to the first level.

Edward and his son stand in the kitchen. The older man looks perturbed. Big Eddie looks on the verge of tears. "I ain't done nothin' wrong," he whines.

I ignore him. "Is there a basement?" I ask.

The older man shakes his head. "No."

I take a moment to make eye contact with both of them. "I'm going to have a deputy take a look around the pasture and field. Is that all right with you?"

"That's fine," says the elder.

"I appreciate your cooperation," I say, and then I'm through the door.

Glock meets me at the Explorer. "Anything interesting in the barn?" I ask.

"Just a girlie magazine up in the loft, Chief."

Rolling my eyes, I put the vehicle in gear and start down the lane.

I've just made the turn onto Township Road 4 when my cell chirps. I tug it out of my pocket, glance at the display. T.J. "Chief, I'm out here at Dick Howard's place on Township Road 14 and Goat Head Road. Dick says he saw a pickup truck he didn't recognize drive past his place right about the time the kid went missing."

My interest surges. That intersection is just down the road from the Schattenbaum place. "Make or model?"

"No and no. Said he glanced out the kitchen window when he was fixing a sandwich and didn't pay much attention."

I think about the tire tread marks. "Full-size pickup?"

"Yeah."

"Color?"

"Light. White or tan."

"Did he get a look at the driver?"

"No, ma'am."

"Tell him to call if he remembers anything else. Glock and I are talking to RSOs. Keep at it."

"You got it."

I tell Glock about the call. "We're on our way to see Lester Nisley," I say. "He's an RSO and Swartzentruber. Still on parole."

"Sounds promising."

"We'll see."

Lester Nisley lives with his parents on a hog farm four miles south of the Schattenbaum place. The smell of manure hits me as I make the turn into the lane. Next to me, Glock mutters something unseemly and rolls up his window.

Most Swartzentruber Amish don't use gravel for their lanes, and the Nisleys are no exception. We bump down a rough dirt road fraught with ruts. A quarter mile in, the lane opens to a turnaround situated between a clapboard farmhouse and two barns. The one to my right is a low-slung hog barn. Farther back is an old white bank barn with its front sliding door standing open. The house is to my left; it's a plain farmhouse with no flowers or shutters or landscaping. An enormous garden encompasses most of the side yard. A dozen or so pairs of trousers hang from a clothesline. A weathered outhouse is situated just off the backyard.

"I feel like I've just gone back in time a hundred years," Glock says as we get out.

"Some Swartzentrubers are more Old Order than others," I tell him, but I'm thinking about the tire-tread marks found in front of the Schattenbaum place. "Keep your eyes open for any sign of a vehicle, tire tread, oil stains, whatever."

Movement at the door of the hog barn snags my attention. I see a man silhouetted against lantern light inside. He's wearing a flat-brimmed hat, standing in the doorway, watching us.

We start that way.

A second man has come up beside him. A younger version of the older man. Neither of them speaks or makes an effort to greet or welcome us. Instead they stand there, legs cocked, and watch us approach. The second man is slighter of build; his beard is of the barely-there variety, his bowl-cut blond hair sticking out from beneath his flat-brimmed straw hat. Father and son, I think.

I've seen the elder Nisley around town, but I don't recall ever speaking to him. His expression reflects a standoffishness I'm no stranger to. One that tells me I'm an outsider and he hasn't yet decided if I'm welcome on his property. He's got angular features, an unkempt beard hanging off the lower half of his face. A thin mouth. A toothpick moving up and down as he works it against his teeth with his tongue. Neither of them looks terribly concerned about the police showing up at eight o'clock in the evening.

Glock and I reach the men. "I'm looking for Lester Nisley," I say.

The elder man jabs his thumb at the younger man. "You found him."

I turn my attention to the younger man. "Lester, is there a place we can speak privately? I need to ask you some questions about your whereabouts earlier today."

The older man straightens, puts his weight on both feet. He's just realized this isn't a routine visit.

The younger man shrugs. "I reckon we can talk right here."

"Where were you between noon and five P.M. today?"

"I was here all morning." Tipping his hat, he scratches his head. "Went to the feed store around noon."

"Were you with anyone?" I ask. "Or were you alone?"

"I went by myself."

"Can anyone corroborate that?"

He looks at me as if he's not quite sure what "corroborate" means. "My *datt*," he says after a moment. "Guy at the feed store. I got a receipt in the house."

The older man nods. "He worked out here in the barn all day, morning and afternoon. Midday I sent him into town to pick up feed."

"Do you know the Helmuth family?" I ask, aware that Glock has quietly made his way into the barn for a look around.

The elder Nisley tilts his head. "Why are you asking us these questions?"

I don't respond; I don't look away from the younger man and repeat the question.

"Ivan and Miriam?" he says. "Yeah, I know 'em."

"Not well," the elder Nisley cuts in. "My wife took a cake to them when Ivan broke his leg last year. I helped when the wind blew their barn down. That is all."

I don't look away from Lester. "What about the children?"

He laughs. "They got a bunch, that's for sure."

"Do you know them?" I ask. "Have contact with them?"

I feel the older man's eyes on me, but I don't look away from his son. I stare at him hard, waiting.

"No."

I add a harsh note to my voice. "You sure about that, Lester?"

"I don't deal with them. I have no use for kids."

"Lester." I lower my voice. "I know you're a registered sex offender."

The young man's eyes widen. "She wadn't no little kid!"

"You were convicted of having a sexual relationship with a thirteen-year-old girl when you were nineteen."

"The *Englischer* police don't understand our ways," the elder hisses.

"Ways?" I say. "What ways is that?"

"They were going to marry," he tells me. As if that makes any difference whatsoever.

I look at Lester. "Let me see your hands," I snap.

Looking bewildered, he puts out his hands, turns them over. "What are you looking for?"

His hands are dirty, but unmarked. No blood or cuts. I don't comment.

The old man's eyes narrow on mine. "Why are you asking my son about the Helmuth family? Why are you interested in his hands?"

I give them the basics of what happened at the Schattenbaum farm, watching them closely for reactions. The elder's mouth falls open. "Mary Yoder?" he gasps. *"Doht?"* Dead?

"Elsie Helmuth is missing," I tell them.

Comprehension flickers in the elder man's eyes; he knows why I'm here. "Someone took a child?" he asks.

I turn my attention to Lester, who has fallen silent. "Lester, did you see any of the Helmuth family earlier today?"

The younger man's eyes dart left and right, as if he's looking for an escape route in case I attack. He's just realized where this is going and he doesn't like it. "No!"

"You were convicted of sexual misconduct with a minor. I'm obligated to ask you about Elsie Helmuth. You are obligated to answer. Do you understand?"

Lester looks at me, mouth open, eyes wide, frightened now. "Yes, but . . . that was different. Edna was young, but . . . we're married now!"

The urge to tear into Lester Nisley is powerful, but I don't. As much as I dislike him on a personal level—as much as I despise what transpired between him and a minor six years his junior—I understand how and why it happened. It was immoral; it was against the law. Unfortunately, some of the Old Order Amish don't see it that way.

The age of consent in Ohio is sixteen. Most Amish couples marry in their late teens or early twenties. Some of the Swartzentruber and Old Order marry younger. Even with Ohio's "Romeo and Juliet" law, which would have protected Lester from prosecution if he was less than four years older than the minor female, the six-year age difference made the so-called courtship a crime, hence his two-year stint in the Mansfield Correctional Institution.

The Amish church district looked the other way for the most part. In the eyes of a few, the only thing Lester had done wrong was have premarital sex. As long as he confessed his sins before the congregation, he was not held responsible. Most of the Old Order supported him. That's one of several Amish tenets I couldn't live with and one of the reasons I never fit in—and ultimately left.

The elder Nisley moves forward. "They're married now, in the eyes of the Lord. Edna is sixteen. A grown woman."

"When's the last time you spoke to Elsie Helmuth?" I ask Lester.

"I don't speak to her at all. I don't even know which one she is." Lester says the words with a great deal of defensiveness, as if my questions offend some moral sensibility. The irony doesn't escape me.

I pause, let the silence ride. Out of the corner of my eye, I see Glock approach from the shadows of the barn. The older man looks over his shoulder at him, suspicious, but he doesn't say anything.

"Mr. Nisley, we believe Elsie Helmuth is in extreme danger. As you can imagine, her parents are worried. If you know something you need to tell me right now."

"We don't know anything," the older man tells me.

"Do you mind if I take a look inside your house?"

"We have nothing to hide."

"Thank you." I send Glock a nod, and he starts toward the house.

I turn my focus back to the men. "Have you seen any strange vehicles or buggies in the area?" I ask. "Anything unusual?"

Both men shake their heads.

Over the next minutes, I take both men through the same questions I posed to the Grabers, but they've nothing to add. By the time I'm finished, Glock has exited the house and joins us.

"If you think of anything that might be important, I'd appreciate it if you'd let me know." I hand the elder man my card.

Neither man says anything, so I nod at Glock and we head back to the Explorer.

"Not very repentant for a religious guy," Glock says as we drive down the lane.

"In the eyes of the Swartzentruber Amish, he did nothing wrong."

"A thirteen-year-old kid?"

I shrug. "As disgusting as that is, I don't like him for the Helmuth girl."

"Yeah." Glock sighs. "I'd still like to beat his ass."

CHAPTER 5

Four hours missing

A missing endangered child is the kind of scenario in which a cop needs to be in a dozen places at once. Searching. Talking to family, witnesses, and suspects. Extracting evidence at the crime scene. Doing something—whatever it takes—to find a child in imminent danger and bring her home. Every minute that passes is another minute lost, and that torturous clock never stops ticking closer to a potentially devastating outcome.

Glock and I spent half an hour talking to registered sex offender Gene Fitch. He's an unlikable individual and a drunken slob to boot, but he had a solid alibi.

I've called upon every law enforcement resource available, including BCI, the Holmes County Sheriff's Department, and the Ohio State Highway Patrol. I've mobilized every member of my own department. The Amber alert has gone out. Tip line has been activated. No one is going home tonight. We're four hours in, and it's as if she's disappeared from the face of the earth.

It's excruciating to know an innocent little girl is out there, frightened and alone and in the kind of danger no child should ever have to face. I don't know what's worse, thinking of her being brutalized—or imagining her little body lying somewhere and growing cold.

I'm consciously trying not to become too entangled in my own emotions when a call comes in from Tomasetti. Dread punches me squarely in the gut, and I brace. *Please don't have bad news. . . .*

"I'm on my way to the Helmuth place," he begins. "I'm with a colleague. She's trained to interview young children. I thought we might have another go at the five-year-old."

"I can be there in a few minutes."

"Hang on a sec." I hear him speaking to someone on the other end, and then he comes back on. "She's wondering if you can bring a toy for the girl. Something a kid her age will like and be comforted by."

"I know just the thing."

I make it to the Carriage Stop Country Store on the traffic circle just as the manager is locking up for the night. Some fast talking gets me in the door and to the toy aisle. I was never a doll lover as a child; much to my *mamm*'s chagrin, I was a tomboy and more likely to be playing ice hockey or riding the plow horse. Still, I manage to find an Amish-made doll I think a five-year-old girl will like.

In keeping with the Amish tradition of avoiding any type of graven image, it's faceless and made of nude-colored fabric. She's wearing a royal-blue dress, a black apron, and a black bonnet, with smooth nubs for hands and feet. I deflect questions from the clerk about the murder and missing girl as she rings up the sale. I put it on my card and then I'm through the door and back in the Explorer.

I pass six buggies as I near the Helmuth farm, Amish men armed with flashlights or lanterns and the resolve to find one of their own. At the mouth of the lane, I raise my hand in greeting to two boys on horseback. It's unusual to see so many out after dark, when most Amish families are winding down for the night or already in bed. These men have organized search parties. More than likely, the women are cooking and cleaning for the Helmuth family. As is always the case, the Amish community has rallied to support those in crisis.

The farm glows with lantern light. The windows. The front porch. Even the barn is lit up. There are four more buggies, the horses still hitched, parked in the gravel off the back door. Tomasetti's Tahoe sits adjacent to a chicken coop, the headlights on, engine running. I park behind the Tahoe and start toward it. I'm midway there when Tomasetti and his passenger get out. He's wearing his usual creased trousers, button-down shirt, and suit jacket with the tie I bought him for Christmas last year. He looks tired, rumpled, and grim.

"Agent Tomasetti." I extend my hand, cross to him, and we shake. "Chief Burkholder."

I turn my attention to the woman standing next to him and offer my hand. She's petite, about fifty years of age, with silver hair cut into a sleek bob. She's wearing the usual agent attire. Khaki slacks. Button-down shirt. Practical shoes. A navy windbreaker embellished with the BCI logo. She's soft-spoken and self-assured, without the in-your-face demeanor I see in so many law enforcement pros.

"Mackenzie Upshaw." She gives my hand a squeeze. "Everyone calls me Mackie."

She's no-nonsense and to-the-point. No makeup. No frills. Discerning blue eyes beneath thick black brows.

"Agent Tomasetti was just filling me in on the case," she tells me. "I wanted to get your take before we speak to the child."

With the niceties out of the way—and kept to a minimum—she's ready to get down to business. I like her already.

Tomasetti motions to his Tahoe and we gather around for a quick huddle. "Kate, Mackie is trained in the forensic-interviewing protocol RATAC—rapport, anatomy identification, touch inquiry, abuse scenario, and closure," he tells me. "It's a questioning process most often used with child victims of sexual abuse."

"It's a terrific protocol," Mackie tells us. "Effective and nonintrusive. It basically means I'll be asking nonleading questions, using terms the little girl will understand. I'll keep it nice and slow since most children that age have pretty short attention spans."

"I talked to Annie immediately after the incident." I relay to her our exchange. "I didn't get as much out of her as I would have liked."

"Kids make for extremely difficult interview subjects, especially when they're younger than six or seven years old." She pauses. "I understand this child is Amish."

I nod.

"Is there anything you can tell me that might help me relate to her?" Mackie adds.

I take a moment to get my thoughts in order. "Amish kids are much like their English counterparts, especially when they're as young as Annie. That said, there are distinct differences." I pause, thinking. "Generally, Amish kids are more sheltered. More disciplined. Religious. They're taught to respect and obey their elders, especially their parents. The biggest difference is that she will probably see you as an outsider, not because you're a cop, but because you're not Amish."

"What do you suggest?"

"Win her trust." I hold up the doll, pass it to her. "Bribery."

Mackie takes the doll and grins. "Cool."

"Works every time," Tomasetti mutters.

"If I sense she's clamming up or becoming uncomfortable," Mackie says, "I want you to jump in. We need to keep her engaged and as focused as possible. Any thoughts on that?"

I shrug. "*Deitsch* might help."

"Excellent." She thinks about something a moment. "Is she shy?"

I nod. "That's my impression."

Mackie looks at Tomasetti. "Would you mind sitting this one out? The fewer people present, the more comfortable she'll be."

"No problem."

"You're a good sport, Agent Tomasetti." Mackie looks at me. "Shall we?"

As we cross the gravel to the sidewalk, I notice the young hostler carrying a bucket of water to the buggy horses. I recognize him as one of the Helmuth children. Even in times of turmoil and stress, the parents keep the kids busy with responsibilities.

I knock and we enter. The aromas of lantern oil, candle wax, and something frying fill the air. We're midway through the mudroom when Ivan Helmuth rushes through the door to greet us. "You bring news of Elsie?"

"We're here to speak with Annie," I tell him.

His brows furrow. For an instant, I'm afraid he's going to refuse. But he knows what's at stake. "This way." He leads us into a well-lit kitchen.

Two Amish women stand at the sink, washing and drying dishes. A third mans the stove, stirring a steaming Dutch oven with a wooden spoon.

Mackie extends her hand to Helmuth and recites her name. "I'm with BCI," she tells him.

"Sit down." He motions to the big wooden table. "I'll get Annie."

Mackie and I pull out chairs and sit. She puts the doll on her lap and sets her hand on it. I nod, letting her know it's going to make a good first impression.

A minute later, Ivan and Miriam Helmuth appear at the kitchen doorway with their daughter. Miriam's hands are on Annie's shoulders. The girl is pale, with circles beneath her eyes. She's wearing a light green dress with sneakers and her *kapp*. Upon spotting us, she turns and buries her face against her *mamm*'s skirt.

"You remember Chief Burkholder?" Ivan asks.

The girl doesn't turn around, but nods.

"You can call me Katie," I tell her in *Deitsch*.

She turns her head, peeks at me out of the corner of one eye. Curious about my use of Pennsylvania Dutch.

"My friend's name is Mackenzie," I tell her, "but everyone calls her Mackie."

Annie turns slightly, her one eye seeking the BCI agent, and she repeats the name, testing it, as if she likes the way it feels on her tongue.

The instant the girl makes eye contact with Mackie, the BCI agent raises the doll. "I'm hoping we can come up with good name for her. Do you have any ideas?"

The girl looks up at her *mamm* as if asking for permission to speak. Tugging out a chair, the Amish woman settles into it, pulls the child into her lap, and wraps her arms around her. Ivan leans against the doorjamb, arms crossed, watching.

"What do you think about Willie?" Mackie says with a mischievous grin.

Annie smiles shyly and presses her face against her *mamm*. "That's a boy's name."

Mackie laughs. "Do you have any ideas?"

The girl nods, but she's not engaged; she doesn't want to talk to us. She doesn't care about the doll.

"I always liked the name Susie," I tell her. "What do you think, Annie?"

For the first time the girl gives us two eyes, dividing her attention between Mackie and me and the doll. "I like it."

"Susie it is then." Mackie looks longingly at the doll, giving an exaggerated frown. "I think I'm a little too old for dolls."

"Annie's just about the right age," I put in.

Mackie perks up as if she hadn't thought of it. "What a great idea! Annie, would you like her?"

Again, the girl looks up at her *mamm*. Asking for permission to accept the gift. The woman nods, encouraging her to interact.

The girl gives an enthusiastic nod. "*Ja.*"

Mackie runs a hand over the doll's head, gives it a big, smacking kiss, and then passes it to the child. "There you go."

A smile whispers across the girl's face as she takes the doll. Something shifts inside me when she looks at the doll, then closes her eyes and hugs it against her.

"Maybe Susie can keep you company until we find Elsie," Mackie says.

Caution enters the child's eyes, but she nods.

"Did you and Elsie find lots of walnuts today?" Mackie asks the question in a nonchalant, casual way, as if it's an afterthought and she doesn't care whether she gets an answer.

"Two bags," Annie says in a small voice.

Good girl, I think. *Talk to us, honey. Talk.*

"What happened while you were picking up walnuts?" Mackie asks.

The girl turns away, sets her face against her *mamm*'s dress, and seems to fold in on herself. Pulling away. From us. From questions she's already been asked too many times and doesn't want to face again. From the memory of her dead grandmother and the knowledge that her sister is gone.

"Was there someone else there?" Mackie asks gently.

The little girl puts her thumb in her mouth and begins to suck.

"I wonder if the stranger was picking up walnuts, too?" Mackie asks of no one in particular.

The thumb comes out. "He was in the house," Annie tells us.

"A man?"

"*Ja.*"

"Hmmm. What happened next?"

"Grossmammi was in the house, too," the girl says.

Mackie casts a look toward me. "'Grossmammi' is 'Grandmother'?"

"Yes." I wink at Annie and whisper, "She doesn't know *Deitsch.*"

Mackie continues. "I wonder why your *grossmammi* went into the house." A pause and then, "Did she hear something? See something?"

"She just likes it because she used to play there when she was little."

"I see." Mackie gives an exaggerated nod. "Did she go in through the front door or back?"

"Back."

"What were you and Elsie doing?"

"Putting walnuts in our bags. We wanted to fill them up so we could play."

"Did you see anyone else outside?" Mackie asks.

"No."

"So you and Elsie were playing and picking up walnuts." Mackie slants her a smile. "Having fun?"

"*Ja.*"

"And Grossmammi was in the house, looking around. What happened next?"

The girl snuggles against her *mamm.* "We heard Grossmammi yelling."

"What did she say?"

"I don't remember."

The agent nods thoughtfully. "What did you do?"

Again, the girl brings her hand to her mouth and begins to suck her thumb. She pulls it out long enough to say, "We thought she fell down or saw a mouse, so we went in to find her."

"What did you see when you went inside?"

A storm cloud of emotion darkens her face. Her breaths quicken. I see her mind dragging her back to what must have been a horrifying moment. "Grossmammi." She buries her face against her mother.

"Where was she?" Mackie asks.

"On the floor. In the kitchen. She was bleeding and . . ." The girl stops speaking as if she doesn't have enough breath to finish.

"Was there anyone else in the kitchen?"

"Not at first, but then the Plain man came out."

"What did he look like?"

The girl takes us through much the same description as the one she gave me. White male. Old—at least in the eyes of a five-year-old child. Brown hair. When she's finished, she turns away, presses her face against her *mamm,* and whispers, "*Ich bin fashrokka.*" I'm scared.

Miriam pats her daughter's back. "God is with you. He will guide you."

Mackie is soft and sympathetic, but maintains a gentle level of pressure. "Everything you tell me might help us find Elsie."

The girl turns to look at her, wipes her face with her sleeve. "Elsie was scared," she whispers.

"I know, sweetie. You're doing a good job." Mackie reaches out and squeezes the girl's hand. "What happened after the man came into the kitchen?"

"We ran out the back door."

"Did the man follow?"

"*Ja.*"

"What happened next?"

"I don't know. I just ran."

"Did he say anything?"

Her brows furrow and she takes a moment to think about it. "He said, '*Sie is meiner.*'"

It's the first time I've heard the words. I stare at the girl, wondering if she got it right, but there was no hesitation in her voice.

Mackie looks at me for translation, raises her brows.

"It means 'She's mine,'" I tell her.

"You're a very brave little girl." Mackie reaches out and pats the girl's hand. "Just a few more questions and we're all done, okay?"

Over the next twenty minutes, Mackie covers every conceivable question with the child. Some the girl answers readily; others she veers away from or curls inward. But Mackie is a highly skilled juvenile interrogator. She has sharp instincts, knowing when to push, when to back off, and she has patience. There's no doubt Mackenzie Upshaw is very good at what she does. Is it enough?

When we're finished, I thank the parents and then Mackie and I walk to the Tahoe where Tomasetti is waiting.

"I feel confident that child told us everything she can recall at this time," Mackie says with a sigh. "It's possible she'll remember new details over the next few days. But I think we got most of it."

"Anything new?" Tomasetti asks.

I nod. "When Mackie asked Annie if the man said anything, she responded with, '*Sie is meiner,*' which basically means 'She's mine.' It's an odd thing for an attacker to say."

Tomasetti grimaces. "As if he feels somehow . . . entitled to her."

Mackie shrugs. "Or he's mentally unhinged. Confused."

"Do you think she's reliable?" he asks.

"I do," Mackie replies. "I believe she was truthful. I think her answers were unembellished. When she didn't know the answer to something, she said so."

"Do you think she's credible enough for us to get a facial composite?" Tomasetti asks.

"I think it's worth a shot."

"I'll get permission from the parents." I look at Tomasetti. "It would be helpful if the composite artist can come here to the house."

"I'll get it done," he says.

I'm still pondering the order of the events that led up to the attack. "Was the killer waiting for them? Was he familiar with Mary's routine?" I say, thinking aloud. "Or was this a crime of opportunity? Did they surprise him? And he panicked?"

Tomasetti watches me closely, nods. "And who was his target? Was this about Mary Yoder? Or was it about Elsie?"

Mackie chimes in. "Most child predators are opportunists. They wait or they stalk; they see a kid alone or one that's in a vulnerable situation, and they move in, either through deceit—the do-you-want-to-see-my-puppy approach—or force."

"The violence of the attack on Yoder is significant," Tomasetti says.

"That degree of savagery indicates a profound level of passion," I say. "Hatred or rage or both."

"He knew her," Mackie says.

"Unless he was focused on the girl and Yoder got in the way," Tomasetti says. "Maybe she tried to stop him, and things went south."

We take a moment, digesting everything that's been said.

I glance at my watch. "I'm going to talk to the Helmuths, find out who Mary Yoder was close to."

"I'll work on getting a composite artist down here." Tomasetti glances at his watch. "Probably first thing in the morning."

Mackie extends her hand to me. "I'll email you a transcript of our interview with Annie as soon as I get it transcribed."

We part ways and I head back into the house. I find Ivan and Miriam and five of their children in the kitchen. Ivan has put on his coat and boots. He's going to do the only thing he can: search for his child, though by now he's realized the effort will be fruitless. I can tell by his expression he can't bear to sit inside and do nothing. Miriam is sitting at the table, her face in her hands, an untouched mug of coffee on the table in front of her. Two of the children have fixed bowls of cereal. They're silent and subdued, knowing that tragedy has invaded their safe and protected home. Both parents look frazzled and exhausted and utterly miserable.

I pull a prepaid cell phone from my pocket and hand it to Ivan. The Amish man doesn't take it. "We do not need a phone," he says. "All we need is our daughter."

"Take it," I say firmly. "If there's an emergency and you need to talk to me quickly."

When he doesn't accept the phone, I go to the counter and set it down next to the sink. "Keep it handy," I tell them.

The Amish woman looks away, but not before I see the assent in her eyes.

"I'm going to look for her." Ivan Helmuth's gaze is defensive, defiant, as if he thinks I'm going to try to stop him. "She's out there somewhere."

I was only gone for a few minutes, but in that short span of time I've reclaimed my position as an outsider. I address both of them. "I know it's been a difficult day. I want you to know . . . I'm on your side. I'm—"

"Why hasn't anyone found her?" Miriam snaps.

"We're looking," I assure her.

"It's going to be cold tonight." She puts a hand over her mouth, tears streaming. "Elsie doesn't have a coat. She'll be cold. I can't bear to think of it."

The image of a shivering, frightened child, all alone—or with someone intent on harming her—tears me up inside. Makes me feel ineffective and powerless because I'm unable to prevent it. Time is like sand running between my fingers.

Rising abruptly, Miriam rushes from the room.

I look at Ivan. "I need to ask you about Mary Yoder."

"I'm finished with your questions. All this talking . . . it's not helping." He buttons his coat and strides to the door, but he doesn't leave. He stands there with his hand on the knob, breathing heavily, looking down at the floor. After a moment, he storms through without speaking.

I become aware of the children sitting at the table. Their spoons have fallen silent. Cereal going soggy. Five pairs of eyes pin me where I stand, expressions apprehensive and confused.

"Mamm says God will take care of Elsie," says a girl of about eight or nine.

"Grossmammi isn't coming back." The youngest girl closes her eyes and begins to cry.

A girl of ten or eleven puts her arm around her. "Shush now. Grossmammi's in heaven with God and all of us are going to be there with her one day."

"No one knows where Elsie is." The little boy speaks up for the first time. "Mr. Miller said someone stole her."

Realizing the conversation is about to go in a more speculative and dark direction, I move to refocus them. "What are your names?" I ask.

The question seems to startle them, but they come around quickly. The oldest girl straightens, sets her hands on the table in front of her. "I'm Irma."

I turn my attention to the child sitting next to her and raise my brows. "How about you?"

A girl with strawberry-blond hair and eyes the color of spring grass squirms beneath my stare. "I'm Becky and I'm seven."

I look from child to child; each mutters their name and age, polite but reluctant. Red-haired and freckled, Elam is eight. Gracie is nine and very pretty. At ten, Bonnie is thin and gangly, already taller than her older sister, and nearly as tall as her *mamm*.

"Luke and Annie are sleeping," Becky finishes as she shovels cereal into her mouth. She's the only one who has resumed eating.

"I'm Katie Burkholder, the chief of police," I tell them. "I want you to know we're doing everything we can to find your sister."

A shower of measured responses sound, but they're uttered with such softness I can barely make out the words. They don't believe me—the *Englischer*—I realize, and the reality of that bothers me more than I want to acknowledge.

Becky begins to cry. "I want Elsie to come home. She always comes to my room and kisses me good night. Sometimes she tickles my belly."

"I'll kiss you good night," Bonnie says. "But I'm not tickling your belly."

"Shush now." Irma sets her hand over Becky's. "We all miss her. It's like Mamm says. God will take care of her. And He will send her back to us."

Elam picks up his spoon, but he doesn't eat. Instead, his moss-green eyes slide from his sister to me. "What if you can't find her, Chief Katie?"

"I'll find her," I tell him.

"Mamm says Elsie was a gift," Becky says.

Bonnie's expression softens. "I've known that since the day Bishop Troyer brought her—" She cuts off the words. Her eyes skate away from mine and back to her cereal bowl. Quickly, she raises a spoonful of cereal to her mouth and begins to chew, staring straight ahead. I look around and notice Irma won't look at me.

It's an odd moment. I almost chalk it up to what has surely been a wearisome day. But in light of today's events, I'm curious what Bonnie had been about to say.

"What about the bishop?" I ask.

Bonnie swallows. "Nothing," she mumbles.

I wait, but she keeps her eyes on her bowl and won't meet my gaze.

Next to me, Irma and Becky exchange a look I can't quite decipher and I sense a strange rise of tension. What the hell?

After a moment, Irma pats her lap. "*Kumma do.*" Come here.

Clenching her spoon, Becky climbs onto Irma's lap, and with two spoons the girls begin to share the bowl of cereal. All the while something I can't quite articulate niggles at the back of my brain.

Miriam enters the kitchen, a girl's coat in her hands, and the moment is gone. She glances toward the door, realizes her husband has left, and lowers it to her side. She looks bereft for a moment, then turns her attention to the children, slips back into her *mamm* persona.

"What are all of you still doing up? Staying up past bedtime isn't going to help us find Elsie now, is it? You'll just be sleepy in the morning."

The Amish woman brings her hands together. "Come on now. Up to bed. All of you." She shakes her head with exaggerated admonition. "Eating breakfast at ten o'clock at night. My word."

Chairs scrape against the floor. Irma takes a final bite of cereal and then gathers their bowls, takes them to the sink. The others clamber to the door. The little boy goes to his *mamm* and throws his arms around her hips, lets his cheek sink into her skirts. "Night."

She sets her hand on his head. "You say a prayer for Grossmammi and Elsie," she says to all of them.

When the children are gone, Miriam goes to the nearest chair and collapses into it as if her legs are no longer strong enough to support her. She raises the coat to her face and breathes in deeply. "Smells like her," she whispers, then adds beneath her breath, "I know God always has a plan. For the life of me I can't figure out what it might be this time."

I pull out the chair across from her and sit. "We'll be searching through the night."

She raises her gaze to mine. Her eyes are tired, the energy behind them depleted. "I don't know what to do, Chief Burkholder. I keep . . . searching the house, going room to room like a crazy person. I go to her room and look in, thinking she'll be there."

I'm still pondering the odd moment with the children a few minutes ago. Something Bonnie said. I look at the Amish woman sitting across from me. "Are Elsie and Becky twins?" I ask. "They're both seven years old?"

"They're not twins." Miriam offers a wan smile. "The children came . . . quickly."

I wait a beat, my thoughts circling back to Mary Yoder. "Was your mother close to anyone in particular? Did she have a best friend? A confidante?"

"Mamm spent most of her time with us, here at home. She was always cooking or baking. But she was a social bird, too, and liked to visit with the widow down the road, Martha Hershberger." Miriam's brows furrow. "She was friendly with the bishop's wife, too. Sometimes the three of them would sew together after worship." She makes a sound that might've been intended as a laugh, but comes out like a sob. "I suspect they did more gossiping than sewing." The words are not unkind and followed by a wistful smile. "Those ladies could talk a blue moon."

I pull out my notebook and scribble the names. "Your *mamm* was a widow?"

Miriam nods. "Going on eight years now." She cocks her head, narrows her eyes on mine. "I don't see how Mamm's friends could have anything to do with what happened, Chief Burkholder."

"It's helpful to know the backgrounds of everyone involved. You never know when something from someone's past can come back to haunt them."

"We're *Amisch,* Chief Burkholder. We've no ghosts to speak of."

Over the course of my career in law enforcement I've heard a thousand variations of those words. Experience has taught me, they're rarely true, even among the Amish.

CHAPTER 6

Six hours missing

There were too many people around—police and Amish alike—for him to risk taking the road, so he cut through the field on foot and ran until he could go on no more. Ivan Helmuth couldn't remember the last time he'd cried. When he was fourteen and broke his leg after jumping from the hayloft and landing on the plow. When his datt *died. Now, alone and under cover of darkness, he fell to his knees and wept like the child he hadn't been for a long time. The tears were a loud, ugly ordeal but, dear God, he'd never felt such agony. He'd never been so frightened in his life.*

Sweet Elsie.

Please deliver her back to us.

He knew God always listened, but His ways were sometimes mysterious. Still, Ivan had always had his faith. It was his strength. The thing he could hold on to during times of trial. This was different. He prayed, of course, but the words didn't come easily. The old lie rang hollow in his voice and he couldn't help but wonder: Was he finally being punished for what he'd done?

Rising, Ivan trudged to the edge of the plowed field, which put him on the township road that would take him to the Troyer place. The bishop had come to them the moment he'd gotten word. He'd been at their farm most of the day. He'd prayed with them. Comforted them. But they hadn't had the chance to talk. Not privately. There'd been too many people around asking too many questions. Ivan needed to be alone with the bishop. He needed to show him the note.

He tugged the handkerchief from his pocket and took a minute to wipe the tears and snot from his face and beard. By the time he reached the house, he'd caught his breath, regained some semblance of control. There was no glow of lantern light inside. They were already in bed. It didn't matter. He went directly to the back door, knocked, and waited.

Around him, the night was restless. The wind ebbed and flowed through the trees. A cow bawled from its pen. In the distance, a lone coyote yipped.

Where are you, my sweet child? *he thought, and he fought another hot rush of tears, the ache that went all the way to his bones.*

He'd just knocked a second time, with urgency, when lantern light flickered in the window. He heard the shuffle of shoes. The door swung open. Bishop Troyer stood there, gripping the walker he used these days, still wearing his sleep shirt. His ancient face was gaunt in the light from the lantern he held, his eyes sunken and owlish and knowing. He'd been the Amish bishop since Ivan was a boy. As the leader of the congregation, he wielded his position with uncompromising authority.

Ivan didn't bother with a greeting. "We must talk," he said.

"You are alone?" Bishop Troyer asked in his old man's voice. "No one followed?"

"I'm alone."

The old man looked past him as if to make sure. "Kumma inseid." Come inside.

Glancing over his shoulder, Ivan Helmuth walked into the house. The two men went to the kitchen. The bishop set the lantern on the table and then lowered himself into the chair. Ivan reached into his pocket, fished out the letter. He knew it was only paper and pencil scratch, but it felt dirty in his hand. Evil. He didn't even want to touch it.

"You have news?" the bishop asked.

Ivan unfolded the note, set it on the table, and slid it over to the old man.

> Anyone who steals must certainly make restitution, but if they
> have nothing, they must be sold to pay for their theft.

Bishop Troyer took his time, seeming to read the note two or three times. Trying to make sense of it. But Ivan could tell by his expression he knew exactly what it was. What it meant.

"Exodus," the bishop said after a moment.

Ivan nodded. "Yes."

"When did you get it?"

"It was in the mailbox this morning." Ivan looked at the note. "At first, I didn't realize what it was. Some foolishness. But now . . ."

"Did anyone else see it?" the bishop asked.

"Miriam."

The old man stared at him, silent, his ancient eyes dark and troubled. "This is the work of the devil," he said.

"Ja." Ivan rubbed his fingers over his eyes. "Someone knows. About that night."

"Unmeeklich!" Impossible! Urgency rang hard in the bishop's voice. "No one has spoken of it. No one!"

The old man clung to the old tenacity, but Ivan saw through the veneer, thick and callused as it was. The truth of that terrified him anew. "All these years." He whispered the words, fighting tears. "I need the truth, Bishop. All of it."

CHAPTER 7

Seven hours missing

I'm behind the wheel and midway down the lane of the Helmuth farm when a set of headlights blind me. An unidentified vehicle barrels toward me at a high rate of speed. Black van. Ohio plates. The driver doesn't bother dimming bright headlights. Satellite dish on top. Media, I think. The driver makes no attempt to move over to let my vehicle by. When we're head-to-head, I cut the wheel, blocking him, and flip on my emergency lights.

Dust billows in the glare between our vehicles as I swing open the door. Grabbing my Maglite, I get out and approach the driver's side. Before I reach it the driver starts to back away, but I raise my hand, ordering him to stop.

It's a news van, a network out of Columbus. I reach the driver's side and the window slides down. I have my badge at the ready. "It's a courtesy in this town to dim your brights when you approach an oncoming vehicle," I say by way of greeting.

"Sorry, Officer," says the young man behind the wheel. He's about thirty years old, with shoulder-length brown hair, a barely-there goatee, and a tattoo of a feather on his neck. He's wearing a hoodie over a Hawaiian shirt and an expression that tells me he's anything but sorry. Next to him, a young woman with platinum-blond hair and dark roots leans over to get a look at me. She's wearing a green suit with a trench coat thrown over her lap.

"Our producer sent us out here to cover the murder and kidnapping," she says, irritated because I'm interfering with their mission.

"This is private property. Unless you have permission from the homeowners, you need to back up and leave." I motion toward the half dozen other media vehicles parked along the shoulder, wondering how they got through. "With the rest of the herd."

"Look, we're just doing our jobs. I know you are, too." The young man is trying to charm me. The antic isn't sincere, which only serves to annoy me.

I don't cut him any slack. "Back up your vehicle. Now. Or I will cite you. Do you understand?"

The woman leans forward and catches my gaze. "Any comment on the murder? Or the missing girl?"

"There will be a press release tomorrow." I point toward the mouth of the lane. "You're in the way so back it up now."

"Fine!" The man throws up his hands. "Jeez."

Before he can get the window up, I hear the woman hiss, "Bitch."

I'm smiling when I get back in the Explorer.

It's midnight when I pull into the gravel lane of the Troyer farm. Despite the hour, I'm not surprised to find the windows aglow with lantern light. The bishop may be getting up in years—last time I saw him he was using a walker—but neither age nor his purported arthritis has slowed him down. I pull up to the house, park next to the bishop's buggy, and start toward the door.

Gas hisses in the lamppost as I take the steps to the small porch.

The door stands open, but the screen is closed, which is odd. I knock, wait a full minute, and tap the wood jamb with my key fob.

"Bishop Troyer?" I call out. "It's Kate Burkholder!"

Another minute passes and I finally hear the floor creak. In the semidarkness, I see a woman's form approach. Freda Troyer shoves a lantern my way and glares at me through the screen. *"En hand foll funn geduld is veaht may vi en bushel funn der grips,"* she mutters in a crushed-gravel voice. A handful of patience is worth more than a bushel of brains.

The bishop's wife may be barely five feet tall and a scant hundred pounds, but the force of her persona adds both height and weight. She's wearing a dark gray dress, a black apron, and a white *kapp,* all of it draped with an oversized cardigan she's thrown over thin shoulders. Both she and the bishop are well into their eighties, but no one—Amish or English—treads on Freda Troyer without the risk of being dressed down—or swatted with the horse crop she's rumored to keep on her kitchen counter.

She's looking at me as if I'm some vermin that's wandered onto her porch from the barn. She's got a crease on her cheek and I suspect I woke her.

"This won't wait," I tell her. "You heard what happened to Mary Yoder?"

"Of course I heard." A shadow of anguish darkens her expression. *"Gottlos."* Ungodly. "You're here for the bishop?"

"Actually, I'm here to speak with you."

Her eyes narrow behind wire-rimmed glasses with thick lenses. "I reckon you ought to come in then."

The Troyer home is a hundred-year-old farmhouse that's typically Amish. Wood plank floors. A big kitchen with Formica countertops, a gas stove, and a propane refrigerator. The aromas of meat roasted earlier in the day, cardamom, and cinnamon lace the air. I take one of six chairs at a rectangular table covered with a red-checkered cloth. A lantern flickers in the center. Salt and pepper shakers in the shape of cats.

"Have you found the girl?" Freda Troyer asks as she shuffles to the stove, where a lone mug sits next to an ancient-looking teapot.

"No."

"Poor, sweet child." Making a sound of distress, she pulls out a second mug. "Would you like tea?"

"I can't stay." I watch her pour, anxious to get what I need and get back out there. "I understand you and Mary Yoder were friends."

"I've known Mary for years. She was a good friend. A good woman. Mother. Grandmother."

She carries her mug to the table and pulls out a chair. She lowers herself into it like a woman who feels every one of the eight decades she's been on this earth. "I can't believe she's gone."

"Can you think of anyone who might've wanted to harm her?" I ask. "Did she have any enemies? Any trouble in her life?"

She shakes her head. "Lord, no. Mary Yoder lived her life the way an Amish woman ought to, full of kindness and faith. She was humble and submitted to God."

"Did she ever mention having any problems with anyone?" I ask. "Any money disputes? Family issues? Disagreements with neighbors?"

"No."

"What about her husband?"

"Benjamin?" She looks at me as if she's surprised I'm aware of his existence. "He's been gone for years."

"What about Ivan and Miriam?"

"They're a good Amish family, Chief Burkholder. Not the kind of people who invite trouble into their lives."

"Any problems with the children?" I ask. "Elsie?"

"They're so young and well behaved. And that little Elsie is just the sweetest thing. That poor, precious child." Shaking her head, she looks down at her hands, folds them. "An *Englischer* did this?"

"I believe he may be Amish."

"Hard to believe. *Maulgrischt.*" Pretend Christian. She closes her eyes as if the words cause her physical pain. "I've been praying for them." She raises rheumy blue eyes to mine and for an instant, I see the pain, the burden of the things she hides behind a tetchy veneer, and for the first time I feel as if I've caught a glimpse of the real woman.

"Even him," she whispers. "*Da schlecht mann.*" The bad man.

"If you think of anything, will you let me know?"

"Of course I will."

"I'll see myself out." I'm midway to the door, everything that's been said running through my head, a fast-moving stream of troubled waters. I stop in the doorway and turn to her. "Mrs. Troyer?"

She raises her head, her eyes finding mine.

"When I was at the Helmuth place earlier, one of the children told me Bishop Troyer was there the day Elsie was born. Is that true?"

She dismisses the statement with a wave. "Those little ones are confused and missing their sister is all."

I wait, thinking she's going to say more. Instead, she raises her mug and takes a sip of tea.

Under normal circumstances, it would be far too late for me to be rousing citizens from bed to question them about their association with Mary Yoder or the Helmuth family. With a little girl missing—ostensibly in the hands of a killer—I don't have a choice.

I call Tomasetti as I make the turn onto Threadgill Creek Road. "Any luck with those impressions?" I ask.

"We got decent plaster on both the footwear and the tire tread," he replies. "Footwear has a waffle-type sole. Probably a men's work boot. Size thirteen."

"Big guy." In my mind's eye, I see Big Eddie standing next to his father. "Same size as Eddie Graber."

I tell him about the size-thirteen boot I saw in the mudroom of the Graber home. "Edward gave me permission to look around, which I did." I tell him about the fresh cut on Big Eddie's hand. "I don't like him for this but he has a history with the Helmuths. I want a warrant."

"I can have one within the hour. We'll confiscate the boots and pick him up." He pauses. "Where are you?"

"I'm talking with Mary Yoder's known associates."

"At midnight?"

"So sue me." Rain begins to patter the windshield, so I flip on my wipers. "What about you?"

"I'm still at the Schattenbaum place. CSU is about to wrap it up."

I hear voices in the background, telling me the place is still bustling, that he's busy, and I miss him. "I'll do my best to make it home tonight."

"Me, too."

I start to say something else, but he hangs up. Smiling, I drop my cell back into my pocket.

Martha Hershberger lives in a mobile home a few miles from the Helmuth place. As I pull into the driveway, I don't see any lights on inside. I hesitate, but I hear that incessant tick of the clock that's taken up residence in my brain since Elsie Helmuth disappeared, and I shut down the engine. Grabbing my Maglite, I throw open the door and hightail it to the covered wood porch.

Rain and wind lash me as I go up the steps. I've just knocked when

I feel something brush against my ankle. Startled, I shift the beam of my flashlight, see a couple of cats come out of a small doghouse.

I'm in the process of shooing them back inside when the door to the mobile home opens.

"What are you doing to my cats?" comes a coarse voice in *Deitsch*.

I rise, brush cat fur from my hands onto my trousers, and pluck my badge from my pocket. "Martha Hershberger?"

She eyes me up and down. "What is it?"

Holding the badge so she can see it in the beam of my flashlight, I introduce myself. "I'm the police chief of Painters Mill. I need to—"

"Do you have any idea what time it is?"

I guess Martha Hershberger to be in her mid-to-late seventies. She's wearing a floor-length flannel sleeping gown with white socks. A blue scarf covers her hair, a silver mane that reaches the midpoint of her back.

Her question tells me she probably doesn't know about Mary Yoder or Elsie Helmuth. "I need to talk to you about Mary Yoder."

She cocks her head and for the first time she looks worried. "Has something happened to Mary?"

"She was killed earlier today," I tell her.

"*What?* Mary? Killed?" Pressing her hand to her mouth, she staggers back. "Oh my goodness. *Mary.*"

The interior of the trailer is dark, so I shine my beam inside, at the very least to keep her from tripping over the cat that's found its way in. The woman stares at me, looking aghast.

"May I come in?" I ask. "I'd like to ask you a few questions."

"Of course." She motions me in, grappling for her composure. "What happened to Mary?" Bending, she turns on a lamp. "Someone hit her buggy? People and their cars," she spits. "Always in a hurry." She shakes her head. "Poor Mary."

Dim light illuminates a small, cluttered room that smells of nail polish and last night's TV dinner. That's when it strikes me she's either left the Amish way or she's not big on all those rules. . . .

"She was murdered," I reply, watching her.

The only thing that comes back at me is complete and utter shock. "Murdered? Oh dear Lord. Mary? Who would—I just can't believe it."

"You were close?" I ask.

She raises her gaze to mine. "I knew her most of my life. She was one of the few who stuck with me after I became Mennonite. I thought the world of her. Loved her like a sister. Oh, poor dear Mary." The grief etched into her every feature intensifies. "How is her family coping?"

I tell her about the missing girl.

"Oh, that just makes me sick. Sick to my bones. Such a sweet child. Who does something like that?"

Neither of us has the answer, so we fall silent. For the span of a few heartbeats the only sound comes from the rain pounding the roof. The *tink!* of water dripping into a pan somewhere down the hall.

After a moment, she seems to shake off the shock that's held her frozen, and she motions toward the kitchen. "You want some coffee?"

"That would be great. Thanks."

I trail her to a tiny, jumbled kitchen. Off-white Formica counters. Flowered curtains. Harvest-gold refrigerator and stove. Every square inch of the countertop surface is strewn with miscellaneous kitchen items. I see bags of cookies and chips. Cookbooks. Coffee cans. Canning jars.

"Sorry about all the junk." She opens a can of Folgers with hands that aren't quite steady and scoops grounds into a stovetop percolator. She's distracted, still trying to come to terms with the loss of her friend.

There's a collage of photos on the wall. Martha Hershberger with four teenage girls. Mennonite, judging from the style of their head coverings. Granddaughters. Heads thrown back in laughter. Happier times. The sight of the photo makes me think about familial connections. The power of those connections. The lengths to which people will go to protect their own.

I wait while she clears the surface of a small bistro table for two and we sit. The coffee is weak, but it's hot and I'm desperate for caffeine, so I drink.

Over the next ten minutes, I go over the same questions I covered with Freda Troyer. Martha Hershberger answers them in much the same way. Everyone loved Mary. She had no enemies. No problems with her family or anyone else.

"How did you meet her?" I ask.

"I've known the Helmuths for years. Back when I was still Amish, we were in the same church district." Her laugh is a sad sound. "I was a midwife, you know, delivered their babies."

I sip coffee. "So you delivered Elsie."

The woman's brows snap together. "Now that you mention it, I think she's the only one I *didn't* deliver."

An odd ping sounds inside my head. "You delivered all their children except for Elsie?"

"Yes."

I nod, turning the information over in my brain. "Is there a reason why you didn't deliver Elsie?"

"Miriam told me the baby came quickly. There was no time."

I finish the last of the coffee. "Did Mary Yoder have any other children?"

"She has a daughter in Indiana, I think."

"What about sisters? Brothers? Extended family?"

"I do recall her mentioning a sister." The Mennonite woman assumes a thoughtful countenance. "Younger, I think. They were close once, but had some sort of falling-out."

I flip the page on my notebook, go to a fresh page. "Do you remember her name?"

"Mary hardly ever mentioned her." She's trying to remember. "Started with an M. Marsha. Marie. Marlene, I think."

"Last name?"

Martha shakes her head. "I don't know."

"Did she live around here?"

"Down south somewhere. I couldn't say for sure. I don't even know if she's still alive. Mary didn't talk about her much and I'm not one to pry."

I nod, disappointed because I'd been hoping for more. For something. Most Amish have large, extended families. Evidently, that wasn't the case with Mary Yoder.

I pluck my card from my pocket and slide it across the table to her. "If you think of anything else, will you get in touch with me?"

"Of course I will."

I rise and she takes me through the living room. I open the door, look down to see one of the cats slip inside. I'm turning up the collar of my jacket when I think of one more question. "Mrs. Hershberger, do you know who delivered Elsie?"

"I'm not rightly sure." The woman bends to pick up the cat, runs her hand over its head. "Miriam never said. They had so many children. I never thought to ask."

CHAPTER 8

Fourteen hours missing

It's seven A.M. by the time I make it home, the sun not yet above the treetops to the east. There's nothing I'd like more than to fall into bed for a few hours of uninterrupted sleep. But with Elsie Helmuth missing and a murderer on the loose, I'm going to have to settle for a shower and food. I park next to Tomasetti's Tahoe and head inside.

The house smells of coffee and toast when I walk into my big farmhouse kitchen. The air is warm, and for the first time the full weight of exhaustion presses down on me. A mug of coffee sits untouched next to a plate scattered with crumbs. Tomasetti's laptop is open and humming. I hear the TV in the living room, tuned to cable news.

He appears in the doorway between the kitchen and the living room, in sweatpants and an ancient Cleveland Division of Police T-shirt. He's carrying a towel; his hair is wet.

"I guess that explains why you didn't answer my call," I say by way of greeting.

"They haven't invented showerproof phones yet."

I nod, trying to settle into a more domestic frame of mind, not succeeding. "Did your forensic guys come up with anything?"

"First things first." He crosses to me, eyes on mine. I smell soap and aftershave as he puts his arms around me, presses a kiss to my mouth.

"You get any sleep?" he asks.

"I just need a shower."

"Uh-huh." He shifts me to arm's length and tilts his head. "Got time for breakfast?"

"Give me ten minutes."

Later, over scrambled eggs and toast, he updates me on everything he's learned since we last spoke. "Sheriff Rasmussen picked up Eddie Graber around one A.M., talked to him for a few hours, and drove him home." He shakes his head. "We're running a comp on the boot tread, but Rasmussen doesn't think he's our guy."

I nod. "Was the lab able to type the blood found in the yard of the Schattenbaum house?"

He grimaces and I know even before he speaks that the news isn't good. "Same as the girls."

I wince inwardly, knowing what that means: that the girl could have been stabbed or cut—or worse.

"We don't have DNA back yet, but the lab matched the type. The kid had a tonsillectomy a couple years ago. She's O-negative—"

"But it's possible the blood belongs to the killer."

"Maybe." He says it for my benefit; he doesn't believe it. "That's not a common blood type. Look, we're running DNA now, but the lab is backed up. It's going to take a few days. I got some things shuffled around, put some other cases on the back burner, so we've got priority."

"What about the footwear impressions?" I ask. "The size-thirteen work boots? Any unique marks on the sole? Leads on manufacturer or retailer?"

"We got tread, but not enough detail to pick up unique marks."

I nod, disappointed, trying not to think about the girl, possibly injured and bleeding, and I feel overwhelmed by all the things I don't know and the sheer volume of things I need to do.

We eat in silence. When I walked into the house twenty minutes ago I wasn't hungry. Now I'm starving and I eat with relish. After the shower and a clean uniform, I feel human again, my mind fresh. As I down my second cup of coffee, my thoughts take me through the conversations I had overnight. The family dynamics. The one exchange that keeps coming back to me is the odd commentary between the Helmuth children, Becky and Bonnie, about their missing sister.

Mamm says Elsie was a gift.

I've known that since the day Bishop Troyer brought her—

When I asked them to clarify, they clammed up. Why? Later, when I asked the bishop's wife if he was there the day Elsie was born, she told me he was not. It's a small discrepancy, but it bothers me enough so that I'm thinking about it. And what about Elsie being the only baby in the family that Martha Hershberger didn't deliver?

"You're thinking about something awfully hard," Tomasetti says as he gathers dishes and takes them to the sink.

"Sorry," I say. "I'm probably not very good company this morning."

"Anything you want to share?"

I set down my mug, give him my full attention, the words looping in my head, a record skip I can't seem to stop. "I think there's something going on with the Helmuth family."

He sips coffee, looking at me over the rim. "The parents?"

I tell him about the girls' comments. "Bonnie, who's ten, cut off midsentence. It was as if she knew she'd broached a subject she wasn't supposed to discuss."

"You think the parents are withholding information?"

"I think they're not telling us something that may or may not be relevant to the case. I don't know what it is or why they'd keep secrets when their child is missing. But those kids aren't very good liars and it was quite an odd exchange."

It's the first time I've said the words aloud. As dubious as they sound, it strengthens my belief that there's something amiss.

I tell Tomasetti about my conversations with Miriam Helmuth and, later, with the midwife, Martha Hershberger.

"She delivered all of Miriam's babies, except for Elsie."

"So what aren't they telling you?" Tomasetti asks.

Between the caffeine, the food, and the shower, my brain has clicked back into place. I look at him, thinking aloud now. "The Helmuths have eight children."

"That's not unusual for an Amish family, though, right?"

"Two of the girls are seven years old."

"Twins?"

I shake my head. "Miriam says no."

"Could be Irish twins. It's technically possible."

My mind is already racing ahead. "Tomasetti, I took the physical description of Elsie. Brown hair. Brown eyes."

"Okay."

"I didn't think much about it at the time. But when I walked in to the Helmuth house and got a good look at the other children . . . Tomasetti, they're strawberry blond and green-eyed. I mean, not all kids look like their parents or their siblings, right? But in light of some of the other things that have been said . . ." I shrug. "There's something there."

I pick up my cell, hit the button for the station, aware that he's watching me with an expression that's part skeptical and part perplexed.

Mona picks up on the first ring. "Hey, Chief."

"Get me vital statistics on the Helmuth children," I say. "Birth dates. Place of birth."

"All of them?"

"All eight." I rattle off the names from memory. "I need it yester-day."

"Warp factor one."

"Who's on duty this morning?" I ask, pulling out my notebook.

"Everyone. I mean, in light of the missing kid . . ."

"I'm heading that way. Briefing in my office in an hour."

"I'll let everyone know."

I glance down at my notebook, flip the page. "Mona, one more thing. See if you can find anything on Mary Yoder's sister. First name is Marlene. I think she lives south of here. No city."

"You got it."

I end the call to find Tomasetti's eyes still on me. A look I'm all too familiar with. "You think I'm barking up the wrong tree," I say.

"I think if those two seven-year-old siblings were born any closer than nine months apart, the parents have some explaining to do."

We fall silent. I see the wheels of his mind working out the time-line, putting all those messy details into some order that makes sense in terms of the crime.

"When we talked to the witness child, Annie, do you remember what she told us the man who took Elsie said?" I ask.

He nods. "'She's mine.'"

"I didn't think of the statement in terms of a literal meaning," I tell him. "Deranged individuals say all sorts of crazy things that don't make sense." I shrug. "Maybe I should have. Maybe it means something."

"Like what?"

"What if, for whatever reason, this male subject *thinks* that girl is . . . his."

"I think there's a higher probability that the son of a bitch is a nut-case."

"I know that. I do. Still, I'm going to do some poking around." I can tell by his expression he doesn't concur. It's not the first time we've disagreed on a case. Fortunately, both of us are confident enough in our respective positions, with our experience and perspectives, to admit it when we get it wrong.

"In the interim," he says, rising, "I'm going to round up that composite artist. She's in Parma, so give me a couple hours."

I get to my feet, pick up my duty belt from the table, buckle it around my hips. "Call me and I'll meet you at the Helmuths'."

"You got it." Leaning close, he kisses me. "Don't spend too much time looking for ghosts."

"Wouldn't dream of it," I tell him, and start toward the door.

One of the pitfalls of being a cop—or one of the advantages, if you're a glass-half-full sort—is that you look at the things people say with a healthy dose of skepticism. You look at the things they *don't* say with suspicion. It's not that you think everyone is a liar; you just happen to know from experience individuals lie with more frequency than most people realize, especially in times of crisis. My general rule of thumb is that if it doesn't make sense or if conflicting information begins to pile up, there's a problem. At the very least it's worth a second look.

I'm thinking about Miriam Helmuth and potential motives for lying when I enter the station. Mona Kurtz, who still spends most of her time working dispatch, stands at her station, speaking into the headset, waving a stack of pink message slips at me. She's still wearing her uniform. Like me, she stayed up all night. Unlike me, she looks fresh and ready to tackle her day. Tugging the slips from her hand, I make tracks toward my office and unlock the door.

I've just booted up my laptop when Mona taps on the jamb. "Chief?"

"Morning," I say as I log in. "Any luck with the stats on the Helmuth children?"

She takes the visitor chair adjacent to my desk. "I talked to the clerk at the Holmes County General Health District. She's going to courier birth certificates and related info for the Helmuth children by day's end." She glances down at the sheet of paper in her hand. "Seven of the Helmuth children were delivered by a local midwife, Martha Hershberger. The midwife followed protocol and filed for birth certificates shortly after birth."

My hand freezes on the keyboard and I give her my full attention. "Is the remaining child Elsie Helmuth?"

Her eyes flash interest. "Get this: There's no birth certificate on file for Elsie. No social security number. No paperwork or documentation was ever filed."

"Well that's interesting as hell."

The majority of Amish women use midwives to deliver their babies at home. In the state of Ohio, most midwives are certified and, as a matter of course, file the appropriate paperwork with the local registrar for birth certificates and social security numbers. Some of the Old Order and Swartzentruber Amish don't bother with registering their newborns for a birth certificate, and sometimes not even a social security number. Those are the babies that sometimes fall through the cracks when it comes time for a first job or even a driver's license during *Rumspringa*—the period in a teen's life before they're baptized, when they have the freedom to break all those Amish rules without too much in terms of repercussions. Those are the ones who have to go through the process of obtaining proper identification as young adults.

The Helmuths are neither Swartzentruber nor Old Order. So why doesn't Elsie Helmuth have a birth certificate?

"Anything on Marlene, the sister?"

"Still looking."

"Chief?"

I glance up to see my first-shift dispatcher, Lois Monroe, standing in the doorway. "Everyone's in the war room," she tells me.

"Be right there."

Lois rushes back to reception, and I turn my attention to Mona. "Have you had any sleep?"

"With everything that's going on . . ."

I've been seeking a third-shift dispatcher for several weeks now. Unfortunately, none of the candidates have been right. "If it's any consolation, you're proving to be a hard woman to replace."

Rising, she grins and heads out the door.

A few minutes later, I'm in the "war room," which is basically a storage room turned meeting room. I'm standing at the half podium Lois has set up on a folding table. She's taped a map of Holmes County to the dry-erase board behind me, with Painters Mill circled in red. A red X demarks the Helmuth farm. A second X marks the Schattenbaum place.

I look out at my team and I feel the part of me that's stressed out and exhausted settle. A missing endangered juvenile is a worst-case scenario for any police department. But I know my officers, and I've no doubt they'll put in the hours and do whatever it takes to find her.

"I appreciate everyone working double shifts." I glance down at my notes, but I don't need them. I outline the basic facts of both cases and where we are in terms of the investigation.

I look at Lois, who's standing in the doorway so she can attend the meeting and still hear the phones. "You get the stats and description of Elsie Helmuth typed up?"

"Right here, Chief."

Mona jumps up from her chair, takes the short stack from her, and passes a single sheet to everyone in the room.

"Since the girl is Amish, we do not have a photo." I glance at my notebook. "We believe the suspect is a white male. Likely Amish. Typical Amish garb. Thirty-five to fifty years old. Brown hair. Size-thirteen shoe, which would likely put him at six two or six three, give or take. Footwear impression indicates he likely wore a work boot with a waffle-type sole. We suspect he may be using a vehicle for transportation."

"Covers a lot of ground," Glock says beneath his breath.

I nod. "None of that is set in stone." I point at the nearest officer sitting to my right. "Reports. Pickles."

Roland "Pickles" Shumaker is seventy-five years old, but you'd never know his age by looking at him—or talking to him. His hair—right down to his neat little goatee—is colored a rich hue of mahogany with no gray in sight. His uniform is creased, his trademark Lucchese boots buffed to a burnished patina. He went part-time a few years ago and spends most mornings and afternoons working the crosswalk at the elementary school.

Pickles is a cop through and through; he's paid his dues and has earned the respect of every person in the room. During the late 1980s he worked undercover narcotics and was instrumental in procuring one of the biggest drug busts in the history of Holmes County.

This morning, he's looking at me with the attitude of a man half his age and the cockiness of a twenty-year-old rookie. "T.J. and I hit every house, every farm, within a five-mile radius of the Schattenbaum place, Chief. That's nine homes. Four Amish. Five non-Amish. We talked to multiple individuals inside each home. Aside from Dick Howard, no one saw shit."

I address T.J. and Pickles. "Before you guys call it a day, I want you to talk to them again. Expand your canvass to ten miles. Hit a few more farms out that way."

"Yes, ma'am."

I look at my female officer. "Mona."

She straightens, all business. "Chief."

"There's a service station two miles down the road from the intersection of Goat Head Road and CR 14. Stop in on your way home and see if they have security cameras. If they do, check the angle, see if it captures the street. If it does, get a copy of the last seventy-two hours."

"I'm on it," she says.

I go to the next man. "Glock."

Rupert "Glock" Maddox is the first African American to grace the ranks of the Painters Mill PD, and he's my most solid officer. With two tours in Afghanistan on his résumé, a calm demeanor, and a boatload of common sense, he's my go-to guy when I need a job done right. Last I heard, his wife, LaShonda, is due any day now with their third child.

"Skid and I cleared the outbuildings at the Schattenbaum place. Didn't look like anyone had been in those old barns for years. No footprints. No disturbed dust. Nothing. CSI with BCI looked around as well and concurred." He glances at his notes. "We set up a grid of the back pasture, drafted a couple of deputies from County, walked it twice, but there was nothing there."

"Anyone go out there with dogs?" I ask.

"County did," he tells me. "No hit in the back of the property, but the dogs *did* hit on a scent in the front, near where you found the tread marks and blood. BCI jumped on it. Took those plasters. Sent blood samples to the lab. County also went over the area with a drone but got nothing."

"I found out this morning that the blood is the same type as the little girl's," I tell them. "We're still waiting for DNA."

A stir goes around the room. Blood from a victim is never good news.

"Glock," I say, "where did the dogs lose the scent?"

"At the road, a few feet from where you spotted those tire tracks."

Which means our subject may have put the girl in his vehicle and fled the scene. The thought makes me sick to my stomach.

I look at Skid. "Get with the IT guy who does the website for our department. Tell him to create another page, something prominent, and put out a call for the public's assistance. Any motorist or pedestrian who was in the area of the Schattenbaum farm yesterday between noon and five P.M., ask them to call. Tell them they can remain anonymous. Use our main switchboard nonemergency number. Or they can use the website to give us any information. There's a five-hundred-dollar reward for information that leads to an arrest and conviction."

Skid nods, thumbing notes into his cell. "You got it."

I look out at my small team of officers. "Glock and I talked to RSOs," I tell them, referring to registered sex offenders, and I turn my attention back to Glock. "I want you and Skid to hit it again today. Talk to the same guys, and then expand the area." I turn to the map and indicate a larger circle. "Talk to all RSOs within a twenty-mile radius."

Glock gives me a two-finger salute. "Yes, ma'am."

I look at T.J., then shift my attention back to Mona. "At some point this morning, you two need to go home and get a few hours' sleep."

"No problem," T.J. mutters.

I consider filling them in on the mystery surrounding Elsie Helmuth's birth certificate, but since I don't have a viable theory yet and nothing has been substantiated, I opt not to muddy the waters. "I'll be speaking with the Helmuths again this morning. My cell is on day and night. Mandatory OT until we find that girl or catch this son of a bitch."

CHAPTER 9

Seventeen hours missing

On the drive to the Helmuth farm, I pass several men on horseback, Amish men and boys who've saddled their buggy horses to search the ditches and culverts and wooded areas near the Schattenbaum place. Men clad in camouflage jackets ride ATVs through open fields and the floodplain that parallels Painters Creek, searching rugged terrain not easily accessed by vehicle or on foot. All of these volunteers have likely been at it since first light. Despite the cold block of dread that's taken up residence in my gut, it warms me to see that the community—Amish and English alike—has come out in force to find a missing little girl.

I've just pulled into the Helmuth lane when my cell erupts. I glance at the display: HOLMES CNTY CORONER.

I take a breath and brace. "Hi, Doc."

"I'm about to start the autopsy on Mary Yoder."

"Anything preliminary you can tell me?"

"The forensic pathologist took nail scrapings. Collected hair. Took swabs. We sent everything to the BCI lab. With regard to her injuries and resulting death, the only thing I can tell you at this time is that she was stabbed twenty-two times. Probably with a large knife. She sustained many defensive wounds."

"She fought back."

"As much as she could."

"Cause and manner of death?"

"I suspect she died from blood loss. That's not official yet." He sighs. "There's no doubt it's a homicide. I'll be able to answer those questions definitively once I get her on the table."

"I'd like to be there." I look toward the back door of the house, where three Amish women carrying grocery bags stare in my direction. "Can you give me half an hour?"

"She's not going anywhere."

The Amish women on the back porch don't speak to me as I ascend the steps; they move silently aside as I enter the house. I find Miriam Helmuth sitting at the kitchen table, head bowed, hands clasped. Silently praying.

Another Amish woman stands at the sink with her back to us, washing dishes. I stand just inside the doorway for a full minute, waiting for Miriam to finish her prayer, getting my words in order. When she finally raises her head, her eyes jump with anticipation.

"You bring news of Elsie?" she asks in a voice that's gone hoarse.

I'm loath to crush her hope, but as is usually the case, I don't have a choice. "No news," I say.

She presses a tattered tissue to her nose and looks down at the tabletop. "What are you doing here, then?"

"Miriam." I go to the table, lower myself to the chair next to her. "I know this is difficult, but I need to ask you a few more questions."

She stares at me for the span of several seconds. Then her face screws up. "I just want her back," she whispers. "Safe and sound. That's all."

I give her a moment, and then I ask, "Do you have a birth certificate for Elsie?"

She stiffens, raises her gaze to mine. "Why would you ask such a thing when a child is missing? Some silly piece of paper isn't going to help you find her, is it?"

"It's part of the process." The words aren't exactly true. But I don't want her to become suspicious of me or my questions at this juncture.

Too late, a little voice whispers.

"I don't have a birth certificate for Elsie," she tells me. "We were going to file the paperwork. You know, the home birth document for the government. But . . . we just haven't gotten around to it yet."

"Where she was born?" I ask.

Her eyes meet mine, misery boiling in their depths. But there's something else there, too. A tangle of uncertainty, fear, and resentment. "Here. At the house."

"You used a midwife?"

"I would have." She looks down at her hands again. "Elsie came fast. There was no time. Mamm was here. She helped me through."

"Which midwife were you going to use?"

"The one I used with the other children. Martha Hershberger."

"Did you get prenatal care with Elsie?"

"These questions are not going to help you find my girl." Impatience flares in her voice.

"Mrs. Helmuth." I say her name firmly, but gently. "I'm not the enemy here. Please. I want to bring her home, too. If there's something you haven't told me—"

"I've told you everything."

I give her a moment to calm down before moving on to my next question. "How well do you know your aunt? Mary's sister, Marlene?"

The woman stares at me as if I've asked her about the weather or some recipe that has nothing whatsoever to do with the crisis at hand. "Aunt Marlene passed away years ago. I don't see what she has to do with any of this."

"Why don't you let me decide what's relevant and what's not?" I say firmly.

She seems to sink more deeply into the chair, looks down at her hands in her lap. "I met Marlene once or twice when I was a girl. She was . . . a delicate thing. Didn't come around much."

"Delicate?" I ask. "You mean physically?"

"That was my general impression."

"Did Marlene have kids?"

"Not that I know of."

"What was your aunt's last name?"

"Her maiden name was Byler, of course, same as Mamm's. If she ever got married . . ." She shrugs. "I wouldn't know."

"Do you have any idea where she used to live?"

"I don't know. I told you. *I don't know!*" She struggles to her feet, staggers, grabs hold of the table.

I reach out to steady her, wondering if she's eaten or slept, but she draws her arm away. "If you really want to find my little girl, Kate Burkholder, I suggest you stop asking all these foolish questions and get out there and look for her."

I call Lois on the way to Pomerene Hospital. "I need you to dig up everything you can find on every member of the Helmuth family. There may not be much out there, since they're Amish. But . . . I need for you to dig around a little, see if anything pops."

"Can you give a hint what I'm looking for?"

"Anything to do with children. Deaths in the family. Marriages. Divorces." I think about that a moment. "I've got Mona looking at Miriam's sister, Marlene. She's deceased, but I have a last name: Byler. Tell Mona to take look, see if there's anything out there. Lois, I want you to take a look at the midwife, Martha Hershberger, too. Check to see if Hershberger has any problems with her certifications."

"I'll get right on it." She pauses. "Oh, before I forget, that courier package from Holmes County General Health District came for you."

Copies of the birth certificates. "Put it on my desk, will you?"

"You got it."

I end the call as I slide into a parking space near the Emergency entrance. I'm distracted, thinking about Miriam Helmuth as I go through the double glass doors and take the elevator to the basement. *What the hell aren't you telling me?* I simply can't fathom why a mother would withhold information from the police when her little girl is missing and in danger. What secret is worth jeopardizing the life of your child?

The question pounds at my brain as I enter the reception area of the morgue.

"Hi, Chief."

I look up to see Doc Coblentz's administrative assistant rise to greet me. "Hey, Carmen."

"I saw the Amber alert on my phone." She extends her hand and we shake. "Any luck?"

"We're pulling out all the stops." I let my eyes slide toward the doors that will take me to the medical side of the morgue. "He in there?"

"He's waiting for you."

I barely notice the smell of formalin that rides the air as I pass through the doors. The autopsy room is ahead. The niche where the biohazard protective gear is stored is to my right. Left is Doc Coblentz's glassed-in office. The mini blinds facing the hall are open. Inside, Doc and a second man clad in royal-blue scrubs are staring at the laptop on his desk.

"Kate."

Doc Coblentz is a corpulent man, about my height, with a balding pate and bushy salt-and-pepper brows. This morning, he's wearing his usual hunter-green scrubs with high-end sneakers and a blue apron that ties in the back.

He looks at me a little too closely as he offers his hand for a shake. "Looking a little worse for wear this morning," he tells me.

I frown, hoping it looks more good-natured than it feels. "Long night," I murmur. "Sorry I'm late."

The other man in his office rises. He's African American, with a tall frame, thinning hair the color of steel wool, and keen, intelligent eyes.

"This is Dr. Larry Blake," the coroner says. "He's the deputy medical examiner for Cuyahoga County and specializes in forensic pathology."

Blake and I shake. His grip is firm, but not crushing. He smiles easily and I wonder how it is that these men can spend so much time with the dead yet remain upbeat and optimistic.

"I'm here at the behest of BCI," Dr. Blake tells me. "I understand you've got a missing child on your hands."

I give him a condensed version of the case. "I'm hoping we'll learn something today that will help us find her."

Doc Coblentz motions toward the alcove where the biohazard supplies are stored. "In that case, let's get started."

The three of us leave his office and walk to the alcove where Carmen has laid out individually wrapped protective gear. A paper apron for me. Face mask. Shoe covers. Hair cap. Disposable gloves. Quickly,

I tear open the packages and gear up. The men don't wait for me. I watch them saunter down the narrow hall and go through the double doors that lead to the autopsy room. Once I'm dressed, I draw a couple of deep breaths and follow.

No matter how many times I make this pilgrimage, no matter how many times I assure myself I'm prepared, the dead are quick to prove me wrong. The air thickens and cools, melding with a darker odor that brings the familiar quiver to my stomach. I think about Elsie and I pray to God I don't have to walk this hall again because her little body is laid out on a gurney.

I've seen many a tough guy cut down to size because he can't bear to look at the body of a child and not think of his own. It's the people who can keep all that outrage and disgust under lock and key that I don't quite trust.

The room is so cold, I half expect to see a coating of frost on the gray subway-tiled walls. I take in the rest of the details while trying not to look too closely. Stark fluorescent lights. Stainless-steel counters cluttered with white plastic containers, gleaming instruments lined up on trays, dual sinks with tall, arcing faucets, and a scale that hangs down, ready to weigh things I don't want to contemplate.

Ignoring all of it, trying hard to keep a handle on my quivering stomach, I follow the men to the gurney where I see a body draped with a pale blue sheet. Doc Coblentz pulls on a headset with a small mike and recites the date and time, nine-digit case number, the names of everyone present, including his own, and the name of the deceased.

He pulls the cover down to her pubis. "Sixty-year-old female Caucasian. One hundred and fifty-three pounds. Five feet, four inches in height."

Mary Yoder's body is mature, etched with years and the scars of life. I see a round, slack face. A nose covered with freckles. Eyes at half mast. Long brown hair streaked with silver. I see flesh that rarely saw the sun. But her hands, face, and neck are tanned. I didn't know Mary Yoder, but I've no doubt she was a modest woman. She wouldn't want anyone to see her like this, and I find myself silently assuring her that it will be over soon. That I will do everything in my power to find the person responsible. That I will bring her granddaughter home.

I've attended more autopsies than I want to think about. I'm invariably astounded at the violence people are capable of. I never stay for the full course of the procedure; I couldn't stomach it. However difficult, seeing a victim beneath the stark lights of the morgue is part of a ritual that will hopefully set me on the path to finding a killer.

"Dr. Blake has taken and preserved all possible evidence present on the body. It has been photographed extensively. Once those things were done, the body was washed and X-rayed." Doc Coblentz looks at me, the goggles making his eyes look huge. "One of the more interesting things we found was that the victim had gravel in her mouth."

I stare at him, surprised. "Any idea how it got there?" I look from man to man. "Could she have fallen in the driveway, struck her mouth on the ground?" Even as I ask the question, I recall that the attack likely happened inside the house.

"No way of knowing for certain," Doc tells me. "It wasn't just a small amount, Kate."

"About four ounces," Dr. Blake says.

"If I were to guess," Doc Coblentz says, "I'd say someone put it there."

"Postmortem?"

"Probably," he tells me. "None of the gravel had been swallowed or ingested."

"Any idea where the gravel came from?" I ask. "The driveway? Did the killer bring it with him?"

Dr. Blake chimes in. "We sent a sample to the BCI lab. They'll run a comparison to the material in the driveway."

I find myself thinking about the note found on Mary Yoder the day she was killed.

Food gained by fraud tastes sweet, but one ends up with a mouth full of gravel.

I make a mental note to see if Tomasetti has the resources to match the gravel to a specific area or to a company that deals in aggregate.

"Moving forward." Doc Coblentz reaches up and repositions the light. "As you can see, the decedent suffered multiple sharp-force trauma."

He indicates the victim's hands. "Defensive wounds present on both hands and arms. Nonfatal superficial incised wounds on the left forearm. Left biceps. Right shoulder." He grips the arm and opens the wound, so that it looks like a gaping red mouth carved into skin the color of ash. "Incised wound cut through the tissue, penetrating to the bone."

"The killer is physically strong." I hear my own voice as if it comes from far away and belongs to someone else.

"I concur," Dr. Blake puts in.

"Do you have any idea what kind of weapon was used?" I ask.

"A knife with a serrated blade. As you can see, the edges of the incised wounds are not smooth. I would estimate the length at six to eight inches. I'm guessing now, but there was probably a guard. Likely some type of hunting knife."

"How are you able to discern the length of the knife and that it had a guard?" I ask.

He looks at me, his eyes large behind the protective glasses. "I examined some of these incised wounds under magnification earlier. My findings were interesting." He indicates a two-inch gash above the navel, below her lowest rib on the right side. "When the knife penetrated, without the impediment of bone, it went all the way to the guard. You can't see it with the naked eye, Kate, but under magnification there was bruising present as well as tissue damage where the guard impacted the flesh."

Looking at the wounds, the sheer number of injuries, and the damage done to this woman's body, I get that tremor in my gut again. Sweat breaks out on the back of my neck. Spit pools in my mouth.

"Judging by the force of these wounds, Kate, I would say this was a frenzied attack. The individual who did this was either out of control or simply determined to maim and kill." He indicates several wounds to the shoulders and upper chest. "I believe it happened quickly. He didn't aim. Several of these wounds struck bone, which impeded penetration."

I wince inwardly, trying not to think of the pain that would have caused. . . .

"I'll know more once I make the Y-incision. But I'm comfortable telling you now, preliminarily, that the cause of death is massive hemorrhage. The manner of death is homicide."

CHAPTER 10

Twenty-three hours missing

You put in the hours. You do the research. You do all the right things. All of it with vigor and hope and heart. Still, a seven-year-old little girl is missing. A sixty-year-old grandmother is dead. A community is on edge. And the cops don't have a fucking clue.

I know it's the exhaustion that's hijacked my frame of mind and dragged my thoughts to a place I know better than to venture. A smarter cop would go home for a few hours of uninterrupted sleep, get a fresh start with a clear head and then get back to work.

Wind and rain thrash my office window. Though it's not yet closing time for most shops and businesses, Main Street is deserted. The first major cold front of the fall season blew through around noon. Weather usually doesn't bother me. This afternoon, I'm cold to the bone. I can't help but wonder if Elsie Helmuth is out there, wet and shivering with cold, frightened out of her mind, and hurting. Or worse . . .

"Chief?"

I glance up to see my second-shift dispatcher, Jodie Metzger, come through the door, a carafe of coffee in one hand, a stack of paper in the other.

I shove my cup toward her. "Thanks."

She pours and sets the stack in front of me. "Ladies' Club of Painters Mill had these flyers printed. Volunteers put out nine hundred of them today all over the county. I thought you might want to see them."

I glance at the top sheet. *Have you seen me?* There's no photo of Elsie Helmuth, just her name and a physical description. *Seven years old. Female. Special Needs. Born: March 14, 2012. Brown hair. Brown eyes. Height: 3'9". Weight: 60 lbs.*

It's well done, with all the right information, including the location of where she went missing, the tip line number, and the numbers for the sheriff's department as well as the Painters Mill PD.

"I think we could probably use a miracle, too, if you've got one handy," I tell her.

She shoots me a sympathetic look, and for the first time since I found Mary Yoder lying on the kitchen floor of the Schattenbaum farm, I feel like crying.

Please don't be dead. . . .

"Anything else I can do?" she asks.

"Check the tip line again, will you?" I ask.

"Sure." Jodie looks at me as if she wants to say something else, but she goes through the door without comment.

Earlier, I talked to Tomasetti about the gravel the coroner discovered in Mary Yoder's mouth. He agrees it's likely some strange extension of the note found at the scene. All he can do at this point is have the lab run a comparison to see if the gravel came from the driveway of the Schattenbaum place, which would likely mean the killer simply scooped it up and, after he killed Yoder, shoved it into her mouth. If the comparison shows the gravel didn't come from the driveway, we start checking with aggregate dealers in the area. It's a long shot, but worth pursuing at this point.

I open the manila folder in front of me and look at my copy of the note.

Food gained by fraud tastes sweet, but one ends up with a mouth full of gravel.

The original is printed in pencil. The lettering inept and juvenile. The words are from Psalm 94, the translation from the King James Bible, which is often used by the Amish, and has to do with the ills of receiving something undeserved through deception. What does it mean in terms of the case?

Tucking the note back in the folder, I look down at the yellow legal pad in front of me. I've filled most of it with stray thoughts and theories and a summary of what I know. I'm a big fan of free writing, turning my hand loose with a pen and clean sheet of paper. Sometimes, it's a good way to open the channel to those thought processes that can get lost in the clutter. This evening, it gives me nothing.

I start at the beginning of the pad and page through, skimming notes I've already read a hundred times. I go to the map, study the red circles that indicate the residences of six registered sex offenders. All of them have been interviewed twice. All but one have alibis. I look at the aerial photos of the Schattenbaum place. The proximity to the creek, which was also searched.

Nothing. Nothing. Nothing.

When the words begin to blur I reach for my reading glasses and keep going. I read the police report again. My description of the girl. Though I wrote the words less than twenty-four hours ago, it seems like a hundred years.

Elsie Helmuth. Age 7. Brn. Brn. Ht: 3′9″. Wt: 60 lbs.

A caution light flares somewhere inside my head. I blink at the page, trying to pinpoint what set it off. I glance at the Missing flyer again. Nothing there. No damn photo. I reach for the envelope from the Holmes County General Health District and, for the second time, I skim through the birth certificates of the Helmuth children. Names. Birth dates. County of birth.

Irma. 5-11-2008. Holmes Cnty.
Bonnie. 8-4-2009. Holmes Cnty.
Gracie. 9-19-2010. Holmes Cnty.
Elam. 11-13-2011. Holmes Cnty.
Becky. 12-27-2012. Holmes Cnty.
Luke. 12-1-2013. Holmes Cnty.
Annie. 11-31-2014. Holmes Cnty.

Why the hell isn't there a birth certificate for Elsie? Miriam Helmuth said the baby came quickly and there was no time for the midwife to arrive. As a result, they never filed the paperwork and simply hadn't gotten around to it yet.

I go back to the Missing flyer, trying to figure out what had caused that weird flutter in my brain. *Have you seen me? Elsie Helmuth. Seven years old. Female. Special Needs. Born: March 14, 2012. Brown hair. Brown eyes. Height: 3'9". Weight: 60 lbs.*

"Wait," I mutter.

A tremor runs through my body when I look at the birth date. March 14, 2012. I stare at the date, take off my cheaters, put them back on. The date stares back at me in black and white. I go back to the birth certificates and look at the birth dates of the other children. If Elam was born in November of 2011 and Becky was born in December of

2012, there's no way Miriam could have given birth to Elsie in March of 2012.

"Jodie?" I call out to reception.

She appears at the door to my office. "Yeah, Chief?"

"Call the Ladies' Club and find out who put together the information for the Missing flyer. I'm specifically looking for Elsie Helmuth's birth date. Find out where they got the information and confirm that it's correct."

"Sure. When do you need it?"

"Five minutes ago."

"Okeydoke."

Leaning forward, I rub my temples, trying in vain to jump-start a brain in dire need of sleep.

I've just finished writing the names of the children and their birth dates when Jodie appears in the doorway. "I just talked to Kelly Hernandez with the Ladies' Club. She got the girl's birth date from Miriam Helmuth."

I pull into the driveway of the Helmuth farm and barrel down the lane. Though it's dark and pouring rain, I pass several men on horseback braving the weather. Half a dozen more are walking along the shoulder; some are wearing slickers and holding flashlights, others are soaked to the skin and carrying lanterns. Despite the fact that they've had no luck, that they've already covered the area a dozen times, they're still looking. I wonder if they know that Miriam and Ivan Helmuth are keeping secrets.

It's possible one or more of the children's birth dates are incorrect—a typo or computer error—but not likely. I didn't take the time to check. If my suspicions are correct, Miriam Helmuth didn't give birth to Elsie. But if not Miriam, then who? Does it have anything to do with the abduction?

I park a few yards from two buggies parked side by side, the horses hunched against the rain, and I hightail it to the door. I enter the house without knocking. The smells of lye soap and bleach greet me as I pass through the mudroom, where two Amish women are operating the old wringer washing machine. A third woman hangs boys' trousers on a clothesline that's stretched across the room. I nod at them as I duck beneath the clothes and I head for the kitchen.

I find two of the children sitting at the kitchen table. Miriam is at the stove, stirring something in a heavy saucepan with a wooden spoon. She looks exhausted and pale, with dark half-moons beneath eyes that don't meet mine.

"Hi, Chief Katie!" Annie calls out.

"Did you bring Elsie?" Luke asks simultaneously.

"Hello back at you." I muster a smile that feels plastic on my face. "We haven't found Elsie yet, but we're looking hard."

"We miss her!"

"She's probably hungry!"

"And cold!"

The words strike like punches to a place that's tender and bruised. I look at Miriam to find her eyes already on me. "I need to talk to you," I say. "Privately."

The woman twists off the burner knob and sets down the spoon. Looking at her children, she brings her hands together. "Pudding's just about done," she tells them. "Go wash your hands and faces. Luke, go get your brother in the barn."

The kids scramble from their chairs. Luke grins at me as he heads for the back door.

"That'll buy us a few minutes." Grabbing a mug, Miriam walks to the table and sinks into a chair. "You bring news?"

I take the chair across from her. I'm hyperaware of that ticking clock that has embedded itself in my brain. An unbearable amount of time has passed since the girl went missing; there's no time for niceties. I'm too tired to make the effort. Worse, I'm pissed off, because I'm pretty sure this woman has been lying to me, so I get right to the point of my visit.

"Elam was born in November of 2011," I tell her. "Becky was born in December 2012. Miriam, there's no way you could have had Elsie in between."

The woman blinks at me. "But . . . she came early, you know. Just four pounds of her."

"When was Elsie born?"

For the first time she looks flustered. "The babies came so close together sometimes I lose track. . . ."

"Stop lying to me." I smack my hand against the table. "Your little girl's life is in danger and all I'm getting from you are lies."

"I'm not. I just . . . I got a little confused on the dates is all."

I rise, go to her, bend, so that my face is less than a foot away from hers. Now that I'm close, I see the telltale signs of sleepless nights and stress piled atop of stress. The whites of her eyes are a road map of capillaries. Lips dry and cracked. Breath that smells of coffee and sour milk. Worst of all is the abiding terror that's got its claws sunk deep into her, a relentless beast devouring her from the inside out.

"Elsie isn't your biological child, is she?" I say quietly.

The woman stares at me, unspeaking for the span of several heartbeats. Then the flesh of her cheeks begin to quiver. Her body follows suit, shaking so violently I'm afraid she's going to vibrate off the chair and fall to a heap at my feet.

"She's mine," she whispers. "She's always been mine. In every way."

Generally speaking, the Amish are stoic when it comes to displays of emotion. That's not to say they don't grieve, or have tempers or feel fear; like the rest of us, they do and just as keenly. But they're not prone to outbursts, not even children.

Evidently, Miriam Helmuth has reached her breaking point. Her child is missing. Her mother is dead—violently murdered. If I'm going to get anything out of her, now is the time to do it, so I push.

"The choice you make at this moment may be the only thing that saves your daughter's life," I say. "Think about that before you lie to me again."

Squeezing her eyes shut, she lowers her head.

"Do you know where she is?" I ask.

"God, no."

"Do you know who has her?"

Closing her eyes tightly, she shakes her head, grappling for control, her emotions teetering on the edge of some bottomless abyss. "I don't know," she cries. "I don't know why they did what they did."

"Who are 'they' and what did they do?" I ask.

A sob escapes her. She puts a trembling hand over her mouth, holds it tightly against her face, and then she doubles over as if she's in physical pain.

I wait, impatience and compassion and anger warring inside me.

After a moment, she sits up and meets my gaze. "They brought her to us," she whispers. "In the middle of the night. This screaming, red-faced little baby."

"Elsie?"

She nods. "She was a tiny thing. Just hours old. Hungry. Frightened. Wanting her *mamm* and some milk."

The reality of what I'm hearing strikes me with the force of a blow. The floor shifts beneath my feet. I almost can't believe my ears.

"Who brought her to you?" I ask.

"The midwife. The bishop from Scioto County."

"I need names."

Scrubbing her fingertips over her eyes, she looks at me through the layers of misery and exhaustion and guilt. "I don't know."

Lowering myself into the chair, I pull out my notebook and stare down at the blank page. I almost can't get my head around what I've been told. What it could mean in terms of a missing little girl and the brutal murder of her grandmother.

"Who's the baby's mother?" I ask.

"No one ever said, and I didn't ask. They were secretive about it."

"Who else was involved?"

"The bishop. The midwife." She hesitates. "Bishop Troyer."

The floor shifts again, violently this time, a small boat tossed about on a raging sea.

"Bishop Troyer?" I echo the name dumbly. A man I've known my entire life. A man of staunch beliefs and resolute faith. A leader admired not only by me, but by the entire Amish community. But he's tough, too. When I was a troubled teen and didn't follow the rules set forth by the *Ordnung,* my parents put me before him. It was an experience I never forgot. It didn't keep me from breaking the rules, but I made certain neither my parents nor the bishop found out about it. Tonight, I can't help but wonder: How is it that a man who had judged me so harshly once upon a time could commit his own sin with absolute impunity?

"Why did they bring the baby to you, Miriam?"

"I don't know. You have to understand, Chief Burkholder, it was the kind of thing that wasn't to be discussed or questioned."

"What can you tell me about the midwife?"

"All I know is she wasn't from around here. She was older. I didn't recognize her. I assumed the bishop brought her along to care for the baby."

"I need more."

The Amish woman shakes her head.

"Surely they told you *something*."

"They said nothing to me, but I listened. From what I gathered, the baby's *mamm* was . . . troubled. I think there was something wrong with her. Something not right in her life. So much that she couldn't care for her own baby."

"Do you mean health problems? Mental problems? Was she dying and didn't have family? What?"

"I wish I knew."

"Was there any paperwork? Or documents?"

"Not that I saw."

I stare at her, trying to come to terms with what was done. The ramifications. What comes next. "Why did you agree to take the baby?" I ask. "Didn't you wonder where she came from? Why she was being given to you? Did you think about the parents? That it might cause problems down the road?"

She raises her gaze to mine. "We did it because the bishop asked us to. Adopt her, I mean. Children are a gift from God, you know, and I knew that little girl was in trouble. She's one of the special ones, you know, with the problems and all. She needed us. I figured her *mamm* might have some problem, too. I thought we were probably helping her, as well." She shrugs. "If she was sick or dying. If she didn't have a husband or family."

"Does Ivan know all of this?"

"Yes."

"Was your mother involved?" I ask.

"I think she knew about it. I don't know how much. I asked later, but she wouldn't speak of it."

"Did Elsie's biological parents agree to relinquish her? Or was Elsie . . . taken? Removed from the home?"

"No one said."

We fall silent, the only sound coming from the tap of rain against the window. The hum of the propane refrigerator. The white noise of our thoughts.

"Miriam, do Elsie's biological parents know where she was sent?" I ask.

Her eyes widen. A wild and primal fear tears across her face. "You think they did this?"

Sie is meiner. She's mine.

"I think it's a possibility we have to consider."

Leaning forward, she puts her face in her hands and begins to sob. "Oh dear Lord, how could this happen? And why now?"

I don't know what to say. What to think. Staring at her as she sobs, I don't even know what to feel. "Is there anything you can tell me that might help me figure this out?"

She straightens, raises her gaze to mine. "The notes." She whispers the words as if she's frightened someone might hear her. "I didn't tell you . . . Ivan thought it best if we didn't say anything."

"What notes?" But I'm thinking about the note found on Mary Yoder's body. A detail that was not made public.

Rising, Miriam goes to the kitchen drawer, pulls out a small devotional book, opens it and pulls out some papers. "Three of them now. The latest this morning. In the mailbox." She unfolds three sheets of lined notebook paper and slides them across the table to me. They look as if they've been folded and unfolded a dozen times. The same type of paper as the note found on Mary Yoder.

Ill-gotten treasures have no lasting value, but righteousness delivers from death.

As I read, I'm thinking about evidence. Fingerprints. The possibility of DNA. Matching the paper to a specific notebook or manufacturer. A retailer. The prospect of CCTV or even a check or credit card. I go to the second note.

The Lord is a God who avenges. O God who avenges, shine forth. Rise up, Judge of the earth; pay back to the proud what they deserve.

And the third.

Anyone who steals must certainly make restitution, but if they have nothing, they must be sold to pay for their theft.

"I should have told you." Miriam begins to sputter. "I was scared. Ivan didn't want to tell. He didn't—"

"Who has handled these notes?" I ask, my voice sharp.

"Me. Ivan. That's it."

"Do the passages mean anything to you?"

The Amish woman shakes her head. "The first is a proverb. The second is a psalm. Ninety-four, I think. The other . . . Exodus."

I stare at her, letting the full force of my anger come through. "What else haven't you told me?"

"That's it. That's everything. I promise. I was just so scared. I didn't know what to do."

"Miriam, listen to me. If we're going to find Elsie. If we're going to find the person responsible, you have to trust me. You have to be honest. You have to tell me everything. Do you understand?"

"I do." She looks down at her hands, where they're knotted in front of her. "Chief Burkholder, I don't know who the mother is. Who the parents are. I don't know where they're from or why they did what they did." A sob escapes her. "All I know is that when I took Elsie into my arms, she was mine. She was home." She goes to pieces. "I want her back. My sweet baby girl. Please. Chief Burkholder, find her for us. *Find her before it's too late.*"

CHAPTER 11

Twenty-five hours missing

My head is reeling on the drive to the Troyer farm. Twice I pick up my cell to call Dispatch to find out if there was a missing child in the area seven years ago; twice I put it down without making the call. I need more information. I need to talk to the bishop, find out if he was, indeed, involved, and get all the facts—if there are facts to be had.

Why would a child be taken from her birth mother and placed with another family? Was the mother afflicted with Cohen syndrome, too? Of course, it's possible she'd passed away or had some other health issue. Usually, if there's some kind of disability—mental or physical or both—the Amish take care of their own without question. But if that was the case, why all the secrecy?

The possibility that the bishop was involved shakes my world. He's been a fixture in my life for as long as I can remember. To the Amish girl I'd been, he was revered and feared in equal measure. Is it possible he played a role in placing Elsie with the Helmuths? That he did, in fact, take part in what boils down to an illegal adoption?

I believe Miriam is telling the truth. In terms of the abduction, it could explain a lot. The big question now is who are the parents? What's their story? Were they knowing participants?

Having grown up Amish, I know that as a general rule, they are decent, law-abiding citizens. They're family-oriented, hardworking, and they consider children a gift from God. Most Amish couples are exceptional parents. Their children grow up with the support not only of their families, but of the community as a whole.

But like all of us mortals, the Amish are not perfect. Over the years, I've heard the whisperings of a belief system and traditions taken too far. When I was fifteen, an Amish girl not much older than me became pregnant out of wedlock. The father-to-be was nowhere to be found. The young woman's mother and grandmother stepped in and conspired to get her married off to an acceptable Amish bachelor. The marriage was rushed. The dates were fudged. The baby was born "early." The young woman's husband—and most of the community— was never the wiser. A happy ending for all—unless you're a fan of the truth. Did some situation with a social stigma attached bring about what happened with Elsie Helmuth?

A hundred questions pound my brain as I park in the gravel area behind the Troyer farmhouse. It's after six P.M., fully dark, and a steady rain falls from a low sky. I discern the glow of lantern light in the kitchen window as I take the sidewalk to the back door and knock.

The scuff of footsteps sounds inside. A moment later the door swings open and I find myself looking at Bishop Troyer. He's always seemed ancient to me, especially when I was a kid. I was as terrified as I was fascinated by him. I like to think I'm long past all that juvenile melodrama. Still, I have to bank a slow rise of nerves.

His hair is silver shot with black. His beard is the same, unkempt, and reaches the waistline of his trousers. He's dressed in black—shirt, suspenders, jacket, and a flat-brimmed hat. He's smaller than I remember, his body a little more bent. I heard he took a fall a couple of months ago. He's using a walker now. None of those things detract from the power that radiates from those steely eyes.

"Katie Burkholder?"

"Bishop Troyer." I look past him to see his wife standing at the kitchen table. By the light of a single lantern, I notice a half gallon of ice cream and two bowls in front of her. "I need to talk to you. Alone. It's important."

He glances past me as if expecting some unsavory non-Amish person at my heels. "*Kumma inseid.*" Come inside.

Gripping the walker, the bishop turns and trundles to the table.

The aromas of lantern oil and green peppers cooked earlier in the evening hang heavy in the overheated air as I follow him into the kitchen.

"*Sie bringa zeiya funn da kind?*" his wife asks, eyeing me with an odd combination of anticipation and suspicion. She brings news of the child?

I give her a hard look. "No."

"*Ich braucha shvetza zu* Chief Burkholder," he tells her. I need to speak with Chief Burkholder. "*Laynich.*" Alone.

The woman lowers her gaze in submission. "*Voll.*" Of course. Draping a kitchen towel over the back of a chair, she leaves the room and disappears into the shadows of the living room.

I make no move to assist as the bishop struggles into a kitchen chair. Before he's seated, I say, "I know Elsie isn't the biological child of Miriam and Ivan Helmuth. I need to know what happened and who was involved. Right now. Do you understand me?"

When the old man is seated, he sighs, then raises his gaze to mine, impervious to the words, my tone. "I don't know what you think you know, Kate Burkholder, but chances are you are wrong."

There were a dozen instances in my youth when my parents were at wits' end about how to handle me and my unacceptable behavior. Several times I was put before the bishop, alone, and left at his mercy. I've always known my mind, and I wasn't easily intimidated, but I can tell you facing off with this man was a fear-provoking experience. Even after all these years I see him as an elder. A man whose decisions are not to be questioned.

"What I know," I say firmly, "is that you and Ivan and Miriam have been lying to me. Elsie's abduction and the murder of Mary Yoder is likely related to what happened with Elsie seven years ago. You need to tell me everything so I can do my job and find her."

"Miriam told you?"

"She didn't have a choice. Neither do you. If you refuse to help me, I will arrest you for obstructing justice. You got that?"

"I can tell you what I know, Katie. It isn't much."

"Start talking."

The old man takes my tone in stride. He isn't shocked or rattled or even annoyed, but for the first time I see the wheels turning behind those cold steel eyes. "Seven years ago, I received a letter from the bishop down in Scioto County, Noah Schwartz. He asked for an emergency meeting. Said it was urgent. I agreed, of course, and the next day he came to me, here in Painters Mill. He said the *Deiner* had made an important decision and they needed my help."

"*Deiner*" is the *Deitsch* word for "servants," which is how the elected officials—the bishop, ministers, and preachers—are referred to. "Tell me about the meeting."

He looks down at the tabletop where his hands, fingers twisted and swollen with arthritis, rest easily. After a moment, he meets my gaze. "Noah asked me if I knew of a couple who could take in a child and raise it as their own."

I tug out my notebook and write down the bishop's full name. "Why would an Amish bishop become involved in something like that?"

"According to Bishop Schwartz, the child had no one. *No one.* She needed a family. Parents. A safe place. A home."

"You didn't question him about the circumstances? Or ask where she came from? Didn't you wonder about the parents?"

"I trusted in the wisdom and goodness of the bishop. I had faith that the Lord would see us through the darkness we were facing. You have to understand, Katie, it was a troubling time and there was uncertainty. Grief, even. And fear. None of the decisions made were entered into lightly or without a great deal of thought."

"Who else was involved?" I ask.

"The midwife."

"What's her name?"

"I do not know."

"Noah Schwartz brought you the baby?"

The old man nods. "Two days later. Noah and the midwife brought the girl child. We took her to Miriam and Ivan late in the night. We prayed. And it was done."

"Who are the parents?" I ask. "What are their names?"

"I do not know."

"Where did the baby come from? What town?"

"Scioto County. That's all I know."

I write it down. Scioto County is in the southern part of Ohio. In the back of my mind, I recall Martha Hershberger telling me that Mary Yoder's sister, Marlene, was from "down south somewhere."

"Do you know Mary Yoder's sister, Marlene?" I ask.

The bishop shakes his head. "No."

"Have you ever heard the name?"

Another shake.

Even as I ask the questions, I struggle to make sense of everything I've been told. "Why did Bishop Schwartz take the baby? Was the mother sick? Injured? Dying? Why did he become involved at all?"

"I did not ask," he tells me. "All I can tell you is that Noah Schwartz did this thing in the name of the Lord and the church."

I stare at him, my heart pounding a hard tattoo against my ribs. I don't want to believe the story I've been told. That two Amish bishops participated in what is at best an illegal adoption. At worst, a kidnapping. But in my heart of hearts, I know it's the truth, however questionable. While Bishop Troyer is not above manipulation in the name of the *Ordnung,* he is not a liar.

"Where do I find Bishop Schwartz?" I ask.

"I heard Noah passed a couple of weeks ago."

Disappointment tings in my chest. "What about the midwife?"

"I do not know."

"Where are they from?"

"Most of the Amish live in Crooked Creek, I think. A few hours south. Down by the river. I'd met Noah once or twice over the years. Scioto County is not part of our church district, but they are in full fellowship with us here in Holmes County. They are of the same affiliation."

"Who else knows about this?" I ask.

"Just the bishop and me. The midwife. Miriam and Ivan. That is all."

"What about Mary Yoder?"

"I can't say for certain, but I think she knew. Noah mentioned speaking to her, but he didn't go into detail. In all these years, Mary and I have never spoken of it."

I close the notebook and give him a hard stare. "Is it possible someone else knows about what happened?"

He shrugs. "I don't know."

"What about the parents of the baby? Do they know what happened? Do they know where the baby was taken? Who took her in?"

"I do not know."

"Does your wife know?"

"She was here that night, of course. As the wife of a bishop, she does not question."

"Bishop, I believe Elsie Helmuth may have been taken by someone who knew about or found out about what happened all those years ago. Her birth parents. A relative. An older sibling. Someone who wanted her back."

"I don't see how, Katie. Bringing that baby here to Painters Mill, it was a solemn and private thing. Done in the night, under cover of darkness. We were careful. It was never spoken of again."

"Someone spoke of it."

He stares at me, silent.

I set my hands on my hips and sigh. "Bishop, you can't just take a baby from one family and give it to another one. Even if your intentions were honorable and you think it's the right thing to do."

"You come here tonight to question our ways? You of all people?"

I don't respond to the jab, but I feel it in a place I thought was immune. "This isn't about me. It's about finding that girl."

"I've told you everything I know."

I shake my head and sigh. "You likely broke the law. What am I supposed to do with that?"

"It was done in the eyes of the Lord. His law is above man's law. You know this, Katie. Or have you strayed so far from your roots that you no longer believe?" He says the words in a voice like iron. "If what we did is against some English law then so be it."

•   •   •

. . . the child had no one. She needed a family. Parents. A safe place.

We took her to Miriam and Ivan late in the night. We prayed. And it was done.

If I hadn't heard the words directly from Bishop Troyer, I never would believe he was capable of something so outrageous and reckless.

I drive back to the station in a state of shock, my conversations with Miriam Helmuth and Bishop Troyer replaying in my head like some tragic song. By the time I park and head inside, I've come up with a loose plan.

I find Mona, still in uniform, sitting at the reception desk, listening to the radio, surfing the internet.

"Oh, hey, Chief."

"Dig up everything you can find on Noah Schwartz. I think he lived in Crooked Creek, Ohio. Scioto County. No middle. He was an Amish bishop. I believe he's deceased."

She's already reaching for a legal pad, jotting everything down. "Got it."

I slide messages from my slot and head toward my office. "Run him through LEADS. Check for warrants," I say over my shoulder. "Get me a list of midwives in Crooked Creek and Scioto County. I think there are some registries out there." Even as I bark out the requests, I realize that because we're dealing with the Amish—many of whom stay off the governmental grid—the information may be hit-or-miss.

"Chief, you still interested in Marlene Byler?" she calls out.

I turn and go back to her station to find her holding out a purple folder. "There's not much out there. I mean, with her being Amish and all. Just a newspaper story and an obituary," she tells me. "That's how I found her. Mary Yoder is listed in the obit."

I take the folder. "Anyone ever tell you you've got a great detective's mind?"

She grins. "All the time."

In my office, I boot up my computer, pour a cup of day-old coffee, and open the file on Marlene Byler. Her obituary is on top, so I read.

Marlene Byler, 29, of Crooked Creek died unexpectedly on March 17, 1990. She was born in Scioto County on May 11, 1961. She was a homemaker and member of the Old Order Amish Church. She is survived by her sister Mary Yoder of Painters Mill.

I go to the next page. It's an article from the *Scioto County Times Record* newspaper dated two days after her death twenty-nine years ago.

SCIOTO COUNTY WOMAN JUMPS TO HER DEATH

Sheriff Kris McGuire tells the Scioto County Times Record 29-year-old Marlene Byler died after jumping from the Sciotoville Bridge into the Ohio River about 5 P.M. Thursday. McGuire said her death is being investigated as an apparent suicide. According to the sheriff's department spokesman, an autopsy will determine if Byler died from the impact, drowned, or died from a combination of factors.

I read the article twice. It's a troubling, unusual story. Not only was Marlene Byler Amish, but she was evidently distraught enough to jump to her death. Is any of it related to the murder of Mary Yoder or the abduction of Elsie Helmuth? What secrets did she take with her to her grave?

Shoving the questions aside for now, I cruise out to the National

Center for Missing and Exploited Children website, seeking information on infant abductions in Scioto County seven years earlier. There's nothing there. I spend an hour scouring every law enforcement and missing-person database I can think of—all to no avail.

At the same time, Mona ferrets through various internet sites for information on Noah Schwartz, the bishop. The only thing she finds is a single piece on the buggy accident that took his life two weeks earlier and an obituary in *The Budget*.

"Here's the list of registered midwives for Scioto County." She passes me a printout from one of the national registries. "None listed for Crooked Creek, Chief. Several from Scioto County."

I take the list. "You got your Google hat with you?"

She grins. "Never leave home without it."

"I'm looking for information on a newborn that went missing seven years ago, give or take. If you strike out in Scioto County, expand your search to contiguous counties. Look at everything, not just law enforcement databases—but blogs and social media sites, too."

"I'm all over it."

For three hours Mona and I probe every crevice of the internet, searching for even the most obscure mention of a missing child, first in Crooked Creek, and then Scioto and surrounding counties. A couple of cases meet our general criteria, but further investigation proves it couldn't have been Elsie. Either the case was solved or the baby was male or the parents were of Asian or African American descent.

At ten P.M., I hit a wall. The words and images on the screen begin to blur. The last thing any cop wants to do when a child is missing is walk away because of something as inconsequential as sleep. But there comes a point when exhaustion becomes an impediment to productivity. I've reached that point.

Elsie Helmuth has been missing for thirty excruciating hours. Every tick of the clock lessens her chance of survival. But it's time to call it a day. Go home. Sleep. Start fresh in the morning. Right.

Tomasetti calls at midnight. "DNA from the blood found in the yard of the Schattenbaum farm belongs to Elsie Helmuth," he says without preamble.

I close my eyes, relieved he can't see the shiver that goes through me. "Damn it."

"As far as we know she could have gotten a bloody nose in a scuffle," he offers, "or fallen and cut herself. Something like that."

Or else the crazy fucker cut her. . . .

Neither of us utter the words, but we're thinking it.

"I hate this," I say.

He sighs. "Yeah."

"What about the notes I gave you?" I ask. "Anything come back? Prints? The paper or notebook manufacturer?"

"We got zilch. No prints. No DNA." A buzz of silence. "Kate, you sound wiped out."

I laugh, but it rings tired and phony. I tell him about my conversations with Bishop Troyer and Miriam Helmuth.

"That changes everything," he says. "Do you think any of this could have something to do with the girl being special needs?"

"I can't imagine. Tomasetti, the Amish consider special-needs children a gift from God. They're never considered a burden. Any Amish person with a physical or mental handicap is well cared for."

"What if, for some reason, the mother couldn't care for her?" He lets the thought trail. "Would that be enough for the Amish to step in?"

"Maybe," I say. "Family."

A pause ensues as our minds work that over. "I'm looking for information on missing infants in Scioto and surrounding counties during that time frame. Tomasetti, there's nothing there."

"You follow up with the sheriff's department down there?"

"They got nothing."

"What about the Amish community?"

"Of course none of them have phones," I tell him.

"Were you able to find Mary Yoder's sister?"

"Dead," I say. "Suicide."

"Shit."

"Tomasetti, the bishop who brought the baby to Painters Mill is dead."

"How?"

"Buggy accident."

Silence ensues. "Kate, why the hell would a bishop get involved in something like that? It doesn't make sense."

"I don't think a bishop would without some . . . compelling reason."

"And what would a compelling reason be to take a newborn baby from its parents?"

"In light of Elsie Helmuth having Cohen syndrome, maybe her mother had been deemed mentally or physically unable to care for a baby. Maybe there was no father in the picture."

It's the most honest answer I can give. Or is it? Would it be more truthful for me to admit that the cultural roots I left behind so long ago still have a hold on me whether I like it or not?

"The footprints found at the scene were male," he reminds me. "What if the mother and her male partner relinquished the child for whatever reason and, at some later point, had a change of heart? Maybe they did some digging and found out where the child was sent."

"But . . . murder?"

"We've seen it happen for less."

Lowering my head, I put my face in my hands and rub my eyes. "These people are Amish. . . ."

"What if they're not? What if the Amish community saw some . . . injustice or wrongdoing and stepped in?"

"There has to be some . . . connection to the Amish," I say. "Or the bishops wouldn't have gotten involved."

"So what are you going to do about it?"

"There's only one thing I *can* do."

"I can't go with you to Scioto County. Not with this girl missing and a task force in place."

"With this being an Amish issue, it's probably best that I go alone anyway," I tell him.

"In the interim, I'll dig around a little on my end." He pauses. "Is the mayor going to give you grief over leaving town?"

"Of course he is. But I'm hired to protect and serve, not please. Besides, I'll only be gone a day," I tell him. "Two, tops."

"Famous last words." He sighs. "If it's not too much trouble, come home and get some sleep before you go."

"On my way."

CHAPTER 12

Forty-two hours missing

Dawn ushers in the first frost of the season, a sky the color of slate, a north wind, and just enough drizzle to keep my intermittent wipers busy. I'd planned on an early start, but ended up spending several hours at the station. I didn't pull out until after nine A.M. to make the four-hour drive to Crooked Creek, which is on the Ohio side of the river half an hour east of Portsmouth. I'm southbound on Ohio 23 just past Chillicothe when the call comes in from Tomasetti.

"The tire-tread plaster casts captured at the scene were viable," he tells me.

"Best news I've had all day."

"And it's still early. Manufacturer is Goodyear. Wrangler radial P 235/75R15 105S SL OWL."

"Does any of that tell us the type of vehicle?"

"Light truck or SUV."

"Pickup truck," I say. "Covers a lot of territory."

"The good news is the tires are worn. The technician says there are markings from wear. In this case, some minor damage, a slice on the outer edge that's unique to this tire."

"So if we produce a suspect, chances are good we'll be able to match the tire."

The silence that follows tells me there's more, that it's probably not good. "Have you talked to anyone at the station?" he asks.

"Not yet," I say. "Do I need to brace?"

"The national media have moved in. Cable networks started running the story last night. They're camped out in front of the police station and on both ends of Township Road 14. They've got people in town, shoving cameras and mikes in front of anyone who'll talk to them, especially if they're Amish."

"Shit."

In some cases, the media can be helpful to law enforcement, especially when there's a missing person. Television and radio can help get the word out and circulate photos. The rest of the time, they just get in the way, passing along misinformation, demanding time no one has, and disrupting the lives of the people involved.

"Might be best if they don't know you're down there," he says. "Especially if you want to keep it low-key."

"I do."

"In that case I'll try to keep it under my hat," he says dryly. "Look, I've got to run. Keep me posted on how it's going. And if it's not too much to ask, stay the hell out of trouble."

Any time a cop pokes around in an outside jurisdiction, it's prudent to check in with local law enforcement to let them know you're in town so I make my first stop in Portsmouth. The Scioto County Sheriff's Office is housed in a newish redbrick building that also accommodates the county jail and communications center. I called ahead, hoping to meet with the sheriff, but he wasn't available, so I spoke with one of the deputies that regularly patrols the Crooked Creek area. I briefed him on the case, some of which he was already familiar with. I asked him to check for reports—official or unofficial—of a missing child six to eight years earlier. He said it didn't ring a bell, but he'd only been with the department a couple of years. He promised to take a look and let me know.

Deputy Martin Harleson meets me inside the reception area with a hearty handshake and welcoming smile. After introductions are made, the duty deputy buzzes us through the secure door and Harleson shepherds me to a small meeting room equipped with a table and chairs, a coffee station, sink, and vending machines.

I lay out the fundamentals of the case. "We believe he may be Amish and has connections to Crooked Creek. I wanted to let you guys know I was in town."

"Any way I can help?" He asks the question sincerely enough, but I see the curiosity in his eyes. Cops are a nosy lot, me included. We like to be in the thick of things, especially when it includes murder.

"Do you know who replaced Noah Schwartz, the Amish bishop who was killed?"

He shakes his head. "No idea."

"Do you have the names of any of the ministers?" I ask. "Or preachers? Elders?"

"We don't deal with the Amish much here in Portsmouth. Most of them live to the east of us. They own a lot of the farms down by the river. A lot of buggies on the road in that area. Bishop Schwartz was the first fatality. Hit-and-run. Let me tell you, it was the worst damn thing I ever saw."

The term "hit-and-run" gives me pause. "What happened?"

"Driver hit the buggy from behind. Had to be doing fifty. Killed

Schwartz instantly." Sighing, he scrubs a hand over his jaw. "I don't think those Amish people realize how vulnerable they are in those buggies."

"You guys make an arrest?" I ask, troubled not only because Schwartz is one of the people who was involved in the case, but because I'm not a fan of coincidence.

"We didn't have much to work with. There were no witnesses. Nothing left behind. Not even a fuckin' skid mark."

I stare at him, aware that my pulse is up. "The driver made no attempt to stop?"

"We assumed he was probably under the influence. Drugs or alcohol or both." Grimacing he shakes his head. "Welcome to the opioid epidemic."

"Where did it happen?"

"River Road area. We call it The Bend. East where the road runs along the river, then doglegs north. Kids go out there all the time to drag-race and raise hell."

"The bishop lived in the area?"

"He actually lived to the east a ways."

"Any idea what he was doing there?"

"No one ever said." He cocks his head. "Why the interest?"

"I think the bishop knew the family in Painters Mill." I shrug, trying to keep it nonchalant. "Did you have a chance to double-check on any missing infants reported six to eight years ago?"

"I did a cross search, expanded the date criteria to four to ten years, and there's nothing there. Had a missing baby five years ago, but it was a domestic thing and resolved within twenty-four hours. Two-year-old boy went missing nine years ago. Deputy found him in a pond, drowned. That's all I got."

He shifts, looking a little miffed because he knows I'm not telling him everything. "Do you mind if I ask why you're interested in missing minor children?"

"The Helmuth family has relatives down here." I shrug. "Since most kidnappings of minor children are perpetrated by a family member or someone known to the family, I thought I'd sniff around."

His eyes narrow on mine. "You think some Amish person from Crooked Creek took that little girl?" He makes no effort to conceal the incredulity in his voice. "Most of the Amish down here are Old Order. Painters Mill is four hours away. That would be a difficult trip to make by buggy."

"They hire drivers when they need to travel a distance not practical to cover by buggy."

"You know a lot about the Amish."

"I was born Amish," I tell him. "I left the fold when I was eighteen."

"Oh. That's interesting." He offers a sheepish grin. "So you know Penn Dutch and all that?"

"I do."

"Huh." He scratches his head, looking amused. "Never met an ex-Amish chief of police."

I smile back, knowing the revelation would earn me some leeway. "I thought talking to some of the Helmuths' relatives might be helpful."

"Wish I could be more help, Chief Burkholder. The Amish keep to themselves down here. The only place I see them regularly is the farmers' market. They're there every weekend with furniture, vegetables, quilts, and whatnot. They do some work for folks around here in Portsmouth. Fences. Sheds. Stuff like that. One of the local guys built a workshop for me last summer. Nice dude and he did good work."

He studies me intently for the span of several seconds. "I think I've got his name and address around here somewhere. Might be a good place for you to start."

"That would be great."

Pulling out his phone, he taps the screen. "Got it right here. Name's Adam Fisher." He recites an address and I thumb it into my phone.

I rise and once again extend my hand for a shake. "Is there a police department in Crooked Creek? Anyone I could talk to there on the law enforcement side?"

"Mayor disbanded the department a couple years ago. They were down to two officers. Lack of funds, you know. Scioto County covers that whole area now."

He looks at me again as if he wants to say something else, but doesn't. "If you need anything from us, Chief Burkholder, you let me know and we'll help out if we can."

I thank him for his time and head for the door.

Driver hit the buggy from behind. Had to be doing fifty. Killed Schwartz instantly. . . .

The deputy's words echo in my head as I drive east toward Crooked Creek. Sadly, buggy accidents are a fact of life in Amish country. They're slow-moving vehicles and, unfortunately, some of the Old Order reject the use of reflective signage and safety lights. Add a driver under the influence to the mix and it's a recipe for disaster. I've investigated my share of accidents over the years; too many of them are alcohol or drug related.

No witnesses. Nothing left behind. Not even a fuckin' skid mark. . . .

While his assertion that the lack of skid marks can indicate an intoxicated driver, it's not the only conclusion that might be drawn. If Bishop Schwartz was involved in the illegal adoption of an infant, who's to say some enraged parent or relative didn't take it upon himself to mete out a little retribution?

Crooked Creek is a tiny village with a population of 623, according to the sign at the corporation limit. The hamlet is nestled in an old-growth forest along the banks of the Ohio River. Set against the backdrop of the foothills of the Appalachian Mountains to the south and east, it's a picturesque setting. But there's poverty, too. On the outskirts of town a smattering of abandoned industrial-type buildings demark what was probably once a bustling manufacturing hub.

The small downtown area is lined with historic buildings, some of which date back to the mid-1800s. As I make the turn onto River Road and idle down the brick-paved street, it becomes even more apparent that hard times have fallen upon this pretty little town. At least half of the once-grand buildings are vacant. Several of the display windows are boarded up with plywood; others are broken, the interiors left open to the elements. There's a sandwich shop called The Fat Catfish that looks open. Dooley's Hardware advertises red-hot deals on potting soil, select hand tools, and Adirondack chairs. Lochte General Store has Folgers coffee and women's housecoats on sale. I see a sign for a pharmacy, but as I drive past I realize it, too, has closed. At the end of town, a sign with an arrow urges motorists to make the turn for Deer Corn and Beer.

I leave the downtown area, drive past a post office and a gas station, and I head east on the Ohio River Scenic Byway. Even in light of the economic downturn, this part of the state is beautiful. Light rain falls from a glowering sky as I drive past massive maple, oak, and black walnut trees. I pass several quaint farms, some of which are Amish. Occasionally I catch a glimpse of the river, a shimmering, muddy blur through the trees.

As I travel east, the houses become sparse. Many are little more than shacks. Mobile homes sit like rusty tin boxes. I can't help but wonder what this place was like at the height of its manufacturing heyday.

A few miles east of Crooked Creek proper, the voice of my GPS tells me to turn left on Stephen Road. Another mile and the name on the mailbox tells me I've reached my destination.

The Fisher farm is set on lush bottomland with a pasture to the east and a cut cornfield on the west side. Farther in, the lane wends through a wooded area. At the top of a rise it veers toward a two-story brick house that's been painted white. Green shutters. A galvanized-steel roof from which a tall chimney juts. There's a bank barn twenty yards from the house. A dozen or so head of Black Angus cattle graze in a pasture. There's a manure spreader heaped with its namesake parked in front of the barn.

I cruise around to the rear of the house, park, and take a pea-gravel walkway bracketed by landscape timbers to the front. I've just stepped onto the porch when the door swings open. I find myself looking at a plump Amish woman of about forty. She's holding a broom in one hand, a dustpan in the other. White apron and *kapp*. Cheap black sneakers.

She startles upon spotting me and drops the dustpan, which clatters to the floor. "Oh."

"I didn't mean to frighten you." I pick up the dustpan and hand it to her. "I'm looking for Adam Fisher."

"That's my husband." She glances at my badge as if she's not quite sure she believes me. "What's this all about?"

"I'm working on—"

"*Was der schinner is kshicht?*" What in the world is going on?

I look past her to see a tall, thin Amish man approach. He's wearing typical garb: blue work shirt, dark gray trousers with suspenders, a navy jacket, and a flat-brimmed hat.

I introduce myself. "I'm working on a case in Painters Mill that involves an Amish family with connections to Crooked Creek." I recap, sticking to generalities, watching him carefully for a reaction. "I was wondering if you could tell me how to get in touch with Bishop Schwartz's widow?"

"That would be Lizzie. Put the house up for sale just last week."

"Do you have an address?"

"The old one." He recites a Crooked Creek address. "Not sure where she moved to."

I pull out my notebook and write it down. I direct my next question to Mrs. Fisher. "Do either of you know the names of the midwives in the area?"

They seem surprised that a midwife would be of interest, but Mrs. Fisher answers readily. "Well, Sadie Stutzman was the only midwife around for years. I used her with our seven children. But she's getting old, you know. Had a stroke a few months back."

"*Narrisch,*" the Amish man mutters beneath his breath. Insane.

His wife bites her lip. "Most of the Amish ladies use Hannah Beachy over to Portsmouth these days. She's *Mennischt,* you know." Mennonite. "She doesn't have as much experience as Sadie, but she's a nice girl, certified by the state, Ohio and Kentucky, and all that."

I write down both names, but I find myself more interested in the former. "Where can I find Sadie Stutzman?"

"The government people tried to get her into that rehabilitation home down to Ironton after the stroke." The Amish woman laughs. "We all knew she wouldn't leave. She's a crotchety little thing. Stubborn, too. Some of the women in our church district take a covered dish or vegetables out to her every week or so. She still lives out to that old house by the river. Lived there with her husband for years."

She rattles off an address and I write it down.

One of the most difficult aspects of information gathering in the course of a case—particularly when the topic is sensitive—is maintaining a prudent level of confidentiality. The Amish may be pious and reject most modes of electronic communication, but they're a tight-knit group, well informed as far as the local goings-on, and like most human beings, they occasionally fall to gossip. If I start asking questions about midwives and missing children, I risk sparking rumors—maybe even hindering my quest for information. I don't want that to happen, especially since I have no idea if I'm right about any of it. But I've come in blind; I need a starting point, so I proceed with caution.

Hoping to get into their good graces, I switch to *Deitsch*. "Mr. and Mrs. Fisher, are either of you aware of a child or baby that went missing from this area in the last eight years or so?"

"A missing child? *Here?*" Mrs. Fisher looks at me as if I've sprouted a third eye. "Not that I know of."

Mr. Fisher stares at me, his expression inscrutable. "An Amish child?"

"I'm not sure," I say. "Could be Amish or English."

"That sort of thing doesn't happen around here," the Amish man tells me. "If it did, it would have been big news. We would have heard."

"You're *Amisch*?" Mrs. Fisher asks.

"I was, but I left."

"We're sorry for you." Mr. Fisher doesn't say the words unkindly.

I don't respond. "Do either of you know Marlene Byler?"

Both assume puzzled expressions. The Amish man shakes his head. "Can't say we do."

I pass him my card. "If something occurs to you about a missing child, will you get in touch with me?"

He takes the card, drops it into his pocket without looking at it. "Have a blessed day," he says, and closes the door in my face.

CHAPTER 13

Forty-eight hours missing

In the early stages of a case, a cop never really knows if the premise they're operating on is right or wrong or somewhere in between. The longer I'm here in Crooked Creek, the more pronounced the feeling that my time might be more wisely spent in Painters Mill. Every minute that passes is one more minute that Elsie Helmuth is gone, that her life is in jeopardy. My gut is telling me I need to be there, at the heart of the investigation, looking for her. Not here where facts are scarce and no one seems to know shit.

The theory that two Amish bishops and a midwife transported a baby to Painters Mill, perhaps against the wishes of the baby's mother or without her knowledge, seems outlandish. The Amish are not in the business of stealing babies. Certainly not the bishops or elders.

But as I pull onto the county road and head south, Miriam Helmuth's words replay in my head. *They brought her to us. In the middle of the night. This screaming, red-faced little baby.*

A baby that may have come from Crooked Creek.

Shoving my doubts aside, I plug the address for Sadie Stutzman into my GPS, but quickly discover that some of the roads aren't on the map. Half a mile from the river, I realize why. The road isn't really a road at all, but a narrow dirt track crisscrossed with tire ruts. The ground is muddy, so I put the Explorer in four-wheel drive and press on.

The first property I pass is an abandoned mobile home that was apparently swept off its foundation at some point by floodwaters and never put to rights. It's green and white, striped with rust, and sits at a cockeyed angle against a huge tree that prevented it from being carried downstream. As I pass by, I realize the power of the current bent the mobile home nearly in half.

Mud pings inside the Explorer's wheel wells as I approach the neighboring property. I see a small frame house covered from foundation to roof with vines. At first, I think the place is abandoned—another casualty of hard times and a river with an insatiable appetite for anything bold enough to stand too close. Then I spot the loafing shed at the rear; a horse and several goats graze in a tumbling-down pen someone has slapped together with stock panels and wire. An Amish buggy sits at the back side of the shed. It doesn't look as if it's been used in a while.

The mailbox slants at a precarious angle, as if the water encroached and tried to push it downstream. There's no name, just two numbers someone smeared onto the post with a finger and some paint. I glance at my GPS. The two numbers match, so I pull in and park next to a big clump of pampas grass, its golden spires jutting six feet into the air.

I take the cracked sidewalk to the steps. Stepping onto the front porch is like entering a cave. Vines cover every surface, climbing up the wrought-iron column like snakes. A storm door hangs by a single hinge, so I ease it out of the way and knock.

I wait a full minute, but no one comes. No voices or the sound of footfalls from inside. Thinking of the animals out back, I resist the urge to check the knob to see if it's locked and I descend the steps. I've just started toward the Explorer when a sound tells me there's someone in the backyard. Pulling up my collar against the wind and drizzle, I walk around the side of the house.

I get my first good look at the river, a vast expanse of shimmering brown water that slides along the muddy bank. A few yards away, a diminutive figure is at work on some earthen project. A woman, I realize. I start toward her.

She's Amish. Small in stature. White *kapp*. A charcoal-colored dress that reaches nearly to the ground. Gray barn coat. Black muck boots. No gloves, even though she's got a shovel in hand.

"Hello?" I call out. "Mrs. Stutzman?"

The woman shovels dirt from a wheelbarrow onto a pile of earth that's about three feet high. Her coat and head covering are soaking wet and spattered with mud, telling me she's been outside for some time. Upon hearing my voice, she stops working and turns to me.

"Who might you be?"

She's barely five feet tall, with a voice like rusted iron. Her face is deeply wrinkled and dotted with age spots, a good bit of facial hair on her chin. Gold, wire-rimmed glasses cover viscous eyes.

I introduce myself. "I'm from Painters Mill. I'd like to talk to you about something that may have happened here in Crooked Creek a few years ago that involves a child."

"Painters Mill, huh? Never heard of it."

She's standing so close I can see the silver glint of the pins she used to close the front of the dress. Her eyes are cloudy with something yellow in the corners. The left side of her face sags slightly and I recall Mrs. Fisher telling me this woman suffered a stroke a few months back.

"Are you sure about that?" I ask.

"If I wasn't sure, I wouldn't say it now, would I?" Hefting the shovel, she jams it into the dirt in the wheelbarrow, and dumps it onto the mound. I'm not exactly sure what she's doing; it's the kind of project a woman her age shouldn't be taking on. That said, she's strong for her size and her age.

"What are you working on?" I ask.

"Levee," she tells me, ramming the shovel into the wheelbarrow. "Storm comin'."

I was raised to respect my elders. You don't talk back to them. You don't let them exert themselves to exhaustion while you stand there and do nothing. "Big job."

"That's why God gave us hands, now, isn't it?" She's breathing heavily as she upends the shovel, dumping dirt onto the pile. Her face is wet. I can't tell if it's rain or sweat.

I watch her work, uncomfortable because a levee is an impossible feat without heavy equipment and I remember Adam Fisher's muttered description of Sadie Stutzman. *Narrisch* . . .

"Can I help you with that?" I ask.

"Only got one shovel." She hands me the aforementioned tool and grins a semi-toothless smile. "Don't mind if I take a breather, though."

I take the shovel, jam it into the dirt-filled wheelbarrow, and toss a glob of mud onto the mound. I'm aware of her stepping back, bending, setting her hands on her knees.

I keep working. "I understand you're a midwife."

"Was till the stroke got me. Don't do too much anymore. There's a new one down to Portsmouth. A nice *Mennischt* girl." Mennonite. "Gotta have all them certifications and paperwork for the government these days. I ain't got the patience for such things."

The handle of the shovel is muddy and wet. I'm not wearing gloves. But the woman is talking, so I keep going. "I understand you knew Bishop Schwartz," I say as I toss another shovelful of earth onto the mound.

151

"Everyone knew the bishop."

"You were close?"

"Close enough." She straightens. "He was the bishop, after all."

"Did you ever travel with him to Painters Mill?"

An emotion I can't quite identify flickers in her eyes. "Can't say I did."

Despite the cold and rain, I'm starting to sweat beneath my coat from the effort of my chore. "Are you sure about that, Mrs. Stutzman? I understand you and Bishop Schwartz transported an infant to Painters Mill."

"Don't recall anything like that." She holds out her hand for the shovel. "Give it here."

I ignore her, keep working. "How long have you been working on the levee?"

"A few weeks now." She doesn't seem to notice that her efforts have garnered little more than a pile of earth that will likely wash away with the next downpour.

"The river floods?"

"Every few years. It's the way things are here."

"Do you know Bishop Troyer in Painters Mill?" I ask.

She looks at me over the top of her glasses. "You think you're pretty smart, don't you, Kate Burkholder? Coming down here and asking all these nosy questions."

I set down the shovel and upend the wheelbarrow, dumping the remaining dirt and mud onto the mound. "I'm asking you questions that need to be answered."

"Go get me some more dirt then." She motions toward a section of the yard that's been inexpertly excavated. The place from which she's getting dirt for her levee.

Holding her gaze, I bend and lift the wheelbarrow, roll it over to the shallow hole. "A seven-year-old little girl is missing," I tell her. "She's Amish. Innocent. Someone took her two days ago. I think it's related to something that happened here seven years ago."

"I don't know anything about that."

I bank a rise of irritation, and put the energy into filling the wheelbarrow. For the span of several minutes the only sound comes from the grate of steel against wet earth, the birds in the trees along with river, the din of rain against the barn roof a few yards away.

"They killed him, you know."

I stop digging, turn to her. "What? Killed who?"

Another flash in her eyes, an unexpected wiliness, a cognizance of exactly what we're talking about and what she's saying. But there's fear there, too. "Bishop Schwartz. That's who we're talking about, isn't it?"

I pick up the shovel and cross to her. "Bishop Schwartz was killed in a buggy accident."

She stares at me as if I'm some dense child. As I regard her, I'm reminded once again of Adam Fisher's words. *Narrisch,* he said. Insane. Considering the project we're working on, I suspect this woman may be well on her way. I don't believe she's arrived at that destination just yet.

"*Was* it an accident?" she asks.

"Are you saying you believe someone did that to him on purpose?"

"I'm saying I knew something wasn't right all along," she whispers in that rusty-steel voice. "Knew it for a long time. Everyone did. Kept their mouths shut like good Amish. Such a terrible thing. Sin piled atop of sin. I couldn't abide by it."

The old woman hobbles to the wheelbarrow, realizes the shovel isn't there, and returns to where I stand. "He said I was never to speak of it. So I held my tongue."

"Mrs. Stutzman, do you know who was driving the vehicle that struck Bishop Schwartz's buggy?"

"The English police said it was druggies that killed him." She hefts a harsh laugh. "That ain't who done it and it wadn't no accident. I told them, but they wouldn't listen. I'm just a crazy old woman after all."

"Who killed him?"

A light enters her eyes, like a smile, only she's not smiling. "The father of the child."

The earth seems to tremble beneath my feet. The doubt I'd felt earlier about being here flees. "Give me a name."

"I may be old, Kate Burkholder, but I still value my life." She looks around, motions toward the river, her eyes scanning, seeking something unseen. "He listens through the water, you know." The old woman lowers her voice. "If he finds out I'm talking to you, he'll kill me, too. Just like the others."

"I need a name," I say firmly.

She tries to take the shovel from me, but I don't release it.

"I can keep you safe," I tell her. "I'm a police officer."

"The way you kept that girl safe? The bishop?"

I relinquish the shovel. "I need your help."

"You can't stop him. No one can. It's in God's hands now."

I'm losing her, so I try another tactic. "Tell me about the baby. Who is her *mamm*?"

"They shamed her. She couldn't handle it. And just look what happened."

"Tell me. Please."

"Those poor babies." The woman makes a sound that's part grief, part disgust.

"What babies?" I ask, the words spiraling in my brain. "Who are you talking about?"

Ignoring me, she jams the shovel into dirt, pushes it deeper with her shoe.

"What about Marlene Byler?" I ask.

"They shamed her to death. That's why she jumped. They shamed her. *Shamed her.*" Repeating the words like a mantra, she begins to dig, frantically. "Like mother, like daughter. One and the same—both were bad eggs." Jamming the shovel into the dirt, tossing it into the wheelbarrow. Again and again.

When I can stand it no longer, I go to her, try to take the shovel, but she won't release it. "Why did they take the baby?" I ask.

The woman tightens her mouth, doesn't look at me.

"Who are the parents?" I wait a beat. When she says nothing, I add a resounding "Please, all I need is a name."

She raises a shaking hand and wipes rain from her face, slings it to the ground. "You speak the devil's name too often and you'll hear the flap of his wings. You'd be wise to remember that, Kate Burkholder."

Throwing down the shovel, she turns away and starts toward the house.

For an instant, I consider going after her. Pressuring her until I get what I need. I'm not above bullying when I want something, when it's important, even if she's old and frail. This is different. I think the stroke must have affected her mental state. Might be better to try again in the morning.

My boots sink into mud as I walk back to the Explorer. The rain is coming down in sheets and I'm soaked to the skin. My coat's wet. My hair. Rain pounds the hood. I sit there a moment, trying to get my head around what just transpired between me and the old Amish woman.

. . . it wadn't no accident.

Is it possible the hit-and-run that killed Bishop Schwartz wasn't some random, tragic accident? Did the sheriff's department interview Sadie Stutzman? Did they listen to her claims? Or did they simply write her off as an eccentric old woman?

"Damn it," I mutter as I pick up my phone.

The last thing any cop wants to be subjected to is some cop from an outside jurisdiction coming in and questioning the way they handled an investigation. Of course, that's exactly what I'm about to do, so I take a moment to get my words in order before punching in the number.

I get put on hold twice and then Deputy Harleson comes on the line. "Hi, Chief Burkholder. What can I do for you?"

"I got plaster on some tire-tread impressions related to the case I'm working on, and I realized I forgot to ask if you were able to pick up any tread on the hit-and-run that killed Noah Schwartz. I thought it might be worth running a comp."

"I hate to disappoint you, but we didn't get any tread marks. There was heavy rain that night. Anything left behind by the driver got washed away."

I make a sound of disappointment. "I was just talking with some of the local Amish. There are some individuals who believe the bishop's death was not accidental."

He chuckles. "Ah, you talked to the Stutzman widow over there on River Road."

Busted. "Yes."

"I should have warned you. She's a nice lady and all, but she's crazy as a loon. Half the stuff she says . . . you can't believe it. Sorry I didn't warn you."

I'm still thinking about the hit-and-run and the Amish bishop whose life was cut short. "Can you tell me where the accident happened?"

"Intersection of Hayport Road and Burkes Lane. Driver blew the stop sign at a high rate of speed. Hit the buggy from behind."

"What time did it happen?" I ask.

"Nine P.M. or so. Schwartz was one of them Amish that don't use slow-moving-vehicle signs."

"He was Old Order? Swartzentruber?"

"I'm not sure what the difference is to tell you the truth. But Schwartz had no lights or reflective signage on the buggy. It was dark. Perfect storm for a wreck." He pauses. "Do you mind telling me what that hit-and-run has to do with your case up there in Painters Mill?"

"I'm not sure just yet," I say honestly. "If I figure it out, you'll be the first to know."

CHAPTER 14

Fifty hours missing

The scene of the accident is four miles from Sadie Stutzman's house, about midway to the address Harleson gave me for the bishop's wife. Chances are, the deputy's assessment of the incident is correct—a tragic hit-and-run—and Sadie Stutzman, with her strange earthen project and nonsensical ranting, is in the early stages of dementia. I remind myself of all of those things as I roll up to the intersection of Burkes Lane and Hayport Road and park on the gravel shoulder.

Rain pours down from a bruised sky as I take in the scene. It's mostly rural, with a few small, generously spaced homes. There's a guardrail along Burkes. Evidently, the bishop was southbound on Hayport and the unknown driver failed to stop and plowed into the buggy. It's an unfortunate reality anytime you put horse-drawn buggies on the same road with motorized vehicles. Add alcohol or excessive speed—and the absence of proper signage on the buggy—and a cataclysmic outcome is almost guaranteed.

I flick on my emergency lights. I'm already soaked to the skin, so I don't bother with my slicker as I get out of the Explorer. Too much time has elapsed for anything of interest to be left behind. Still, it's usually helpful to see an accident scene in person, to get a feel for it, a better perspective.

The area is wooded. The homes are on good-size lots—an acre or two—and most are relatively private from their neighbors. If someone were planning something nefarious and didn't want to be seen, this would be a good place to do it.

My cell chirps as I'm sliding behind the wheel. I try not to groan when I glance at the display. I don't quite succeed. "Hi, Auggie."

"Kate, I'm glad I caught you. Look, I just took a call from Council-woman Fourman and she's shitting bricks. Someone told her you went out of town. Is that true?"

Auggie Brock is the mayor of Painters Mill. He's a good mayor and a nice man—most of the time. He's well liked, a born politician, and an ally when it's convenient to his agenda. This afternoon, I have a feel-ing my being here is going to be a huge inconvenience.

I tell him where I am, wondering who the stool pigeon is. "I'm fol-lowing up on a lead, Auggie. You know I wouldn't have left at a time like this if it wasn't important." I roll my eyes as I speak, because I know he's not going to buy it.

"Well, has anything panned out?" he asks, exasperation ringing in his voice.

"I'm working on it."

"Kate, you're in the midst of a murder investigation, for God's sake. A little girl is *missing*. People are freaking out. They're scared. I've taken a dozen calls just today from citizens wanting to know what's happen-ing and what we're doing about it. Some parents didn't send their kids to school today. Tourists are canceling their reservations at the B and Bs. That's how bad it is. I don't see how your traipsing down there to some river town is going to help solve this case up here."

I'm not exactly traipsing, but I refrain from pointing that out. Instead, I lay out the scenario as explained to me by Miriam Helmuth. "Auggie, most abductions are committed by family members. I believe Elsie Helmuth has family here in Crooked Creek, and I think they may have been involved not only with the kidnapping, but the murder of Mary Yoder. None of this is for public consumption."

"What the hell am I supposed to tell Janine?"

Several choice words float through my brain, but I behave myself. "Tell her I'm following up on a lead. Let her know Agent Tomasetti is handling the task force, and I should be back inside of twenty-four hours."

He sighs, appeased, but barely. "I'll cover for you as best I can, Kate, but I suggest you return with something to show for your time."

"I'll do my—"

He hangs up on me.

The house where Bishop Schwartz had once lived is vacant, with a for-sale sign in the front yard. I call the Realtor's number, and after being put on hold twice, I get the address for the widow, Lizzie Schwartz.

It's a scenic drive that takes me over a covered wooden bridge, past picturesque farms and forest, to a narrow patch of asphalt that ushers me to the doorstep of the Lake Vesuvius Recreational Area. The mailbox is well marked, so I make the turn onto a nicely maintained lane. The residence is a sunny yellow farmhouse with a bold red door and a wraparound porch jammed with potted plants and a wood swing.

I park in the gravel pullover at the side of the house. Two huge black dogs, tongues lolling despite the chill, bound up to me and begin to bark. Their tails are wagging and they look like they're enjoying the rain, so I take a chance and get out. Luckily, the dogs are friendly, and they accompany me onto the porch.

I knock and take a moment to scratch one of the dogs behind a floppy ear. The door opens and I find myself looking at a pretty Mennonite woman. She's wearing a pink print dress that falls to just below her knees, with a white apron and a high-end pair of sneakers. I guess her to be about forty years of age. She's got freckles, bright red hair pulled into a ponytail, and eyes the color of a mossy pond. She's not a classic beauty, but she's attractive. Even though her clothes are rumpled, her hands stained with something that looks like paint, she's comfortable in her skin.

She looks from me to the dogs and grins, revealing crooked teeth that somehow add to the allure of her face. "You lost?"

"I hope not." I show her my badge. "I'm looking for Lizzie Schwartz."

"I'm Rachel, her daughter." Her smile falls just a little. "Is this about the buggy accident?"

"In part," I say honestly.

She looks at me thoughtfully. "After Dad was killed, my husband and I brought Mom here. We've got a big house. The kids are grown—only two for me, thank you very much. I don't know if you saw it when you pulled in, but we've got that cute little *dawdi haus* out back."

"*Dawdi haus*" is *Deitsch* for "grandfather's house," which is basically a cottage some Amish build next their home so their elderly parents can live nearby and they can care for them during their golden years.

I follow her through the living room and kitchen and out the back door. The *dawdi haus* cottage is more Victorian than Plain, but somehow exudes the best of both worlds. White board-and-batten siding, Galvalume shingles on a steeply pitched roof, wood shutters stained a dark walnut, and a tiny stone porch crowded with clay pots overflowing with sweet rosemary and fall mums.

"Mama?" Rachel doesn't knock, but calls out as she enters.

"In the kitchen!" comes a spry female voice.

Rachel glances over at me and sniffs the air. "She's making apple butter."

We find Lizzie Schwartz at the counter, peeling apples, a dozen or so mason jars lined up on the counter, and a big pot sitting on the stovetop.

"Didn't know we had company." The woman turns to us. She's substantially built and clad completely in black, which will be her color of choice for the next months or even a year, since she's in mourning.

"She's a police, Mama. Here to talk to you about Datt."

A shadow darkens her expression. "You caught the man who hit him?"

"No, ma'am." I tell her about Mary Yoder and Elsie Helmuth. "I want to talk to you about something that happened a few years ago."

A few minutes later the two of us are seated at the table, a cup of steaming cider in front of each of us.

"Noah was a good bishop," she tells me. "A good man. Father. Husband." She sips cider, swallows a little too hard.

"Did he ever travel to Painters Mill?" I ask.

"I believe he did, in fact."

"How long ago?"

"Years, I think."

"Did he know Sadie Stutzman?"

"Anyone who's had a baby around here knows Sadie." She looks at me over the rim of her cup.

It's the longest run of straight answers I've received since I've been in Crooked Creek. "Did your husband transport a baby to Painters Mill?"

Her eyes flick away, then return to mine. "Maybe."

"That's an interesting answer." I set down my cup. "Do you know the circumstances?"

"No." She folds her hands in front of her. "But I probably know more than I should." She gives me a sage look. "The little girl you were telling me about. The missing one. Do you believe they're one and the same?"

"I think that's a possibility."

Bowing her head slightly, she rubs at her temples. "Oh good Lord."

"Mrs. Schwartz, do you know who the parents are?"

"I do not," she tells me. "But I overheard something I never forgot. I knew it would come back to haunt me. I just had this feeling . . . that it was *wrong*."

"Your husband told you about it?"

"Not exactly." Her smile is sad. "You know, it's a momentous occasion for an Amish man to become *Deiner*. For most, it's a burden. A weight they bear. But it's also a calling and they serve with joy." She purses her lips. "Noah took his position as bishop very seriously. He was a sensitive man. He felt things . . . deeply. Too deeply perhaps. But he was strong, too. He never talked to me about the things he dealt with. He never burdened me with knowledge of the things that troubled him."

"How did you find out about the baby?"

This time, her smile contains something akin to shame. "I eavesdropped on a conversation that was none of my business. Between Sadie Stutzman and my husband. I'm not proud and it bothered me for years. What I heard kept me up nights."

"Tell me about the conversation."

Her mouth tightens. "Sadie Stutzman came to our door. It was late. The middle of the night. She was . . . crying and distraught. That was odd for her because that lady is tough as leather, coolheaded, and not prone to high emotion. She was a midwife, you know. To see her so upset . . . I assumed one of her young mothers had lost a baby. I was wrong."

The Amish woman wraps her hands around her mug. "Noah went out to the porch and they spoke in low voices for a long time. I went to the kitchen and made coffee, but when I took the cups to them, I heard Sadie say something about taking a newborn from its *mamm*."

"Did she mention a name?" I ask. "Do you have any idea who the parents are?"

The Amish woman shakes her head. "You have to understand, Chief Burkholder, I only caught bits and pieces of the exchange." Anguish flashes in her eyes. "The thing that surprised me the most—aside from the whole conversation about taking a baby—was that Noah already knew about it. They'd discussed it before. He was the one who suggested Painters Mill. I think he knew someone or had someone in mind for that poor little baby."

She closes her eyes. "God knows, I knew better than to stand there and listen, but I couldn't stop. I just couldn't imagine what could have happened that would prompt Sadie to take an innocent newborn baby."

"Did you have some sense as to why they did it?" I ask.

"All I can tell you, Chief Burkholder, is that there must have been a good reason. That, I know for certain."

"Like what?"

She shrugs. "I couldn't say. But I knew my husband and he was a good and decent God-loving man. This must have been . . . an urgent situation. If the baby wasn't being fed or cared for. Something like that."

"Did you ask your husband about it?"

"I did." Shame flashes in her expression. "I told him I'd overheard part of the conversation." She chokes out an awkward sound. "It's the closest I ever came to lying to him." Another flash of pain. "He wouldn't speak of it. Said he didn't want to burden me. He told me some things are better left unsaid."

She raises her gaze to mine. "He went to Painters Mill the next day. Came home very late. I knew they'd done it. I never broached the subject again."

We sit in the silence of the kitchen, the smells of cinnamon and cider lingering, the words that passed between us adding unpleasant weight to what should have been an enjoyable moment.

"Do you know if the baby was Amish or English?" I ask.

"I'd always assumed she was Plain." Her brows furrow. "Why else would an Amish bishop be involved? An Amish midwife?"

"Did you ask Sadie Stutzman about it?"

"I put it out of my mind is what I did." She shrugs. "Noah said the knowledge would be a heavy burden. That was enough."

She raises her gaze to mine as if something new has occurred to her. "Chief Burkholder, do you think my husband's death is somehow related to . . . what happened with that child? All those years ago?"

"I think it's a possibility."

Tears glimmer in her eyes, but she doesn't let them fall. "Why now? After all this time?"

"I don't know," I say honestly.

Another cumbrous silence and then I ask, "Mrs. Schwartz, do you know of any women who were *ime familye weg* in the weeks before the conversation you overheard?" "In the family way" is the Amish term for "pregnant." "Anyone you can think of?"

"I wondered, of course. Was she unmarried? Was she too young? Unable to care for a baby?" She gives another shake of her head. "I didn't dwell."

I think about everything that's been said and what it could mean in terms of finding Elsie Helmuth. "Do you know Marlene Byler or Mary Byler?" I ask, using Mary's maiden name.

"I didn't know either of them, but I heard about what happened to

Marlene. What she did all those years ago. Jumped off that big bridge up near Portsmouth. I don't know if it's true, but I heard she took her infant daughter off that bridge with her."

A rush of interest engulfs me. "A baby?"

"Less than a year old. The police never found the body so no one knows if it's true."

"What can you tell me about her?"

"Not much, really." The woman shrugs. "She was Amish. Had some mental or emotional issues, I think. There were rumors."

"What kind of rumors?"

"Hush-hush stuff. Boiled down to her not being able to follow the rules. The Amish put up with it for a long time; some tried to help her. But eventually the bishop excommunicated her."

"Do you know why?"

She shakes her head. "She killed herself shortly afterward and people stopped talking about it."

"Did your husband keep a journal or write things down while he was bishop? Anything like that?"

"Noah kept everything in his head." She presses her hand to the left side of her chest. "Or here, more like. In his heart."

"Who's the new bishop?" I ask.

"They just nominated Melvin Chupp."

"Do you know where he lives?" I ask.

"Near Wheelersburg, I think."

I reach into my pocket and set my card on the table in front of her. "If you think of anything else or if something comes to mind that you forgot to tell me, will you let me know?"

"I will." Giving me a sad smile, she reaches out and pats my hand. "You'll do the same, Kate Burkholder?"

"Bet on it."

. . .

I make the drive to Wheelersburg, but there's no one home at the Chupp house so I head back to Crooked Creek. I find the one and only motel and pull into the lot. The Sleepy Time Motel is a mid-century modern dive. I suspect even back in 1960 the place was low-budget. The years haven't been kind. A tangle of chain-link surrounds what was once a swimming pool. An earthquake-size crack splits the concrete where the drain had been. The restaurant in the space next to the office is boarded up with plywood, the single remaining plate-glass window hastily patched with duct tape. I'm desperate for a shower and a bed, so I park and check in.

The room is exactly what I thought it would be. There's a swayback queen-size bed with a tattered headboard and spread. Bad wall art from the 1970s. The bathroom fixtures are rusty, loose tiles on the floor, the grout stained with a couple of decades' worth of mold. But the room is clean, and will do just fine for a shower and sleep.

I brave the shower and crawl into a lumpy bed that smells of scorched cotton and a mattress well past its prime. A mix of rain and sleet pounds the window like handfuls of pea gravel tossed against the glass. Outside, the temperature has dropped twenty degrees in the last hour. The room is cold despite the fact that I've cranked the heater up as far as it will go. I've got my wet jacket draped over the back of the desk chair to dry.

Pulling the spread up to my waist, I fire up my laptop. I run a few searches on Cohen syndrome, but there's not much out there. The symptoms include a host of problems—developmental delay, intellectual disability, muscle weakness, eye problems. It's a rare disorder, caused by a gene mutation, and slightly more prevalent among the Amish. Both parents have to have the gene, but usually don't show signs of the disorder themselves.

If that holds true, it rules out my theory that the mother may have been physically or intellectually unable to care for her child due to Cohen syndrome.

It's eleven P.M. when I call Tomasetti. I summarize my conversation with Lizzie Schwartz. "She overheard most of it. Bishop Schwartz and the midwife conspired to bring a newborn infant to Painters Mill."

"You talk to the midwife?"

I take him through my exchange with Sadie Stutzman. "She danced around most of my questions. Tomasetti, she suggested Bishop Schwartz's death wasn't an accident."

"Did you look at the police report?"

"I talked to the deputy who investigated the accident. They have no idea who was responsible and attributed it to a drunk driver."

"Was the midwife able to make a case?"

"That's the problem. She's . . . eccentric. She'd suffered a stroke recently and the general consensus is that she may be in the early stages of dementia."

"Is she completely diminished mentally?" he asks.

"Not so much that I felt I needed to discount everything she said. And I got the distinct impression she's afraid."

Tomasetti falls silent, digesting; then he asks, "What's your gut telling you? Do you think it's possible someone killed him because of what happened with the kid seven years ago?"

"I think the timing of it and the circumstances are suspect."

"Why now?" he asks. "After so much time?"

"Maybe the parents or a parent or even a family member recently found out what happened and who was involved, and they decided to . . . take back what had been stolen from them." I pause, thinking about the notes. "Look, I'm going to try the midwife one more time tomorrow before I leave, talk to the new bishop, then I'll head back."

SHAMED

After hanging up with Tomasetti, I go back to my search engine, using a multitude of criteria for a missing child five to ten years ago, but nothing comes back. I strike out with the law enforcement databases, too. No newspaper stories. I even spend some time floundering around some of the social media sites. Nothing. Nothing. Nothing.

I go back to the file I brought with me, rereading every report, every interview transcript, every form, and my own personal notes. One name that keeps popping up is Marlene Byler, Mary Yoder's sister. I think about familial connections. The rumors surrounding her death. Is there some nexus I'm not seeing? I flip the page, look at the crime scene photos, desperately seeking something—anything—I missed before, all to no avail.

By the time midnight rolls around, I can't keep my eyes open. I shut my laptop cover, turn off the TV, and exhaustion drags me into a hard sleep.

CHAPTER 15

Sixty-four hours missing

The river moved with an uneasy restlessness. Wind whipped the surface into waves more befitting a lake. The brown current boiled with turbulence. The eddy near the bank formed a whirlpool, sucking leaves and debris into the depths. The family of muskrats that had been living in a push-up near shore had moved to the marsh across the road. Even the red-shouldered hawk that had nested in the birch tree had left for higher ground.

Something coming, she thought.

Sadie Stutzman stood on the back porch and watched the water slither past the muddy bank. Dawn teased the horizon above the treetops to the east. Snow pattered the brim of her winter bonnet and dampened the shoulders of her shawl, but she barely noticed the cold or wet.

She loved the river. The sight of it. The smells. She loved the land with its fickle ways and hidden threats. She'd been born here, raised in this very house. She'd been married in the old barn, which had been swept away by the river going on thirty years ago. She'd lost her husband here a decade ago. Somehow, she'd grown old. This morning, watching the water that was as cloudy and troubled as her own mind, she knew she would probably die here, too. Such were the joys and agonies of life.

Taking a final look at the river, she pushed open the door that took her into her small kitchen. In anticipation of the snow, she'd pulled the last of the mint from the little patch that grew along the side of the house. Tearing off a few leaves, she dropped them into a mug and poured hot water from the teapot she kept simmering on the stove. Mint tea always calmed her. This morning, with her mind in turmoil, she figured she might need two cups.

She couldn't stop thinking about the English policewoman who'd come to her, asking questions, digging up things she had no business digging into. The woman had no idea what she was doing. If she wasn't careful, Kate Burkholder was going to unearth something awful. Something dangerous. Dummkopp, *she thought.* Idiot. *It was a harsh judgment; the woman was just doing her job. She had no way of knowing that the truth would only make things worse. That some questions were best left unasked.*

The exchange haunted her throughout the night. If only she could hurl the memories into the water and let them be sucked into one of those eddies to be buried in the mud and darkness. Perhaps the stroke had been one of God's tender mercies. In His eternal kindness and wisdom, He would erase the memory of that night, of what she'd done. What they'd done. He would ease her pain. Forgive her. Restore the peace she'd lost seven years ago.

Thanks to Kate Burkholder, it was all coming back.

Clutching the mug of tea, Sadie shuffled through the kitchen, down the hall, and entered her bedroom. She set the cup on the night table next to her bed, lit the lantern, and opened the drawer. The sight of the notes sent a shiver through her. She picked them up anyway and read.

> *It is mine to avenge; I will repay. In due time their foot will slip;*
> *their day of disaster is near and their doom rushes upon them.*

The Bible quote was from Deuteronomy 32:35. She'd found it in her mailbox the morning after Bishop Schwartz was killed. Most people would

have laughed at such a thing, imagining some harebrained teenager play-
ing tricks. Not Sadie. She'd known right away it was no joke. She knew
who'd written it, and she knew why.

She flipped to the second note.

> *If a thief is caught breaking in at night and is struck a fatal*
> *blow, the defender is not guilty of bloodshed . . .*

The threat was not lost on Sadie. The question foremost in her mind
was: How did they find out? Only a handful of people knew what had been
done. None of them would have talked about such a thing. Not by choice.

A seven-year-old little girl is missing. She's Amish. Innocent.

Those were the words she couldn't get out of her head. The words that
were a knife to her heart. Sadie cursed Kate Burkholder for saying them.
She cursed herself for what she'd done. For what she'd let happen. For not
having the courage to tell the truth.

"You are with me, Lord, so I won't be afraid. What can human beings
do to me when I have You?" She recited the psalm from memory as she
tucked the notes into the envelope. Untying the strings of her winter bon-
net, Sadie slipped it from her head and set it on the rocking chair in the
corner. Picking up her mug, she blew out the lantern and left the bedroom.

She knew the English policewoman would be back. Kate Burkholder
didn't have a timid spirit. Next time, Sadie would tell her the truth. She
would end this. Deliver that sweet child from evil—if it wasn't already
too late.

Sadie was midway down the hall when she felt the cold air wrap around
her ankles. She stopped, listening, her heart jumping in her chest. Door's
open, she thought, *and she knew.*

"Du dauerte iahra," came a whispered voice from the living room. You
took her.

SHAMED

She saw him then, a silhouette in the dim glow of lantern light. A mountain of a man, standing there, stone still. Eyes like tiny fires.

"I saved her life." Despite the fear crawling over her, Sadie held her ground. "You'd best take her home."

"She is home." He started toward her. Purpose in his strides. Intent in his eyes.

Dear God.

Sadie turned and ran. But she was old. Two steps and he was upon her. A predator on prey. No chance of escape.

"I was trying to help you!" she cried.

The first blow fell upon her, sent her to her knees. Pain streaked across her scalp. The cup flew from her hand, warm tea splashing on the wall, her dress, her legs. Then she was on the floor, the carpet scratchy against her cheek. Head reeling, she looked up at him. "Please don't hurt her!"

"Thou shalt not steal," he said.

Before she could retort, he raised his foot, brought it down hard, and the night swallowed the day.

CHAPTER 16

Sixty-five hours missing

I wake a little before seven A.M. to two inches of snow and a sunrise of monochrome gray. By eight A.M. I'm back on the road. I swing by a small grocery store, grab a cup of coffee, and an extra for Sadie Stutzman along with a dozen blueberry muffins; then I take the county road south toward the river. I'm not above plying a potential witness with food and caffeine.

I drive past the same properties as yesterday. Something about the snow makes them look not quite so dilapidated. Muddy tire tracks mar the driveway of the Stutzman place. As I pull up to the house and shut down the engine, I wonder who's already been here so early. She doesn't seem like the kind of individual who gets a lot of visitors.

Grabbing the cardboard tray containing the coffee and muffins, I wade through snow and mud and take the steps to the front porch. A dusting of snow on the concrete reveals footprints. None are clear, but judging from the size, they belong to a male and they haven't been there long.

I move the storm door aside and knock. "Sadie?" I call out. "It's Kate Burkholder."

I wait a full minute. There's no sound from inside and no one comes to the door. Undeterred, I head around to the rear in case she's up early and working on her earthen levee project. The horse whinnies at me from its pen. Waiting for hay, I think, and I wonder why it hasn't yet been fed. I glance toward the mound of earth Sadie was working on yesterday, but the snow hasn't been disturbed. I take the steps to the tiny porch to knock. A thread of worry goes through me when I find the door open a few inches.

"Sadie? Hey, it's Kate Burkholder. Is everything all right?"

No answer.

I stand there, holding the cardboard tray, thinking about the tire tracks in the driveway, the footprints on the porch, debating. I call out her name again, but no one answers.

"Damn it." Setting the tray on the concrete, I push open the door. The interior is dimly lit and so quiet I can hear the wind whistling through the eaves. The smell of something burning and overripe bananas float on cold air.

"Sadie?"

I step into the kitchen. It's small. Lots of clutter. Something sizzles to my right. There's a low-burning blue flame beneath an old-fashioned teapot. The water has boiled over. The source of the smell. Evidently, it's been burning for some time. I twist off the gas.

The house is a boxy structure with narrow doors and low ceilings that lend a slightly claustrophobic ambience. I pass through the kitchen, pause in the doorway that opens to the living room. Like the rest of the house it's a small, messy space. Lanterns, paperback books, bundles of yarn, and various knitting projects are scattered atop a rustic coffee table. An orange and green afghan that looks as if it's been mauled by a pride of cats is draped over a sofa the color of pea soup. A hook rug covers threadbare carpeting. There's a darkened hallway to my left.

"Sadie?"

Shadows fill the room, so I go to the front window and open the curtains. Dim light seeps in. I glance into the hallway to my left. The thread of worry I'd felt earlier augments into an adrenaline punch when I see the Amish woman lying on the floor, a small heap, unmoving.

"Oh, no."

I go to her and kneel. She's sprawled on her right side with her left arm above her head. Wearing the same dress as yesterday. A mug lying on its side. Urine has soaked into her skirt and puddled on the floor. Something dark smeared on her *kapp*. I know she's dead even before I see her face. Cloudy eyes open and staring. Mouth sagging. Darkish tongue hanging out between hit-or-miss teeth.

"Oh, Sadie." I press my fingers to her carotid artery, but there's no pulse. A chill coils at the base of my spine when I realize her flesh isn't yet cold to the touch.

I have no way of knowing what I've walked into. Sadie was an elderly woman, a stroke victim, and well into her eighties. She could have fallen during the night and broken a hip. She could have had another stroke or a heart attack. Any number of things could have happened. But I can't stop thinking about the tire tracks in the driveway. The footprints on the front porch.

Rising, I step back, slide my .38 from the holster. The hallway is dark; with my other hand I tug the mini Maglite from my jacket pocket. No movement in the bedroom or bathroom beyond. In the periphery of the beam, the old woman's flesh is colorless. Her lips dry and nearly purple. The smear on her *kapp* snags my attention. Blood, I realize. A dribble of it runs from her ear to the crease of skin at her throat. Something not right about her face. . . .

I shift the light. Horror burgeons when I realize one side of her skull has been crushed.

"Shit. Shit."

Every sense attuned to my surroundings, I back away, retrace my steps. The floor creaks behind me. I spin, catch a glimpse of the rocking chair an instant before it crashes into me. The curved slat strikes my temple. Pain sears across my scalp. The armrest slams against my left shoulder. The force sends me to my knees. My .38 clatters to the floor.

A jet engine of adrenaline roars through me. A dozen thoughts register at once. My attacker is male. Tall. Heavily built. Beard.

I dive for the .38. An instant before I reach it, a hand slams down on my shoulder. Fingers dig into muscle and skin, yank me backward with such force that I spin, land on my back. He comes down on top of me, straddles my midsection, draws back to punch me.

I bring up both knees, drive them against his spine. He rocks forward, unfazed, but it buys me an instant. I ram the heel of my hand into his face. The cartilage in his nose crunches. His head snaps back.

His fist careens off my left cheekbone. Stars scatter in my peripheral vision. Pain zings. I'm at a huge disadvantage, weight and strength and position. We're in the hall, hemmed in by the narrow space. I do the only thing I can and bring up my right leg, hook it over his head, my heel against his throat, and send him backward. He growls like an animal. He's off balance now, halfway off me. I bring up my other leg and stomp his chest. The force drives him back. Not for long. He lunges at me, throws a wild punch.

"I'm a cop!" I scream. "I am armed! Get the fuck off me!"

His fist bounces off my knee as I bring it up. I kick at him with both feet. My right heel glances off his chin. He grabs my ankle, but I punt his hand away with my other foot.

Kicking, wildly and without aim, I roll, launch myself at the .38. My hand finds the butt.

He comes down on top of me, a boulder slamming against my back. I'm facedown, my right arm extended, gripping my weapon. A fist comes down on my head like a sledgehammer. My chin slams against the floor. My teeth clack together. My finger is inside the guard. . . .

"Get off me! I'm armed! I will shoot you!"

My screams fall on deaf ears. He's straddling the small of my back. A second punch lands between my shoulder blades. Pain tears the breath from my lungs. His fist slams against the right side of my head. Red and white lights flash. My ear rings. Hands fumble, find my neck. Viselike fingers clamp around my throat, squeezing.

He pulls me backward, lifts the top part of my body off the floor, then shunts my head down. My forehead and nose slam against the floor. Another round of stars. Pain climbs up my sinuses. The warmth of blood on my lips. The copper taste of it in my mouth.

I yank the .38 toward me, bend my arm at the elbow, aim as best I can over my shoulder, and I take a blind shot. The explosion rocks my brain.

My attacker goes rigid. An animalistic howl tears from his throat. I pull the trigger again. He rolls off me. I twist, crabwalk back, bring up the gun. "Police! Get on the ground! Get on the ground!"

I see his silhouette against the window, coming toward me, and I pull off another shot. I hear a whoosh! A piece of furniture flung at me, something heavy hitting my arm. Another zing of pain. A damn chair. . . .

I kick it aside, hear it clatter across the floor. He's nowhere in sight, but I hear him moving around in the living room. "Get your fucking hands up!" I scream. "Get them up! Get on the ground or I will shoot you dead! Do it now!"

The chair flies at me from the mouth of the hall. I block it with my foot. I catch a glimpse of him as he sprints to the kitchen.

I scramble to my feet, dizzy, stumble right, hit the wall with my shoulder. "Police! Stop!"

I follow, round the corner, see him go through the back door. "Police! Halt!"

The man jumps from the porch, streaks across the yard. Then I'm through the door. I level my .38 at the man.

But he's gone.

The deputy with the Scioto County Sheriff's Office arrives on scene in fourteen minutes. I'm sitting in the Explorer, which I've moved to the road's shoulder in front of the house. I was able to preserve some of the tire-tread imprints, but not all of them, and the snow is melting quickly. The prospect of capturing plaster impressions doesn't look good.

The deputy isn't happy with me. For pulling into the driveway. For letting myself into the house. For touching the victim and corrupting a crime scene like some backwoods rookie. He's not shy about letting me know. I don't blame him, so I let him take his jabs. In my defense, I had no way of knowing what I was walking into.

"You make a habit of walking into other people's homes when they don't answer the damn door?" he asks.

"She was elderly. She'd recently had a stroke. I figured a welfare check was in order."

It's a pretty good reason to enter a residence. He's still not pleased.

"Do you need an ambulance?" he asks.

"I'm fine."

Within minutes, another deputy arrives on scene, followed by an ambulance from Portsmouth and a fire engine from the Ironton Fire Department. I'm standing next to my Explorer on the shoulder of the road in three inches of mud when a trooper with the Ohio State

Highway Patrol pulls in. In the last two hours, I've been questioned by three deputies and a female trooper. I've relayed the turn of events half a dozen times. I expect I'll be retelling it a dozen more before I'll be allowed to proceed with what I need to get done.

"Chief Burkholder."

I turn to see Deputy Martin Harleson approach. He's frowning at me, but his hand is outstretched so I shake it.

"You've certainly had a run of bad luck since you've been here in Crooked Creek," he says.

"I'm not sure it has much to do with luck."

I tell him everything I know about the case, my suspicions about an infant being taken from the area seven years ago. I don't know if I can trust him, but in light of what happened to Sadie Stutzman, I don't have a choice. I hold nothing back.

"That's why you were asking about missing kids," he mutters almost to himself.

I nod. "And Noah Schwartz."

He scratches his head. "You think that hit-and-run has something to do with all this?"

"I do."

"Holy cow." He blinks at me. "So are we talking about a stolen baby?"

"Or an illegal adoption of sorts involving Noah Schwartz and Sadie Stutzman."

"And now both of them are dead."

I nod.

"Shit." He scrubs a hand over his face. "Any idea who?"

I shake my head. "A relative. Biological parent or parents." I shrug. "Someone close to the family."

We watch a white Suburban with SCIOTO COUNTY CORONER emblazoned on the doors pull into the driveway.

"Maybe I ought to take another look at the hit-and-run that killed Noah Schwartz," he says after a moment.

"I'd appreciate it if you did." I watch the technician open the rear door of the Suburban and roll a gurney out of the back. "I thought I might talk to the new bishop before I head back to Painters Mill. See if he can shed some light on any of this."

He nods, interested now, his eyes level on mine. "You think he knows something about this?" He motions toward the house.

I give him the only answer I can. "I don't know."

"Look, I'll do what I can to send you on your way, but someone in our investigations division is going to want to talk to you; they're going to want a statement." He motions toward my sidearm. "They're going to need your weapon, too."

I don't relish the idea of being without my .38 for the remainder of the trip, especially after what just happened, but I don't argue. I sigh. "That's fine."

"Hang tight, Chief Burkholder, and I'll get things rolling."

Bishop Melvin Chupp lives on a dirt track off of Hansgen Morgan Road near Wheelersburg. It's a pretty piece of land with an old brick farmhouse and two big red bank barns in the back. The woman who answers the door tells me I'll find her husband in the barn. She hands me a paper plate heaped with a dozen or so oatmeal cookies to take to him and tells me I should eat as many as I can because he "eats like a starved horse."

Carting the plate, I take a barely-there stone path to the barn. The big sliding door stands open, so I take the ramp and go inside. The pleasant smells of horses and hay and leather greet me like old friends. "Hello?" I call out. "Bishop Chupp?"

"Who wants to know?" comes a whispered voice.

"Chief of Police Kate Burkholder."

"I like the sound of that name. Come on back."

Balancing the paper plate of cookies in my right hand, I start toward the sound of the voice. I find the bishop in the first stall I come to. He glances at me and puts his finger to his lips. "Shhh."

I look past him to see a goat in the throes of kidding. For an instant, the case and all its darkness and urgency fall to the wayside. I forget about the death of Sadie Stutzman, the ambush this morning, and for a short span of time, I'm living in the moment, enthralled, watching three tiny creatures enter the world.

As the doe begins to lick the afterbirth from her offspring, I find myself thinking of the bond between a mother and her offspring. I think about the woman who gave birth to Elsie Helmuth and I wonder: How far would a parent go to get their child back?

I look at the bishop and motion toward the aisle outside the stall. "*Kann ich shvetza zu du e weil?*" I ask. Can I talk to you awhile?

"*Kannscht du Deitsch schwetze.*" You can talk Dutch. The Amish man grins, as pleased as he is amused. "That's two miracles in one day," he exclaims. "First triplet goats and then an *Englischer* speaking *Deitsch*!"

Breaking into laughter, he follows me from the stall. Once we're in the aisle, I hand him the cookies. "From your wife."

Smiling down at the plate, he rubs his fingers together and selects the biggest one. "She's stingy with the sweets."

"Probably for your own good."

"It is."

Narrowing his eyes, noticing the bruises on my face, he proffers the plate. "You look like you could use a little kindness."

I take a cookie without answering and we eat in silence for a moment. I don't know this man from Adam, but I find myself liking him. He's got gentle eyes filled with jollity and a discerning intelligence.

"I understand you're the newly ordained bishop," I say.

"The voice of the church spoke, and I was struck by the lot," he says, referring to the Amish practice of selecting their bishop from the ordained leaders by lot.

"I'm working on a case, Bishop, and I need your help." I tell him about the murder of Mary Yoder and the kidnapping of Elsie Helmuth.

His expression sobers. "I will pray for them," he says quietly.

"I think Bishop Schwartz may have been involved in . . . an unofficial adoption of a newborn infant seven years ago."

"Unofficial adoption?"

"I have reason to believe a baby born here in Scioto County was, for unknown reasons, taken from her mother and transported to Painters Mill to be placed with another Amish family. Bishop Schwartz and a midwife, Sadie Stutzman, were involved." I pause, grapple with the words. "As you know, Bishop Schwartz was killed a couple of weeks ago. Sadie Stutzman was murdered sometime this morning."

"Sadie? *Mein Gott.*" My God. The Amish man steps back, presses his hand to his chest. "You know this for certain?"

I nod. "I just left the scene."

He looks down at the ground, troubled, his brows knitting. "*Sis en gottlos ding.*" It's a godless thing.

I watch him carefully, gauging his responses, trying to discern if he's already familiar with the information I've relayed. The only emotions that come back at me are shock and the grief of a man who already bears a heavy load.

"I believe someone living in this area knows what happened seven years ago," I tell him. "I believe that person traveled to Painters Mill, murdered the girl's grandmother, and took the child. I think this individual may be a family member or parent. That little girl is in grave danger."

The bishop lowers the cookie he'd been nibbling and sets the plate on a bale of hay next to him. "I will pray for her safe return."

"Does the name Marlene Byler mean anything to you?" I ask.

He sags, as if the memory is a physical weight on his shoulders. "Her story is a sad and terrible one." He raises his gaze to mine. "It was a long time ago. Do you think what happened to Marlene has something to do with this missing child?"

I tell him what little I know. "She was Mary Yoder's sister."

The bishop sighs, resigned. "I didn't know Marlene, but I heard the stories. She was . . . disturbed." He taps his temple with a fingertip. "Here. She suffered with headaches and fevers. Thought she was possessed by the devil. *Narrisch,* you know." Insane.

"Did she seek treatment?"

"From Amish healers mostly. A local chiropractor. I heard she went to the *Brauch-Doktor* in Pennsylvania a couple times."

"*Brauch-Doktor*" is the *Deitsch* term for "powwowing," which is basically faith healing, using incantations, amulets, or charms to heal. The rituals are mysterious, often used as a last-resort type of treatment. Most Amish today condemn the practice; many of the young aren't even aware of its existence.

"There were all sorts of rumors," he tells me.

"What kind of rumors?"

"About men. English, Amish. She wasn't living a godly life."

"Does she have any children?"

"Rumor had it when she jumped from that bridge, she took her last child with her."

It's a tragic, haunting tale. The question foremost in my mind is:

Does it have anything to do with the abduction of Elsie Helmuth and the murder of her grandmother?

"Do you know if Bishop Schwartz kept any writings or letters?" I ask.

He shakes his head. "I've not seen such a thing. Noah's death came so suddenly . . . no one was prepared. You've checked with Lizzie?"

I tell him as much as I can without revealing anything she wouldn't want disclosed.

The smile that follows is so heavy and filled with grief that I feel the weight of it in my own heart. "There's a saying among the Amish. *Wu schmoke is, is aa feier.*" Where there is smoke, there is fire. "I will ask around, look for the answers you need. If I find something, I will let you know."

CHAPTER 17

Seventy-four hours missing

It was nights like this that tested a man's faith. Nights that were as dark and cold as the devil's heart—if indeed, the beast possessed any semblance of a heart at all.

Bishop David Troyer didn't think so. Mary Yoder was dead. The little girl was probably gone, too. He didn't know how it had come to this. He didn't know what he could have done to stop it or change it. He'd prayed for God to send him the wisdom and the strength he needed to make things right. Somehow, he'd failed. He'd failed all of them. God. Himself. The Helmuth family. He'd especially failed little Elsie.

He left the Helmuth farm just ten minutes ago. Miriam and Ivan had spent most of the day praying for the safe return of their daughter. They'd prayed for Mary Yoder. For their children. The bishop thought maybe they should pray for forgiveness, too—all of them—but he didn't say it. That was on him and he would bear the load alone—even if it crushed him.

His faith was the one thing that had always made him strong, given him joy in times of sorrow, light when there was only darkness. He held his faith dear and he used it to serve. It made him a better man, a better father and husband; it made him a better bishop. His faith in the Heavenly Father was his whole heart. It was his peace. His guidance.

SHAMED

This evening, Bishop Troyer was troubled and questioning decisions he'd once been so certain of, namely the decision he'd made seven years ago regarding the fate of an infant at risk. Had he done the right thing? Had he been honest with God? Had he been honest with himself? The questions pummeled him and yet he had no answers.

Clucking to the horse, he snapped the lines against the gelding's rump and sent the animal into an extended trot. Around him the early evening was windy, cold, and damp. The kind of cold that seeped to the bone.

"God, this hidden sin eats away at my heart." He whispered the words from memory. "I have no peace because of it. Help me to give it to You."

At the intersection of County Road 150 and Township Road 104, he made the turn toward home and headed north. The clip-clop of the horse's shoes echoed among the treetops. A gust of wind made the branches clatter like bones.

He was thinking about the notes, about a little girl who might have left this world all too soon, when a tremendous slug of pain exploded in his side. He thought he heard a crack of thunder. The breath left his lungs. Fire burned and spread, hot wax boiling in his chest.

He slumped forward, reached out, tried to break his fall. The strength leached from his muscles. One of the reins slipped from his hands. Then he was falling. His right shoulder struck the floorboard. An earthquake of pain in his chest. The cold grit of dirt and wood against his face. Blood on his hands, running like rain.

The buggy stopped. Cold silence all around. The hiss of the wind. A volley of pain with every drumbeat of his heart. He couldn't move. Wasn't sure what had happened.

Footsteps sounded, heavy on the asphalt. The labored breaths of someone nearby. The scuff of shoes. The bishop opened his eyes. Relief washed over him when he saw the Plain man. He tried to speak, but there was too much blood, and he managed little more than a gurgle.

The man came to him. Hands touching his arm, his coat. "If thou do that which is evil, be afraid; for he beareth not the sword in vain," *the man said in* Deitsch.

Only then did the bishop realize the man wasn't there to help. Words flared in his brain. He had to stop this terrible thing he himself had helped put into play. "Forgive them," *he ground out.* "For they know not what they do."

"Avvah shpoht," *came the voice. Too late.*

"Kumma druff!" *The man slapped the horse's rump.*

The buggy leapt forward.

The bishop listened to the horse's shoes against the ground, frightened and moving fast. Take me home, my heavenly Father, *and he tumbled into the waiting darkness.*

CHAPTER 18

Seventy-five hours missing

I'm eastbound on US 62 west of Killbuck when my Bluetooth jangles. Glock's name pops up on the display screen, so I hit answer.

"Auggie didn't send out a search party for me, did he?" I ask.

The beat of silence that follows lasts an instant too long, and I know the news is bad. "Chief, I'm out at David Troyer's place. He's been shot. Wife found him twenty minutes ago. It's bad."

The words hit me like the blade of a shovel in my chest. "Shot?" I repeat dumbly. "Bishop Troyer?"

"He's alive. Ambulance just left. He's en route to the hospital. I'm here at their farm, trying to figure out what the hell happened. Tomasetti's on the way."

"My God." I almost can't wrap my mind around the notion of Bishop Troyer becoming a victim of violence. He's been a constant in my life—for better or worse—for as long as I can remember. He's larger than life. Untouchable. Impervious to all the ills that plague us mere mortals. In the back of my mind, a little voice reminds me that he was there the night Bishop Schwartz and Sadie Stutzman brought a baby to Painters Mill.

"I'm ten minutes out." I hit my emergency lights, crank the speedometer to eighty. "What's the bishop's condition?"

Another hesitation. "I don't know yet. But it's serious, Chief. Get here as quick as you can."

I arrive at the Troyer farm to an ocean of emergency vehicles. The road in front of the house is blocked off on both sides by Holmes County Sheriff's Department cruisers. A deputy sets out flares. I yank out my badge, roll down my window. He motions me past and I speed by without speaking.

As I barrel up the lane I see an Ohio State Highway Patrol Dodge Charger. Two more cruisers from Holmes County. Tomasetti's Tahoe is parked at an odd angle behind a buggy to which a horse is hitched. There's an ambulance and a fire truck with the Painters Mill volunteer fire department. Glock's cruiser is parked a few yards away. Half a dozen cops mill about.

I park behind the Tahoe and throw open my door. I'm out and running before I even know where I'm going. I spot Glock standing next to Sheriff Mike Rasmussen. Both men give my bruised face a double take as I stride toward them.

"Chief?" Glock says, looking concerned.

"What happened to Troyer?" I ask.

"Kate." Rasmussen's expression is grim. He's looking at me as if he isn't quite sure he can give it to me straight, so I make an effort to tone it down, yank back my emotions, stuff them back in their hole.

"All we know is that he was shot," the sheriff tells me.

He motions toward the buggy a few feet away. "Wife said he was over at the Helmuths'. He was late getting home. She walked out here and found him in the buggy. Troyer was slumped over, unconscious.

We're still trying to figure things out, but it looks like he was shot elsewhere and the horse brought him home."

"His wife ran half a mile to the neighbors, and they called 911," Glock adds.

Beyond him, I see Tomasetti; he's talking to a trooper, but he's caught sight of me. Abruptly, he ends his conversation and heads my way. "Chief Burkholder."

I start toward the buggy. I'm midway there when he sets his hand on my shoulder, turns me around. Concern sharpens his features, tightens his mouth. "What happened to your face?"

"I got jumped," I say. "I'm fine."

"Kate . . ."

"I can't talk right now."

"You need to see this," he snaps.

I waver, turn to him. I watch as he reaches into his coat pocket and pulls out a clear plastic bag. There's something inside. A smear of blood on the plastic. The ground swells and dips beneath my feet when I recognize the eyeglasses inside. They're small and round with thick lenses. Lenses that are cracked and covered with blood.

The sight is a jab to my solar plexus that takes my breath. For a moment, I can't speak. Finally, I manage, "They're Elsie's. Where did you find them?"

"Buggy. On the seat." He shakes his head. "We don't know if Troyer had them for some reason or if the shooter left them."

"He left them for us to find," I say. "The son of a bitch."

"I'm going to rush them to the lab. Have the blood analyzed, check for latents."

"Dear God if he hurt that child," I hear myself say, trying to breathe, get oxygen into my lungs.

He grimaces, looks away. "I'll have Ivan confirm the glasses belong to the girl."

It's not going to be easy. I want to be there, I realize. But I can't leave. "I need to talk to the bishop's wife."

"Go," he says. "I'll take care of this."

I start toward the buggy. I'm ten feet away when I spot the pool of blood on the gravel. There's more inside the buggy, dripping down the side. Someone has set up mini orange cones demarking the pool. I walk around the buggy, taking in details. There's an afghan on the seat, also stained with blood. A thick smear on the seat front. Dear God . . .

I look over my shoulder toward the men. Glock and Rasmussen have followed me over. "Where did this happen?" I ask.

"We're trying to figure it out," Rasmussen says. "We've got a trail of blood. Deputies are tracing it now."

"Where's his wife?" I ask.

"Inside," Rasmussen says. "I talked to her. She didn't see anything."

Outrage thrashes inside me, expands in my chest. I think about Sadie Stutzman and Noah Schwartz. I think about Mary Yoder and now David Troyer. I think about Elsie Helmuth, terrified and alone and in terrible danger—if she's still alive. And now the bishop's wife, a woman who likely knows more than she's letting on, has nothing to say.

"Mike, did you question her?" I ask.

"Of course I did."

"I want a go at her."

The sheriff's eyes narrow. "You think she's not being forthcoming?"

I lay out my theory, hating the quaver in my voice. That I'm angry and upset. As implausible as all of it seems, I know I'm right. "I think Bishop Troyer was involved with this . . . adoption."

"If there was a newborn stolen, why wasn't it reported to the authorities?" he asks, incredulity thick in his voice.

"Because they wanted to handle it on their own. Because they didn't want to involve Children Services. They knew someone would try to stop them. All of the above."

"Look, Kate, we'll certainly take a hard look into all that, but—"

"The bishop in Crooked Creek was killed in a hit-and-run buggy accident two weeks ago, Mike. The midwife who was part of this was murdered in her home early this morning." I motion toward the buggy. "Now Bishop Troyer has been shot. I believe they were targeted. I believe the person who abducted Elsie Helmuth is responsible. And I don't think he's finished."

"Let's not get ahead of ourselves here. That determination will be made after we look at all the facts."

I like Mike Rasmussen. He's a good cop and a friend. He's a decent sheriff who knows how to run his department. He's not overly political, but he's not opposed to scratching the occasional back to get what he wants. He knows how to get things done. He's easygoing. Reasonable. I never have to wonder if he has my back; I know he does. None of those things come close to convincing me I'm getting ahead of myself.

I turn away from him and start toward the house.

"Where are you going?" he asks.

"I'm going to talk to Freda Troyer."

"She's already been interviewed, Kate. That poor woman is trying to get to the hospital to be with her husband."

"I'll take her," I say without breaking stride.

"Damn it, Kate."

I turn so abruptly, the sheriff nearly runs into me. He sets his hand on my arm, but I shake it off. "You need to trust me on this, Mike."

"That works both ways."

"I'm right about this, so back off."

"This is my jurisdiction."

It was the one thing that didn't need to be said. In the years I've been chief, Mike and I have never argued about turf. We've never had to. We work together well. My department covers county as much as it does Painters Mill. The certainty that I'm right won't let me back down.

"Freda Troyer knows more than she's letting on," I tell him. "I'm going to talk to her because I want answers and I damn well want them now."

I walk into the Troyer home to find Freda pacing the kitchen. She's wearing a charcoal-colored dress, a black cardigan, practical shoes. She's put a black winter bonnet over her prayer *kapp*. Dinner plates and flatware have been set out on the table. A cast-iron skillet sits atop the stove, filled with fried chicken in grease that's gone white. Evidently, she'd been holding dinner for her husband.

"Freda?" I say as I enter.

She startles and turns to me. "Kate." I see anguish in her face. Worry etched into her every feature. Dried blood on hands she didn't think to wash. "How is he?" she asks.

"I don't know. Ambulance took him to the hospital." I approach her, trying to read her frame of mind. Calm on the outside, coming apart on the inside. Struggling for strength. Hanging on by a thread.

"Get your things," I say. "I'll take you."

"Our neighbor is going to take me. He's harnessing the buggy horse now."

"I'll ask one of my deputies to let him know you got a ride." When she hesitates, I add, "I'm going anyway; you may as well ride with me. I'll get you there a lot faster."

While Freda gathers her things—a canvas bag filled with what looks like knitting supplies, a small devotional book—I radio Glock and ask him to tell the neighbor that I'll be driving the bishop's wife to the hospital.

"You guys figure out where the shooting took place?" I ask him.

"Deputy followed the blood trail," he tells me. "Looks like it happened where County Road 150 intersects with Township Road 104."

I know the area. It's rural, not many houses. The perfect place for an ambush. "Anyone see anything?"

"We're canvassing now."

"Tire marks? Anything like that?"

"Still looking around, Chief."

"I'll be there as soon as I can."

I drop the cell into my pocket, turn to see the bishop's wife standing in the doorway, clutching her bag, staring at me. "Let's go," I say.

She follows me outside. I feel the stares track us as I make my way to the Explorer, but I don't make eye contact with anyone. I open the passenger door for her, and then I round the front of the vehicle and get in. I don't see Tomasetti anywhere. I put the vehicle in gear and we start down the lane.

I raise my hand to the deputy at the road, then make a right and head toward Millersburg. I only have a few minutes to ask the questions that need to be asked. I have no idea what we'll find when we arrive at Pomerene Hospital. Glock had said it's bad. The one thing I am certain of is that this woman may hold the key.

"I know Bishop Schwartz from Scioto County brought a newborn baby to Bishop Troyer seven years ago," I say as I pull onto the highway. "I know the baby was taken to Miriam and Ivan Helmuth."

She looks over at me, anguish churning in her eyes. "I don't know what that has to do with what's happened to my husband."

"It has everything to do with it, Freda, and if you know anything

195

at all that will help me get to the bottom of it, you need to speak up right now."

I tell her about the eyeglasses, my trip to Crooked Creek. "Freda, look at my face. I was ambushed and beaten. Bishop Schwartz is dead. The midwife who helped bring that child up here was murdered this morning. Now your husband has been shot. If you care one iota about that little girl, you need to start talking."

The Amish woman stares straight forward, frozen, except for the occasional tremor that runs through her. For the first time I see tears on her cheeks. But she doesn't make a sound.

I push harder. "What if he kills little Elsie Helmuth?" I shout. "What if he goes after Miriam and Ivan or their children? Is all that holier-than-thou-art silence of yours worth it if someone else is killed?"

"Don't you dare speak to me in that manner, Kate Burkholder. You of all people. Backslider. *Maulgrischt,*" she hisses. Pretend Christian. "Your mother didn't know what to do with you and you broke her heart."

She's getting herself worked up. Maybe because it's easier to be angry with me than it is to be terrified for the life of her husband.

I keep my voice level. "This isn't about me."

She's not finished. "*Mer sott em sei eegne net verlosse; Gott verlosst die seine nicht.*" One should not abandon one's own; God does not abandon his own. "You did just that, Katie. And now look at you, talking to me as if I'm somehow to blame."

I've heard the words a hundred times since I came back to Painters Mill. I want to believe they no longer affect me. That I'm immune. Above it. But even after all this time, the small part of me that is Amish—that will always be Amish—recoils from the sting.

"That's enough," I snap. "I know you're hurting and afraid, but I need your help and I need it right now. I'm trying to do the right thing. Do my job. Do you understand?"

Turning her head, she looks out the window, shutting me out.

I hit her with the coup de grâce. "If Elsie Helmuth is killed, it's on your shoulders, Freda. You got that?"

Silence reigns for the span of several minutes. I make the turn onto US 62 and head north. Neither of us speaks until I'm stopped at the traffic light at Jackson Street in Millersburg. The courthouse is to my right, the old Hotel Millersburg to my left.

"You have to understand," she says in a strangled voice. "Being the bishop's wife . . . I see things. I hear things. That doesn't mean I'm told what's going on."

"Tell me what you know."

"I was there the night they brought her," she whispers. "David told me I was to never speak of it. I took those words to heart."

"Who brought her?"

"Bishop Schwartz and a midwife. They brought her here to the house. A tiny little girl. Hours old. She was desperately hungry. I fed her, held her in my arms . . ."

"Do you know who the parents are?" I ask. "I need names."

"No." She shakes her head adamantly. "They did not say, and I did not ask. It was a night filled with worry and tears and many things left unsaid."

"Why did they do it?"

"There is a saying among the Amish." She looks at me. *"Die besht vayk zu flucht eevil is zu verfolgen goot,"* she whispers. The best way to escape evil is to pursue good.

"The bishop, my husband, and that midwife were pursuing good, Katie. All they wanted was to place that innocent baby in a loving home, where she would be safe, and so she would be raised Amish."

"The baby came from an Amish family?"

She shrugs. "I assumed so. Why else would they do such a thing?"

"Freda, why did they take her?"

"I don't know, Katie. They were . . . secretive about all that." The woman shrugs. "I suspected there was something wrong in the home. Some . . . problem."

"What kind of problem?"

"Something bad, or they never would have done what they did. I know my husband. He is a good man, a godly man, and a good bishop. He does not overstep. If there is something I need to know, he will tell me." She shakes her head. "Katie, it would have been unseemly for me to ask questions at such a time. Some of the things the bishop does are . . . delicate. You know, private."

"Was the baby brought here with the blessing of the family?"

"I do not know."

Everything she's told me grinds in my head like shards of glass in a kaleidoscope. I already knew or suspected most of it. What I need more than anything is a name. That's when it occurs to me that Crooked Creek is four hours away by car. There's no way they would have transported a baby in a buggy.

"Freda, did they use a driver?"

She nods. "They came in a van."

"Did you see the driver?"

"No. He stayed outside."

As I make the turn into the hospital parking lot, the Amish woman tosses me a knowing look. "You believe the parents or some relative of the baby are responsible for the bad things that have been done?"

"I do."

She thinks about that a moment. "I'm glad I told you, Katie. It was the right thing to do. God willing, David will give you the name you need when we talk to him."

. . .

According to the emergency room physician, Bishop Troyer was rushed to surgery upon arrival. He sustained a single gunshot wound to his abdomen; it's a life-threatening injury, the seriousness exacerbated by his age. All the doctor can tell us at this point is that the bishop is in extremely critical condition and not yet stable.

I walk with Freda to the surgical intensive care waiting area, where a family with small children stares at the television tuned to some mindless sitcom. I leave Freda there, find a vending machine down the hall, and buy two coffees. When I return, she's sitting in the same place, her head bowed in prayer, tears streaming.

I've known Freda since I was six years old and she smacked my behind with her horse crop when I clobbered one of the other Amish kids. She has always been a strong woman, is much respected by the community, and nearly as formidable as her husband. Tonight, seeing her like this, touches a place inside me I don't want prodded.

Steeling myself against the sight of her broken and weeping, I approach and hand her the steaming cup. "Fortification," I say, offering a smile.

She takes the paper cup and sips. "Good Lord, that's the worst coffee I ever had."

"That's only because you haven't been to the police station."

We exchange a look and then we fall silent. I'm not happy with Freda Troyer or the bishop. They were involved in something malapropos seven years ago. Even after the murder of Mary Yoder, and the abduction of Elsie Helmuth, they didn't come forward. Even after I asked, they held their silence—and possibly information that might have prevented this most recent tragedy. With the bishop's life hanging by a thread, I'm hard-pressed to castigate her.

"I can't stay," I tell her. "I have to get back out there and try to find the person responsible."

The Amish woman nods. "Thank you for bringing me to be with my husband."

She may be alone at the moment, but I know she won't be for long. Word of the shooting and the bishop's condition will spread through the Amish community like wildfire. I know that even as we speak, half a dozen buggies are already en route.

"Freda, is there anything else you can tell me that might help me find the person who did this?"

She shakes her head. "I've told you everything I know."

I walk away, leaving her with her anguish, her fear, and the knowledge that the shooting of her husband isn't the only tragedy that must be dealt with.

CHAPTER 19

Seventy-eight hours missing

I arrive at the intersection of County Road 150 and Township Road 104 to find Glock's cruiser blocking traffic, his emergency lights flashing. He's set out flares, but he's nowhere in sight. A quarter mile ahead, a Holmes County cruiser is parked in the same fashion. The deputy is setting up a reflective wooden horse.

I tug my cell from the console and call Skid. Last I heard, he'd gone home to get some sleep. I'm loath to call him back to work, but I can't spare him.

He answers with a groggy "Yeah."

"Sorry to wake you."

"I wasn't asleep." We laugh because we both know it's not true.

I tell him about Bishop Troyer.

"Damn, Chief, the *bishop*? Is he—"

"He's alive, but critical. The problem is I don't know if the son of a bitch who shot him is finished. I need you to go out to the Helmuth place and keep an eye on things. Keep your radio handy. Wear your vest."

A thoughtful silence and then, "You got it."

I end the call and I'm reminded that I'll need to pick up another sidearm when I get back to the station. Around me, the area is heavily treed, except to the south where yellow cornstalks shiver in a brisk north wind. The temperature is falling fast and I suspect it'll dip into the twenties by morning.

Hitting my emergency lights, I park behind Glock's cruiser, grab my Maglite, and go in search of him. I spot the cone of a flashlight just inside the tree line and start that way.

I call out to him. "Find anything?"

Glock motions toward the road where there's a smattering of tiny orange cones. "Got blood on the road there, Chief. Starts right there where I'm parked. I'm pretty sure this is where the shooting took place."

"Brass?"

"Nada."

"Anyone else on scene?"

He motions toward the deputy at the end of the road. "County arrived a few minutes ago. Pickles and T.J. started a canvass."

We both know with so many trees and the neighboring houses set back from the road and separated by miles of fields, the chances of finding a witness are slim.

We reach the cones. Glock shifts his Maglite. The yellow beam reveals the red-black gleam of blood on the asphalt; additional spatters the size of half-dollars stand out against the yellow line. A few larger pools. Too much, I think, and I pull the mini Maglite from my pocket and kneel. Our beams merge.

"A lot of blood," he mutters. "How's the old guy?"

"They just took him into surgery."

"He able to tell you anything?"

I shake my head. "I don't think he's going to be talking any time soon."

We study the blood for a moment, our beams sweeping left and right, from puddle to puddle, trying to figure out exactly where the shooting took place.

"According to his wife," I say, "the bishop was on his way home from the Helmuth place." I set my beam on the ground, find a spot of blood that's been run over by a buggy wheel. Glock drops a cone next to it.

"He would have been traveling north," I tell him.

"That helps." Setting his hands on his hips, Glock pauses, looks around, motions with his eyes to the woods where the trees are thick. "If I wanted to ambush someone and I thought they might be coming this way, I'd take cover in those trees over there."

I follow his gaze to the place where I'd found him when I arrived. "He would have had decent cover."

"And a clean shot," he adds.

We traverse the ditch and reenter the woods. Though most of the trees have lost their leaves, the trunks are close together and the underbrush is thick, making it difficult to maneuver. The ground is spongy beneath my boots, layered with fallen leaves and rotting foliage. We reach a clearing and split up, moving slowly, our beams sweeping left and right as we make our way more deeply into the forest.

It's so cold I can see my breaths puff out in front of me. I take my time, keeping my eyes on the ground, looking for the gleam of a cartridge or ground that's been disturbed. I check the trees and brush I pass by for broken branches or threads from clothing. Any sign that someone has been here recently. My beam illuminates wet leaves, fallen branches, dozens of naked saplings. I don't venture too far from the road. Chances are, whoever shot Bishop Troyer stood just inside the tree line or possibly a clearing. Well covered, but not seen . . .

"What did you leave for me, you son of a bitch?" I whisper.

I step over a rotting log, veer left toward the road. I notice something light-colored on the ground to my right. My beam illuminates a rock the size of a tire. I hear Glock moving through brush behind me, heading in the opposite direction. I keep going, seeking anything that looks out of place.

I've gone about twenty yards when a speck on the ground snags my attention. I stop, set my beam on it. A tiny white scrap of what looks like tissue paper or fabric is nestled beneath a bush. I go to it, kneel for a closer look, and my heart begins to pound.

The piece of paper is about the size of a dime. It's actually gray in color. Darker and tattered around the edges. Burned, I realize. Wet from the drizzle. It's the kind of thing most people wouldn't notice. Not even a cop. Nothing more than a piece of litter. But I've seen these scraps of paper before. My *datt* was an avid hunter and put venison on our table twice a year. His rifle of choice was a muzzle-loader.

I hit my shoulder mike. "Glock, I got something."

"On my way."

I stand, shine my beam in a circle. I find a freshly broken branch on a sapling. A tuft of grass that's been crushed beneath a shoe or boot. Six feet away, there's a narrow patch of earth where rain has washed away most of the leaves. Sure enough, the faint mark of a shoe imprint with a waffled sole. It's a partial, the rear half set in an inch or so of rotting leaves.

Brush rustles as Glock approaches. "Brass?"

"Partial shoe imprint." I shift my beam to the scrap of paper.

"What the hell is that?" he asks. "Wrapper of some sort?"

"Wadding from a muzzle-loader," I tell him.

He laughs. "Damn good find, Chief."

We kneel for a closer look. "My dad had a muzzle-loader," I tell him. "I saw plenty of those little scraps of paper when I was a kid. Or else I wouldn't have recognized it."

His eyes meet mine. "So our shooter is probably Amish."

"We figured as much, but this is one more indication that we're right." I stand, look around, and sigh. "It isn't much, but more than what we had."

"I wonder if there's any way we can use that wadding to ID the weapon," he says.

"Firearms guy at BCI might know."

He pulls an orange cone from his coat and sets it on the ground next to the scrap of paper. "Hopefully, it'll help us stop this motherfucker."

It's ten P.M. and the Painters Mill Police Department bustles with frenetic activity. Everyone except Skid and my off-duty dispatcher is here, including Tomasetti, Sheriff Mike Rasmussen, and a trooper with the Ohio State Highway Patrol. The task force is meeting and I'm five minutes late, so I snag my legal pad off my desk and head that way.

"Any word on the bishop?" I call out as I pass the dispatch station.

"They won't tell me much, Chief, since I'm not family," says Jodie. "All she could say is that he made it through surgery, he's on a respirator, and is in the intensive care unit in critical condition."

I proceed toward the meeting room, think better of it, and go back out to the reception area. "Thanks for pulling a double shift," I tell her. "I appreciate it."

She beams a grin at me and I'm reminded how young she is. That she probably has better things to do. "Happy to fill in, Chief."

I enter the war room to find John Tomasetti standing at the head of the table, the half podium shoved aside, the mike tucked out of the way. He nods at me when I enter, his eyes lingering an instant too long.

"The technician was able to lift a plaster of the shoe imprint out at the intersection where we believe the shooting took place," he says. "Preliminarily, we got a men's size thirteen. Tread matches the plaster taken at the scene of the Yoder murder and the abduction of the

Helmuth girl. Lab is running a comp now, which is forthcoming, but I think it's safe to assume we are dealing with the same individual. We believe he is a white male. He may be Amish or presenting himself as an Amish person. Judging from the shoe size, well over six feet tall." He looks at me again. "I believe Chief Burkholder will be giving you a more detailed description."

He flips a page and frowns. "We did not get DNA from the killer at the Schattenbaum farm. Both sets belong to Yoder and the Helmuth girl. The tire tread was identified, as most of you know. We believe this individual drives or has access to a pickup truck or SUV."

He looks at me again. "Chief Burkholder, you want to talk about that wadding you found at the scene of the Troyer shooting?"

I speak from my place at the door. "We believe David Troyer was traveling north on Township Road 104 when he was shot. The wadding was in the woods east of the road, about ten yards in. That's where we think the shooter stood and took his shot. The wadding is consistent with a muzzle-loader or black-powder-type rifle. For those of you not familiar with that kind of weapon, they do not use regular cartridges. According to the surgeon who removed the projectile from Troyer, the projectile was a lead ball, which is commonly used and has been sent to the BCI lab. What's significant about the muzzle-loader is that the Amish use that type of rifle for hunting. While we can't say for certain he's Amish, this strengthens my belief that he is or was at some point in his life."

"Makes sense in light of the victim and abducted girl being Amish," Sheriff Rasmussen puts in.

"Unless someone wants us to *believe* he's Amish," Tomasetti adds.

I nod in agreement and continue, summarizing my theory about the illicit adoption of an infant seven years ago and hitting the highlights of my trip to Crooked Creek. "The two people from Crooked Creek who I believe were involved, Bishop Noah Schwartz and the midwife, Sadie Stutzman, are both dead."

A barely discernible stir goes around the room.

I relay the details of my being ambushed and follow up with a physical description of my attacker. "Male. Six-three. Two twenty. Dark hair. Beard, which of course could be altered if he wishes to change his appearance." I look at my audience. "I don't believe the timing of any of this was coincidental."

"You believe the bishop and midwife were targeted because of what they knew?" the trooper asks.

"Or because of what they did," I reply. "I think the hit-and-run that killed the bishop in Crooked Creek and the murder of Stutzman are directly related to the crimes here in Painters Mill and were perpetrated by the same individual."

"Why would an Amish bishop—*two* Amish bishops—and midwife take a baby?" Rasmussen asks.

"No one I've talked to has been able to give me an answer," I tell him. "What they have told me is that the people involved must have believed they had a good reason."

"Good reason?" he says. "You want to expand on that a little, Kate?"

I frown at the sheriff, realizing he's still miffed at me. "I'm operating on theory here, Mike. Just like you."

"Unlike the rest of us you've got some insights into the Amish mindset. What possible scenario could prompt them to plan and execute some sort of . . . illegal adoption?"

I shrug. "If they were concerned about the safety of the baby, for example. Or if, for whatever reason, the mother was unable to care for a newborn. The bishop and/or the midwife may have stepped in to help." Even as I say the words, it feels as if I'm defending what is basically an indefensible action—regardless of the objective—and once again I'm reminded that while I have an intimate understanding of the Amish ways, my cohorts do not.

"Can't help but wonder why someone—the mother or father or family members—didn't go to the police," Rasmussen says. "I mean, if someone took their kid it seems to me that would be their first stop."

"We just don't know," I tell him. "We don't even know if the mother is still living."

"Did you check deaths in the area during that time frame?" Tomasetti asks.

I nod. "There's nothing there that stands out."

"What about the timing of all this?" Glock asks. "Seven years is a long time."

"We don't know," I say.

"So these murders are likely revenge-motivated," Tomasetti says.

"Probably." I nod my head. "As far as the abduction of the girl, I believe we have to operate under the assumption that they wanted her back."

"Is there a possibility Mary Yoder was part of it seven years ago?" Tomasetti asks.

"According to Miriam Helmuth her mother knew about it. I don't believe she was a major player."

"What about Ivan Helmuth?" Tomasetti asks. "He's been keeping a low profile."

"We've gone easy on the parents due to the circumstances," Rasmussen adds. "I mean, the missing kid. Maybe it's time we stepped it up."

Tomasetti nods in agreement. "We can pick up Ivan first thing in the morning, bring him in for formal questioning. Apply some pressure. See if he can tell us something we don't already know."

"I'll take care of it," Rasmussen says.

"Bear in mind they have children," I say. "They're in crisis. You might want to—"

"I got it covered, Kate."

I nod, let it go.

Rasmussen isn't finished. "Look, I know they're your people, Kate, but come on. This couple . . . they're brought a newborn *baby* in the middle of the night and they didn't question it? Didn't tell anyone?"

"According to Miriam Helmuth, they *did* question—"

"They did nothing about it," he snaps. "That's my point. I don't understand how you can defend that."

I take a breath, bank a rise of temper. "Look, all I can say is that most Amish trust their bishop implicitly. In most cases, whether they agree or not, his word is final." I look out across the group, trying to gauge their receptivity. "Yes, the Amish are insular. They prefer to handle problems themselves. They're more apt to rely on each other or their community rather than law enforcement, certainly some government child welfare agency. But it's not done for deceitful purposes."

"That remains to be seen," the sheriff says. "Potentially, we're talking about a federal crime."

"We get it, Mike," Tomasetti growls. "Let's move on."

I don't respond. Mainly, because he's right and I'm on the losing end of a battle I don't want to fight. If my premise is correct, what those two bishops and the midwife did is not only indefensible, but criminal. That the Helmuths did nothing makes them an accessory. It doesn't matter that the issue is probably a hell of a lot more complicated than any of us realize.

I close my notebook and look out over the group. "We're hoping that as David Troyer recovers, he'll be able to give us a name. As it stands now he's in extremely critical condition and on a respirator."

I nod at Tomasetti to let him know he has the floor.

He stands. "I spoke with Sheriff Dan Pallant down in Scioto County at length earlier. He's on board with the task force and taking a second look at the hit-skip that killed Noah Schwartz as well as the murder of Stutzman." He gives me his deadpan expression. "Chief Burkholder and I are going to head down that way first thing in the morning."

"Do you think the Helmuth girl is being held in Scioto County?" Rasmussen asks.

"We don't know," Tomasetti says. "But in light of everything we now know, I think there's a possibility we'll find some answers there."

The sheriff shifts in his chair. "Look, I'm not going to get into the whole jurisdictional thing, but I'd like County involved in that, too, John."

"You're welcome to come along or send a deputy, Mike. The reason Chief Burkholder got drafted for this is because she knows the Amish, and she's already made some contacts down there." He shrugs, nonchalant, then looks at me. "You game, Chief?"

I nod.

Sheriff Rasmussen sighs. "Look, just keep me updated."

"Bet on it," Tomasetti says, and the meeting is adjourned.

CHAPTER 20

Seventy-nine hours missing

Miriam Helmuth sat at the kitchen table by the light of the lantern and sobbed. When she had no tears left, she bowed her head and prayed. She knew God listened. She knew He heard. That oftentimes His ways were simply not understood. Tonight, she couldn't shake the sense that the God she loved with all her might had abandoned her.

Please return her to me O Lord God.

It was the first time she'd been alone all day. The first time she didn't have to put on a brave face. The police had left half an hour ago. The last of her Amish brethren had gone home. The children were finally sleeping. Ivan, unable to bear the waiting, had saddled the plow horse for the second time that day. He'd been gone for hours with no food or water.

For the thousandth time she wondered about her sweet Elsie. Was she warm and dry? Had she been fed? Was she crying and afraid and missing her family? She thought about the shattered glasses found in the bishop's buggy and she couldn't help but wonder if someone had hurt her—or worse. The not knowing tore at Miriam like some clawed animal trapped in her chest and trying to dig its way out.

"Lord, I put my hope in You, for Your love never fails." She uttered the

words on a sob, in a voice hoarse with exhaustion. "I need you, God. I can't handle this on my own."

Even as she said the words, she couldn't help but wonder if she was being punished for what they'd done all those years ago. If this was God's way of telling her they'd taken the wrong path.

"Please forgive me my sin, Heavenly Father, for I didn't know—"

The shattering of glass followed by an odd thwack! *tore her from her prayer. Miriam got to her feet, looked around, her heart beating hard against her ribs.*

"Ivan?" she called out.

She strode to the mudroom, but her husband wasn't there. She went back through the kitchen to the hall, glanced up the stairs to the landing where the children sometimes sat when they couldn't sleep, but the stairs were bare.

Where had the odd sound come from? What had broken?

Miriam went back to the kitchen and looked around. The sight of the hole in the refrigerator froze her in place. She didn't know much about guns, but her datt *had been a hunter; she'd been around enough shooting to recognize a bullet hole when she saw it. The realization slammed into her like a jagged block of ice.*

Frightened, she ran to the living room. The curtains were open, darkness peering in. A hole the size of her thumb marred the glass. And she knew he'd finally come for them.

Spurred by panic, Miriam bolted to the stairs, ascended them with the speed of a woman half her age. At the top, she darted left, tore down the hall, threw open the first door and dashed to the beds. Bonnie and Irma slept soundly, snoring softly.

"Miriam?"

Gasping, she spun, saw her husband silhouetted against the door, still wearing his coat. She rushed to him, went through the door, closed it behind her. "Someone shot through the window," she said.

"What?" His eyes widened. "When?"

"Just now."

Even in the dim light of the gas lamp, she saw his face pale. "The children—"

Not waiting for him to finish, Miriam hurried to the next room. Her legs went weak with relief when she found her two sons sleeping and completely unaware.

Ivan met her in the hall, his eyes frightened and large. "The girls are fine," he said. "Sleeping."

"It's him," she whispered. "He's come for us."

Ivan stared at her, saying nothing. He didn't have to. He knew, just as she did.

"Lock the doors and windows." He started toward the stairs.

Miriam choked out a sob, set her hand over her mouth. "Go to the phone," she whispered. "Call Chief Burkholder."

I'm on my way home for a shower and a few hours of sleep when the call comes in. I'm expecting Tomasetti; uneasiness ripples through me when I recognize the number of the prepaid cell I left with the Helmuths.

"Chief Burkholder!" Ivan. I can tell by the breathless cadence of his voice that something's happened.

"Someone shot into the house," he says. "We need you to come."

"Is anyone hurt?" I ask.

"No, but we're afraid. The children!"

"I'm on my way," I tell him. "Stay inside. Stay away from the windows."

I make a U-turn. The engine groans as I crank the speedometer to sixty and blow back through town. I call Skid. "I got shots fired at the Helmuth place."

"Holy shit. Chief, I'm there. Goat Head Road. Didn't see a damn thing."

"I'm ten-seven-six," I say, letting him know I'm en route. "Drive the block. I'll meet you."

"Roger that."

I pick up my radio. "I've got a ten-forty-three-A," I say, giving the ten code for shots fired. I recite the address. "Ten-seven-six. Expedite."

It takes me three minutes to reach the Helmuth farm. I barrel up the lane fast, slide to a halt a few yards from the back door, and I hit the ground running. Ivan stands on the porch, a lantern thrust in front of him.

"Get inside," I tell him as I take the steps two at a time to the porch.

He leads me through the mudroom and into the kitchen. Lantern light reveals terror on their faces. I spot the hole in the refrigerator door before Ivan can point it out.

While a stray shot is always dangerous, in Painters Mill most often it's from a hunter. In light of recent events, I don't believe that's the case this time.

"How long ago did this happen?" I ask.

"Less than five minutes. There's a hole in the front window." Miriam is already striding that way.

Ivan and I follow. The window covering is open about a foot. Sure enough, a bullet hole big enough for me to put my finger through stares back at me. The surrounding glass is cracked, but not broken, typical of a gunshot.

I check the angle, realize it could have come from someone sitting in a vehicle on the road in front of the house. Or more likely the woods across the road.

"Where were you when this happened?" I ask.

"Kitchen table," Miriam replies.

"I was walking in from the barn," Ivan says.

"Were the curtains open?"

"Yes," Miriam tells me.

Which means the shooter likely saw her, but she couldn't see him.

"Stay away from the windows." I start toward the kitchen. "Do not go outside until I give you the go-ahead. Do not turn on any more lanterns. I'll be back."

I go out the back door, slide into the Explorer, and pick up my radio mic. "Skid, what's your twenty?"

"Township Road 14. Went around the block. I got nothing."

"Looks like someone shot through the front window. Drive around to the back of the property. You see anyone, make the stop. I got the front."

"Roger that."

I zip down the lane, too fast, eyes left and right, and head east on the county road. Amish country is dark as sin at night. No porch lights or streetlamps. Just acres of fields separated by greenbelts thick with trees and the occasional stream.

The woods across the road are an ocean of impenetrable blackness. I stop in front of the Helmuth farmhouse, which puts me a hundred yards away, and I get out. Around me, the night is dead quiet. No movement. No hiss of tires or rumble of an engine. The only sounds come from the sigh of the wind through the trees and a dog barking somewhere in the distance. All the while I'm keenly aware that there's likely someone nearby with a rifle, intent on doing harm.

My replacement .38 presses reassuringly against my hip as I look toward the house and the window through which the bullet passed. I think about the angle to the kitchen. If the projectile went into the refrigerator, the shooter likely stood exactly where I'm standing now or else just beyond in the woods.

I turn, scan the darkened forest on the other side of the fence. The vague outline of the Schattenbaum farm down the road. I speak into my lapel mike. "County?"

"I'm ten-sixty," comes a male voice—the sheriff's deputy, meaning he's in the vicinity.

"Can you ten-eight-five?" I say, asking him to look for an abandoned vehicle.

"Copy that."

Tugging out my Maglite, I shine the beam on the gravel shoulder, looking for tire tracks, footprints, or spent casings, but there's nothing there. I cross the road, check the other side, but the gravel is undisturbed. The shooter could have parked right here, turned off his headlights, and fired from inside his vehicle.

Turning off my Maglite, I cross through the ditch and climb the tumbling-down wire fence. Chances are, the shooter made the shot and fled in a vehicle. But the woods would be an advantageous position. He would have a clear view of the house, close enough to make the shot, and yet be hidden within the cover of the trees—where he wouldn't have to worry about being spotted by Skid.

That's when it occurs to me he could have parked on the county road south of here and walked through these woods unseen. After taking the shot, he could have run back through the woods and reached his vehicle in two minutes.

Darkness closes around me when I enter the woods. There's just enough light filtering through the clouds for me to avoid a collision with a tree trunk or low branch. The trees are bare, but tall and tightly packed. I do my best to tread quietly, but leaves crunch beneath my boots. Fifty feet in, I stop, listening. I can just make out the silhouette of the Helmuth farmhouse behind me. It would take a good marksman to make the shot from this distance, but I've no doubt it could be done.

I'm reaching for my shoulder mike to hail Skid when something rustles in the leaves. I see movement twenty yards ahead. I freeze, squint into the darkness. I can just make out the silhouette of a man. He's stone still, looking at me. I don't see a weapon, but that doesn't mean he's not armed. For an interminable second, we stare at each other.

"Police! Get your hands up!" Sliding my .38 from its holster, I start toward him. "Do not move! Get your hands up now! Slowly. Get them up."

The man spins and runs.

I hit my lapel mike, give the code for suspicious person. "Ten-seven-eight." Need assistance.

"Stop! Halt! Police!" I sprint after him, dodging trees, plowing through bushes and saplings. All the while I shout into my lapel mike. "Ten-eighty! Subject is on foot! Southbound, approaching County Road 79. Male. Dark coat."

I'm no slouch when it comes to running, but the man is faster and putting space between us at an astounding rate. I skirt a brush pile. Brambles claw at my coat and trousers. Branches whip my face. I fling myself over a fallen log, splash through a shallow creek. I'm thirty yards from the road when I see the flash of a dome light.

"Police!" I scream. "Stop!"

An engine roars. I hear the screech of tires. I see the glint of a vehicle through the trees. Moving fast.

I hit my shoulder mike. "Subject is in a vehicle," I say, breaths puffing. "Eastbound. No headlights."

My police radio lights up with a dozen codes and voices. Word of a possibly armed suspect has garnered the attention of every law enforcement agency in the county. The sheriff's department. The Ohio State Highway Patrol. My own department. Still, Holmes County is large—a labyrinth of highways, back roads, dirt roads, and plenty of woods.

I burst onto the road, my breaths labored; I see the red flash of taillights to my left. I sprint another twenty yards, trying to keep him in sight, see which direction he goes next. But the vehicle disappears into the night like a ghost.

CHAPTER 21

Eighty-seven hours missing

When you're a cop and working a missing-child case, the last thing you want to do is give up hope. The expectation of a positive outcome is the thing that drives you forward when you're exhausted beyond your limit, uncertain of your path, and besieged by bad news and dead ends at every turn. The longer the case drags on, the more difficult that precious hope is to hang on to, no matter how tight your grip. But cops are realists; when the time comes to give it up, your focus turns to finding the son of a bitch responsible, bringing him to justice—or maybe just bringing a small body home to rest.

I didn't get much sleep last night. I spent most of it with the Helmuths and on the roads surrounding the farm. The sheriff's department searched for the shooter and, later, collected what little evidence they could find, which boiled down to a single tire-tread mark that may or may not have been from the perpetrator's vehicle. There was no brass. No sign anyone had been in the woods with a rifle at all. Still, in light of the threat, I've permanently stationed one officer at the Helmuth farm twenty-four seven. I'm working with a skeleton crew to begin with; I don't know how I'll sustain the manpower. I'll find a way.

Tomasetti and I are on our way to Crooked Creek. We've spent most of the drive talking about the case, the players involved, their motives, brainstorming the possibilities and different scenarios.

Our first stop is the Scioto County Sheriff's Department. It's nine A.M. when Sheriff Dan Pallant ushers us through the secure door and into the same interview room where I met with the deputy two days ago.

Pallant is a middle-aged African American man with a quick smile and a booming voice. He's neatly dressed in khaki slacks and a navy pullover. A salt-and-pepper goatee covers his chin. A slightly receding hairline and heavy-framed eyeglasses lend him a studious countenance. He's cordial, but once the niceties are out of the way, he's ready to get down to business.

"I pulled some files after speaking with you last night, Agent Tomasetti." He sets a stack of folders on the table, opens the one on top. "The hit-and-run that killed Noah Schwartz. We originally wrote it up as a hit-skip, possibly involving an intoxicated driver. I went through every report and email and piece of paper in the file, and there's nothing there to indicate otherwise. No skid marks, no tire-tread imprints, no CCTV cameras in the vicinity, no witnesses, and no suspect. Only interesting thing I ran across was a homeowner who claimed to see a light-colored pickup truck in the vicinity a few minutes before it happened."

Tomasetti inclines his head at me. "Pickup truck fits with the type of vehicle that left the tire-tread imprint we took at the Schattenbaum place."

"Dick Howard on Goat Head Road says he saw a light-colored pickup truck—white or tan—in the area around the time Mary Yoder was murdered and the girl taken," I say.

Tomasetti looks at Pallant. "Any more description on the truck? Long bed? Crew cab? Anything like that?"

The sheriff shakes his head. "Deputy talked to the homeowner again last night and got nothing. I'm sure you know we got a lot of pickup trucks in this part of Ohio and Kentucky."

"I'll get the ROs of all vehicles matching that description, starting in Scioto County, expand from there, and see if anything pops," Tomasetti says.

The sheriff rattles off the contiguous counties. "Adams. Pike. Lawrence. Jackson." He pauses, rubs his palm across his chin. "Might check Greenup County in Kentucky, too."

Tomasetti thumbs the information into his phone.

"I had my night clerk make you guys copies of everything." Pallant shoves a green folder across the table to us.

"Anything new on the Stutzman case?" I ask.

"We don't have much." Pallant slides a second folder toward us, then opens the official file in front of him and looks down at it. "Initially, we investigated the incident as a probable home invasion–robbery. Some scumbag looking for money or drugs or guns. Sadie was eighty-three years old. Ninety-two pounds. She would have been seen as an easy target."

He makes a sound of disgust. "There were no signs of forced entry. That means she either left the door unlocked or she knew him." He looks down at the file, flips the page. "There were signs of a struggle, but some of that occurred when Chief Burkholder was attacked later. Overall, the place wasn't too torn up."

"Prints?" I ask.

He smiles. "Just yours."

"Autopsy complete?" Tomasetti asks.

"Coroner hasn't officially ruled on cause or manner yet, but her skull sure as hell didn't get bashed in without help."

I curb a rise of outrage at the thought of such a brutal attack on an elderly woman.

The sheriff's chair groans when he leans back. "I appreciate your sending the BCI crime scene unit," he says to Tomasetti. "As you can imagine our department is strapped, so it was a big help. Your guy photographed and videotaped everything. Dusted for prints. Tried to get plaster on the tire treads, but snow melted too fast. He did, however, get a shoe imprint."

"Men's size thirteen?" I ask.

The sheriff's eyes narrow on mine. "Yes, ma'am."

"You guys have anyone in mind?" Tomasetti asks.

Pallant shakes his head. "We're looking at the usual suspects. Talked to a few of them. Ruled out a couple of guys who had alibis. Right now we're eyeing a small-time dope dealer lives down the street from the Stutzman residence. He's a piece of shit. Violent felon. We picked him up, mainly just to sweat him a little. I got nothing and can't hold him, but seriously I don't think he's involved."

He divides his attention between the two of us. "In light of your case, I might be right." He taps the folder with his index finger. "That's everything we got on Stutzman."

I open the folder, page through the police report, an incident report, and several dozen crime scene photos. "The house was searched?" I ask.

"I had a couple of deputies go in and look around. The woman was somewhat of a hoarder. The place was so damn messy, we couldn't tell if it had been ransacked. We basically looked for drawers that had been left open. Stuff like that. Old Sadie didn't have much of value, so our search was basically inconclusive."

I recall walking into the house through the back door. Every conceivable surface had been cluttered. "So you were unable to tell if anything had been taken?" I ask.

The sheriff nods. "Nothing obvious." Frowning, he scratches his head. "You know, we made an effort to contact family, but she doesn't have any living relatives."

"Did she have a will?" I ask.

"Don't think so," he replies. "Whatever's left will go through probate. Without any relatives, chances are that little house'll get auctioned off to pay for funeral expenses."

And the house will likely join the dozens of others that have been abandoned and forgotten. It's a sad, depressing thought.

Leaning forward, the sheriff goes to the final two folders, slides one across to me and opens the original. "That brings us to Marlene Byler. Had to dig into the archives for this one."

I open the file to find a short stack of bad copies from what looks like microfiche—police reports, an autopsy report, witness statements. The print is scratchy, dark, and difficult to read.

Tilting his head back, the sheriff squints at the paper through his bifocals. "Twenty-nine years ago, twenty-nine-year-old Marlene Byler jumped from Sciotoville Bridge, killing herself. Death was ruled a suicide. Cause of death drowning. Witness said she had a baby with her. Sheriff's department searched the river, but the infant's body was never found."

He looks from Tomasetti to me. "Do you think that case has something to do with what happened up there in Painters Mill?"

"Marlene is the sister of the woman who was murdered," I tell him.

"A lot of tragedy for one family," he says.

We fall silent. Everything that's been said, the information that's been passed along to us running through my head. I find myself thinking about Sadie Stutzman. A tiny old woman, using a shovel to build a levee because she didn't quite have a grip on reality. No children. No family to bury her. Her only legacy is a mystery she'll likely take to the grave.

"Sheriff Pallant, would it be possible for us to go back to the Stutzman home and take a look around?" I ask.

"The scene's been processed. Crime scene guys have come and gone. We've got everything we're going to get." He leans back in the chair and crosses his arms, dividing his attention between the two of us. "You mind telling me what you're looking for exactly?"

I give him the rundown of Sadie Stutzman's involvement in the Elsie Helmuth case. "We're hoping she kept something—letters or a diary— that might help us fill in the blanks."

"A lot of damn blanks." He heaves the sigh of a man with a heavy weight on his shoulders. "Abduction of a kid adds a whole new sense of urgency."

He jots a set of numbers onto a sticky note and passes it to me. "Deputy put a combination lock on the back door to keep out the thieves. I heard some of the Amish are going to go out there tomorrow and clean up the place. You need to let me know if you find anything pertinent to either case."

"You got it," Tomasetti tells him.

The sun plays hide-and-seek behind cumulus clouds the color of charcoal when we pull into the driveway of the house where Sadie Stutzman lived. The woman has been gone for only a day and a half, but already the place looks abandoned, sitting in its pretty spot by the river.

"This was probably a nice area once upon a time," Tomasetti says as we get out.

"Welcome to the intersection of rust belt and opioid epidemic," I mutter as I close the door.

We move to the front of the Explorer and look around. A blue jay screeches at us from a buckeye tree behind the house. The driveway is filled with ruts from the tires of official vehicles—the sheriff's department, first responders, the coroner. The yellow caution tape that's strung around the front porch flutters in a breeze coming off the water. It's cold and humid and I find myself thinking about my final conversation with Sadie Stutzman.

They killed him, you know.

"Everyone thought she was crazy." I look at Tomasetti. "She was astute enough to know the bishop had been murdered. She knew someone was coming for her."

He tilts his head, gives me a thoughtful look, waits for me to continue.

I look around, feel the uncomfortable press of loneliness, of isolation. "I talked to her the day before she was killed. Maybe I should have—"

"You did your best," he cuts in. "You talked to her. You listened. You offered her protection. Aside from camping out in her backyard, there wasn't much else you could have done."

I nod, knowing he's right. The knowledge does little to loosen the knot of conscience in my gut. "She knew more than she let on. She would have eventually opened up and talked to me."

"That may be why he killed her." Frowning, he motions toward the back of the house. "Let's go inside and see if she left us anything."

We make our way around to the back of the house. The horse and goats are gone, the pen gates left open. A few yards away, the wheelbarrow she'd been using lies on its side, next to a pile of dirt and the shovel.

We climb the steps to the porch. Bending, Tomasetti works at the combination lock. I look out across the yard toward the river, thinking about the old woman, hearing her voice, her words.

I knew something wasn't right.

Everyone did. Kept their mouths shut like good Amish. Such a terrible thing. Sin piled atop of sin.

The lock snicks open. Shooting me a half smile, Tomasetti pushes open the door and we go inside.

The kitchen looks much the same as the last time I was here. Cluttered. Slightly dirty. Several of the drawers stand open, as if someone looked inside, found nothing of interest, and didn't bother closing them properly. Muddy shoe prints mottle the floor. Dozens of people have been in the house since Sadie was killed. Deputies. First responders. Crime scene technicians. The coroner. The stink of garbage hangs in the air, mingling with the unpleasant pall of mildew and a house that's been closed up for too long.

I go to the living room and look around. It's too dark to see much and I'm reminded that, like most Amish, Sadie didn't use electricity. I cross to the window that looks out onto the front porch and open the drapes. Dust motes fly in the crepuscular light that pours in.

I hear Tomasetti moving around in the kitchen, opening and closing cabinets and drawers. "There's a little pantry to your right," I call out to him.

"Kinda hate to disturb the mouse chowing down in the box of cereal."

I roll my eyes. "We're looking for clues, Tomasetti, not mice. I'll take the bedrooms."

I smile when he doesn't respond, and I glance left toward the hall where I found Sadie's body. It's a narrow, dark space. A rust-colored stain the size of a dinner plate mars the beaten-down carpet. Blood, I realize. A hole the size of a coaster has been cut out of the carpet, probably by the crime scene technician to send a sample to the lab for testing.

"I set out the garbage."

I startle at the sound of Tomasetti's voice, turn to find him standing in the kitchen doorway, looking at me. "Thank you," I say.

He looks past me at the stain and the cutout in the carpet, doesn't say what he's thinking. "Any idea what we're looking for?"

I can tell by his expression he doesn't believe we're going to find anything of value. He's going through the motions for my benefit. If I wanted to be honest about it, I don't think we're going to find anything either. Nothing's ever that easy. The house has already been searched by Scioto County deputies as well as BCI. Even so, they probably weren't looking for the same sort of thing that I'm interested in today.

"No," I confess, but I'm thinking. "Most Amish correspond with letters. Any kind of writing. A diary. If we're lucky, she kept some kind of record of the babies she'd delivered over the years."

"I'll take the kitchen." He retreats in that direction. "With the mouse. Let's make it quick."

I go to the first bedroom, push open the door. The room is about ten feet square, darkened, the curtains drawn. There's a twin-size bed covered with a ratty blanket. A closet. A pair of sneakers tossed into a corner. A desk with a single lantern, its globe black with soot. I look around, check under the bed, beneath the mattress, but there's nothing there.

I'm more interested in Sadie's bedroom, where she likely kept personal items, so I move on to the next room. I know immediately this is where she slept. Where she hoped and dreamed and lived out her last days.

I cross to the window, spread the drapes, try not to inhale dust. There's a full-size bed with an iron headboard. A night table contains a lantern set atop a doily, a small book titled *Prayers for Difficult Times*, and a votive candle that's burned down to nothing. A faceless Amish doll sits in a rocking chair in the corner along with a black winter bonnet. Across the room a narrow chest is piled high with newspapers. The drawers are open. A sock hangs out of the top drawer. I wonder if the mess was left behind by Sadie or law enforcement—or someone else.

I kneel next to the nightstand. The candle smells of sandalwood. I open the top drawer, find a Beverly Lewis paperback novel, a tube of lip balm, a package of saltine crackers, a half-eaten chocolate bar. Evidently Sadie Stutzman was a reader and a snacker.

The next drawer is filled with books and newspapers in seemingly no order. I see an ancient-looking German Martin Luther Bible, a tattered copy of *Ausbund,* which is a songbook used during worship, and dozens of newspapers and clippings from *The Budget, The Connection,* and *The Diary* out of Lancaster County. All are Amish publications. Some of the newspapers are folded and intact; some have had pages torn out, stories or advertisements that have been cut out.

I page through the newspapers first, checking the dates—which go as far back as last summer. I find nothing of interest.

"Come on, Sadie," I whisper.

The final drawer contains a stack of handwritten recipes that have been paper-clipped together. Lydia's Date Pudding. Pickled Asparagus. Rachel's Chow Chow. Mommie's No Bake Cookies. I page through all of it and find a frayed manila folder at the bottom of the drawer. I flip it open, glance inside. Dozens of newspaper clippings stare back at me. Most are missing the date; there's no indication of which publications they came from. I leaf through them. Obituaries. Births. Accidents. Church happenings.

I'm about to close the drawer and move on when I spot the brown envelope in the back. I reach for it. My heart stutters when I see the familiar crinkled white notebook papers inside.

"Good girl," I whisper.

Pinching the corner of the papers, I pull out two notes and carefully unfold them.

> *It is mine to avenge; I will repay. In due time their foot will slip; their day of disaster is near and their doom rushes upon them.*

I go to the second note.

> *If a thief is caught breaking in at night and is struck a fatal blow, the defender is not guilty of bloodshed . . .*

Though I still don't have a name or suspect, for the first time, I can definitively tie the murder and abduction in Painters Mill to at least one murder in Crooked Creek.

CHAPTER 22

Ninety-one hours missing

After leaving the Stutzman place—the manila folder and a boatload of newspapers, tear sheets, and cutouts in hand—we head north toward Wheelersburg. As we make the turn onto Hansgen Morgan Road, I tell Tomasetti about my conversation with Freda Troyer. "The night they brought the baby to Painters Mill, they used a driver. Freda remembers seeing a van parked in her driveway."

His eyes latch on to mine. "Does she have a name to go along with the van?"

"She didn't see the driver, but some of the Amish drivers, fondly referred to as 'Yoder Toters,' are hired out on a regular basis and are well known by the Amish community. The bishop is usually well connected. I'm betting we can get a name."

"You thinking this driver overheard something?"

"Or he might be able to give us a name we don't already have."

We park in the same spot as last time I was here. I notice the barn door standing open, so we forgo a trip to the house and head that way. We find Chupp mucking stalls, a wheelbarrow full of wood shavings and manure in the aisle.

"You're back," he says by way of greeting, and his eyes slide to To-masetti. "With a friend."

Tomasetti introduces himself and extends his hand.

"Any luck finding that missing girl?" the bishop asks.

I shake my head. "Did you have a chance to ask around to see if anyone is aware of what may have happened with the newborn seven years ago?"

Sobering, the bishop sets the pitchfork on the ground and leans. "I spoke with several people, Chief Burkholder. Reliable people who've lived in Crooked Creek all their lives. No one knows of an infant. If Bishop Schwartz and Sadie Stutzman were involved in such a thing, they did not speak of it."

Disappointment takes a swipe at me, but I block it and move on to my next question. "I think Bishop Schwartz and Sadie Stutzman may have hired a driver the night they traveled to Painters Mill. Do you know of someone who was driving for the Amish about that time?"

The bishop's eyes widen slightly. "Elmer Moyer has been driving the Amish around for as long as I can remember. He's a nice fellow. A Mennonite. A real talker, if you know what I mean. I've hired him a few times myself." Chupp looks from me to Tomasetti and back at me, his expression grave. "Chief Burkholder, I heard just last week that El-mer Moyer left town."

My heart does a weird patter against my ribs. "Do you know where he went or why he left?"

He shakes his head. "Word around town is that Elmer had some debt." He lowers his voice. "A tab at the feed store. A bunch of credit cards. It was common knowledge he was having money problems."

"How long ago did he leave?" I ask.

"Recently." He shrugs. "A couple of weeks maybe."

"Do you have any idea how to get in touch with him?"

The bishop shakes his head. "Cell phone is disconnected. Several people I know have tried to contact him when they needed a ride. Elmer hasn't returned a single call."

"Sounds like he doesn't want to be found." Tugging his cell from his pocket, Tomasetti thumbs something it. "Let me see if he's in the system."

"Does Moyer have family in the area?" I ask the bishop. "Friends? Someone who was close to him?"

"I don't believe so. Not in Crooked Creek, anyway. He courted the waitress down to the diner for a while. Patty Lou. But I don't think they ever married. She still works there. Little place on Buckeye Street downtown called Foley's."

The bishop's eyebrows furrow as if he's troubled by the things we've discussed. "You don't think something bad has happened to Elmer, do you?"

"When's the last time you saw him?" I ask.

"He drove me to Cincinnati for a doctor's appointment a couple of months ago. We stopped for lunch on the way back. I bought him a burger and a shake." He shrugs. "Didn't know that would be the last time I saw him."

When we're back in the Explorer, Tomasetti says, "Elmer Moyer is not a missing person. He's not in any of the databases. No warrants."

"Record?"

"One conviction on misdemeanor drug charges two years ago. Possession of a controlled substance. Paid a fine. Did probation. No time served. Speeding ticket last summer."

"So he's not Scarface," I say. "I guess the question now is: Did he leave of his own accord? Or did someone do away with him?"

Tomasetti takes it a step further. "Or is he somehow involved in the abduction?"

I think about that a moment. "Moyer used to date the waitress down at the diner. You hungry?"

"Frickin' starved."

CHAPTER 23

Ninety-five hours missing

Foley's is more bar than diner and has Hard Times written all over its redbrick facade. It's nestled between a parking lot riddled with knee-high yellow grass and a vacant space that was once Uhlman's Department Store. I park the Explorer in the lot next to a pickup truck the size of a tank and we head inside.

The interior is a dimly lit, narrow space with booths to the right and, on the left, an ornate bar that's probably as old as the building itself. The air smells of onions, week-old grease, and spilled beer—all of it infused with the redolence of decades-old cigarette smoke. Two men in brown duck coveralls sit at the bar, sipping beer, watching a TV tuned to cable news with the volume muted. A couple sits at a booth by the window. An old Crosby, Stills & Nash rocker blares from a juke-box in the corner. No one looks up when we walk in, so we make our way to the nearest booth and sit.

I'm thinking about Elsie Helmuth and the fateful trip that took her to Painters Mill seven years ago when a woman wearing snug jeans and a fuzzy purple sweater hustles up to the booth. "Evening, folks," she says in a tough voice. "Can I get you something to drink?"

She's tall and thin, with a face that had once been pretty. She's a fast mover, a woman used to getting things done quickly and being on her feet for hours at a time. I'm betting she's waitress, bartender, and manager and she's probably run this place for quite some time.

"I'll have a Killian's Irish Red," Tomasetti tells her.

"Same." Before she can turn away, I ask, "Can you tell us where we can find Patty Lou?"

She spins, her gaze alternating between curiosity and caution. "You guys cops or what?"

Good eye, I think as I lay down my badge. "We're looking for Elmer Moyer."

She looks at my badge a moment too long, not reading, but getting her response in order. "What makes you think I know where he is?"

"You're a friend of his."

"Was. Past tense." Her eyes scan the room, the bar, the booth. Checking on her customers. Making sure they have everything they need. Tips are important to her.

"He left, so I guess we're not friends anymore," she tells me.

I'm aware of Tomasetti settling against the seat back, letting me know this is my show. "When was that?" I ask.

"Little over two weeks ago." She narrows eyes swathed with makeup that doesn't quite conceal the shadows beneath them or the crow's-feet at the corners. "What'd he do?"

"We're just trying to find him."

"Uh-huh. Right. And I'm here because I like the benefits. Give me a break."

"How long were you friends?" I ask.

"Ten years, on and off." She rethinks her answer. "Mostly on toward the end."

"Can you tell us why he left?" I ask.

"Hell if I know. One minute he's Mr. Let's-Get-Married and the next he's just fucking gone." Her tough veneer cracks and for a split second I catch a glimpse of the woman beneath, the one who'd once been happy and hopeful for a future with a man she loved. "If you figure it out, let me know, will you? I'll be back with your beers." She turns and goes back to the bar.

"Sounds like she wasn't expecting Mr. Perfect to skip town," Tomasetti says.

I look at him. "What do you think?"

"I think I want to find Elmer Moyers."

"Suspect? Witness? Victim?"

"All of the above, but I'm leaning toward witness." He lifts a shoulder, lets it drop. "Sounds like he flew the coop right about the time Noah Schwartz was killed."

The waitress returns to our booth, sets two beers in front of us, and slaps down a couple of menus. "Turkey and gravy is the special," she says as she pulls out her order pad. "Chicken fried steak is better."

"I understand Elmer did some driving for the Amish," I say.

She lowers the pad. "Yeah, they hired him sometimes. You know, for long trips. He wasn't exactly raking in the cash, but they paid him well."

"Did he work anywhere else?" Tomasetti asks.

"Worked over to the hardware store for a while. But he was on disability. Hurt his back when he was working construction. Couldn't lift much over ten pounds."

"Where did he live?"

"Little furnished apartment above the furniture store. Landlord has already rented the place."

"Did he ever make a trip to Painters Mill?" I ask.

"Not that I know of."

"Did he ever take a trip with Bishop Schwartz?"

Something flickers in her eyes. Some memory she hasn't thought of in a long time. "I think he did. Like, a long time ago."

"How long?"

"Years?" Curiosity glimmers in her eyes. "Why are you guys asking all these questions about Elmer?"

"Did anyone else go with them on that trip?" I ask.

"Look, I don't know anything about it. I just remember him mentioning he was going to be driving the bishop somewhere. It was a long drive and the old man paid cash."

"Did anything unusual happen during that trip?" I ask.

"He didn't say." She swipes at a tuft of hair that's fallen onto her forehead. "Y'all have me pretty curious, though."

"Can you sit a moment?" I slide over to give her room.

She throws a glance toward the door that leads to the kitchen. "Can't. Owner usually pops in about this time of day."

Tomasetti sets three twenty-dollar bills on the table.

"I reckon I can spare a five-minute break." Reaching for the bills, she stuffs them into her jeans pocket and lowers herself into the booth. "What's this all about? Is Elmer all right?"

I give her the basics of the case in Painters Mill, not relaying any information that isn't already available to the public. "We think Elmer may have driven Bishop Schwartz and Sadie Stutzman to Painters Mill."

Her mouth opens. I see something click into place in her eyes. For the first time since we arrived, she gives me her undivided attention. "Sadie Stutzman," she whispers. "My God, that old lady who was murdered the other night?"

I nod. "Bishop Schwartz is dead, too," I tell her. "Killed in a hit-and-run accident."

She falls silent, sets her elbows on the table, looks down at her hands, then back at me. "What does that have to do with Elmer?"

"Do you remember what day Elmer left town?" I ask.

"The twentieth of October."

The day after Noah Schwartz was killed.

"How was Elmer acting before he left?" I ask.

Her eyes sweep from me to Tomasetti and back to me. "He was fine. I mean, I was working double shifts. I was busy, stressed. But he seemed . . . the same as always." Even as she makes the statement, I hear the hesitation in her voice.

Tomasetti steps in. "Patty Lou, did he seem upset or worried about anything in the days and weeks before he left?"

"Or scared?" I add.

Patty Lou doesn't answer right away. I see the wheels of thought spinning. She's thinking, remembering. Despite her tough-as-nails exterior, she's not very good at keeping her thoughts and emotions hidden from view.

After a moment, she blinks and looks down at her hands. "I figured there was another woman. I mean, we were getting along great. I wasn't expecting him to just pick up and freaking leave me."

"Did he—" I start to speak, but she cuts me off.

"Look, he was . . . weird the last couple of days." She heaves a defeated sigh. "Elmer was a talker. Man, he could carry on a conversation all by himself for days. Except for when he was worried and then he just kind of clammed up."

"Any idea what he was worried about?" Tomasetti presses.

She looks away, checks her customers, the door leading to the kitchen. Shoring up, I think. Then turns her attention back to us. "I thought he was going to pop the question. I figured he was nervous. Big step and all. After he left, I thought . . ." She shrugs thin shoulders. "I figured he was preoccupied because he'd been planning his big disappearing act."

She chokes out a laugh that holds not a smidgen of humor. "I figured he had another woman in another town. Dumped me and all his bills in one fell swoop."

"Any idea where he went or how to get in touch with him?" I ask.

"His phone is disconnected." Tears fill her eyes. "Yeah, I know. I'm pathetic. I tried to call him." She slides from the booth and gets to her feet, swipes at her face with the backs of her hands. "Jesus. Look at me. I gotta get back to work. You guys know what you want to eat?"

We're nearly to the motel when the call comes in from Dispatch. I know even before answering that the news isn't good. I have a sixth sense when it comes to the many faces of disaster and I find myself bracing.

"Hey, Chief," comes Mona's voice. "Any luck down there?"

I hear gloom tucked behind her sanguinity, just out of sight, concealed from most, but not me. I feel Tomasetti's eyes on me so I address her question, keep my eyes on the road, as I tell her about Elmer Moyer.

"We're not sure if he's part of this, a witness, or a possible victim, but we're going to take a hard look at him," I tell her.

A too long pause then, "Chief, I thought you should know . . . Bishop Troyer lapsed into a coma a little while ago. The doc is giving him a fifty-fifty chance of making it through the night."

I close my eyes briefly, grip the wheel a little harder. Remind myself I'm no longer Amish. That Bishop Troyer is as old as the hills and he's lived a long, good life. None of it helps.

"How's Freda holding up?" I ask.

"T.J. swung by their place earlier. He said the Amish are holding vigil at the hospital. Her family is there, too."

She clears her throat. More comfortable cursing some dipshit who's run a traffic light than being the bearer of bad news she knows will affect me on a personal level.

I keep my mind on the business at hand. "Skid still out at the Helmuth place?"

"Glock relieved him so he could grab some sleep and dinner, but he'll be back out there at midnight when he comes on."

"Tell him thanks, will you?"

"Sure."

"You, too, Mona."

I lean forward, punch off the button, slant a look at Tomasetti, and I'm profoundly relieved the cab is dark and he can't see my face.

"I don't think the bishop is going to make it," I whisper, and I rap my palm against the steering wheel.

"I'm pretty sure you told me once he's too damn mean to die."

I choke out a laugh. "Whatever punishments he doled out, I probably earned it."

"You've had a complicated relationship."

"And then some, for a lot of years."

It will sadden me in a profound way if Bishop Troyer dies, especially if his death is caused by an act of violence. While the Amish are certain he will be going to a better place to rejoin loved ones and be with God, I'm not quite so certain. At times like this, the loss of that kind of faith is hollow and cold.

"He's been tough on you," Tomasetti points out.

"I was what the Amish call 'disobedient' and never the apple of his eye. When I was a teenager I thought I hated him."

"Don't be too hard on yourself. Teenagers aren't exactly the smartest of God's creatures."

"I broke a lot of rules," I tell him. "I committed some serious transgressions—in the eyes of the Amish, anyway—and I got into a lot of trouble. I didn't realize it at the time, and I sure as hell didn't appreciate it, but Bishop Troyer never gave up on me. He never wrote me off as a lost cause. Not even after I left."

"So don't give up on him." He reaches across the console and I put my hand in his. "He's a strong man. If he still has something important to do before he checks out—like save your soul from eternal damnation—that might just be enough to get him through this."

I can't help it; I laugh. "Thank you for that perspective."

"Anytime, Chief."

CHAPTER 24

One hundred and four hours missing

I should have known this would be the night my old friend insomnia drops in for an unexpected visit. For two hours I lie beside Tomasetti, staring into the darkness and listening to the sounds of the Sleepy Time Motel, trying to quiet a mind that has no intention of cooperating. I can't stop thinking about an innocent little Amish girl whose life hinges on my finding her, the possibility that I may not succeed, and the reality that it may already be too late.

At one A.M. I slide from the bed, make my way to the desk, and open my laptop, along with the files I've amassed over the last few days. Twice, I take my cell into the bathroom and close the door to speak with Mona—trying not to wake Tomasetti. I read the files on the deaths of Noah Schwartz and Sadie Stutzman given to us by Sheriff Pallant, but neither file offers anything in the way of new information. I reread my own files, trying to see things with a fresh perspective, but there's nothing there.

Frustrated, I shove my laptop in its case and go to the cardboard box where I stowed the pile of newspapers and clippings and the manila folder we retrieved from Sadie Stutzman's bedroom. I'm not optimistic about finding anything new as I pull out the first stack and set it on the desktop.

Since I'm not sure what I'm looking for, I begin by sorting the newspapers by date. I spend twenty minutes looking through copies of *The Budget*, *The Connection*, and *The Diary*. I look for highlighted areas or paper-clipped sections, but there's nothing marked. I skim the local news sections, looking for familiar names or stories that could be related to the Helmuth family or a missing child—anything that doesn't sit right. I'm hoping I'll recognize it when I see it.

Finding nothing of interest, I set the August editions aside and go to September. There's a story about a buggy-accident fatality, but it's out of Lancaster County, Pennsylvania. I pull out my yellow legal pad and write down the name anyway. I pay particular attention to births and obituaries, but none of the names, dates, or circumstances mean anything to me.

At three A.M., I've gone through four months of newspapers, all to no avail.

"Shit," I mutter. Leaning forward, I rub my eyes, thinking about going to bed, trying to sleep. If I don't get some rest, I'm not going to be worth a damn in the morning. But I can still feel that guy-wire tension in my chest, the clench of fear that I'm going to fail and an innocent kid is going to die because of it, and I know sleep will not come. . . .

Scooting my chair back, I dig into the box, spot the folder at the bottom, and pull it out. Dozens of newspaper cutouts spill onto the desktop. MENNONITE THRIFT STORE OPENS IN SCIOTO COUNTY. AMISH COMMUNITY RALLIES FOR INJURED TRUCK DRIVER. AMISH SCHOOL TO BE REBUILT AFTER FIRE. They're in no particular order; some aren't dated. Most of the articles are old, the paper yellowed with age. I page through them, trying to determine if they are relevant or could somehow be helpful in terms of the case.

Nothing.

I skim the last article and shove it back into the folder. That's when I notice the dozen or so obituaries and birth notices that slipped out and scattered on the desktop. Tiny cutouts, just an inch or two in length, most with no date or even the name of the publication. Beneath the obits is a folded half-page tear sheet from the *Portsmouth Daily Times*. The paper is crinkled and yellow with age. I unfold it and skim. There's an advertisement for a local funeral home. Another for a new hospice center going up in Sciotodale. A few more obits, which I scan.

> Nettie Mae Detweiler was born on March 14, 2012 at 3:32 A.M. and passed peacefully in the loving arms of her parents. She entered the house of the Lord at 6:53 A.M. Nettie was the daughter of Rosanna and Vernon Detweiler.

It's the first obituary for an infant I've found. Not a stillbirth, but the newborn survived just a short time. Something about it gives me pause. I look at the date.

> . . . born on March 14, 2012 at 3:32 A.M. and passed peacefully in the loving arms of her parents. She entered the house of the Lord at 6:53 A.M.

A resonant *ping* sounds in my brain. My exhaustion falls away. The mental clutter in my head grinds to a halt. I stare at the date, knowing it's somehow significant. I've seen it before. But where?

Energized, I spin, go to my laptop case, pull out the file on Elsie

Helmuth. I set it on the desktop and page through. My fingers freeze on the Missing flyer published by the Painters Mill Ladies' Club.

Have you seen me? Elsie Helmuth. Seven years old. Female. Special Needs. Born: March 14, 2012. Brown hair. Brown eyes. Height: 3'9". Weight: 60 lbs.

I go back to the obit and look at the date. March 14, 2012. I'm too cynical to believe in coincidence, especially when it comes to kidnapping and murder. This is noteworthy, but what does it mean? My mind scrolls through the conversations I've had over the last few days.

They brought her to us. In the middle of the night. This screaming, red-faced little baby.

They're Miriam Helmuth's words, recalling the night the two bishops—Troyer and Schwartz—and midwife Sadie Stutzman brought them a baby from Scioto County.

Is it possible Nettie Mae Detweiler and Elsie Helmuth are the same girl?

"Holy shit." Rising abruptly, I grab the file and tread to the bathroom. I'm hitting the speed dial for Dispatch even as I close the door.

"You're up late," Mona says.

"Get me everything you can find on Rosanna and Vernon Detweiler." I spell the last name. "Check Scioto County. See if you can find an address. If there's nothing there, try the adjoining counties. Run them through LEADS. Check for warrants."

"Got it."

"Mona, check with the Scioto County Auditor website. Do a property search to see if they own property. A house or acreage."

"You got a town? Or middle initials?"

"Negative."

"I'm on it."

"Mona?"

"Yeah, Chief?"

"Any news on Bishop Troyer?"

"Holding his own."

Ending the call, I swing open the door. I startle at the sight of To-masetti standing there, looking rumpled and grumpy. He frowns at me as if he's thinking about laying into me for working in the middle of the night, for waking him when both of us should be sleeping, but he doesn't.

"You're looking bright-eyed and bushy-tailed for a woman who's been up all night," he growls.

"I think I found something," I say.

He groans. "Lay it on me."

Half an hour—and four large coffees—later, Tomasetti and I are sitting at the desk, my laptop humming in front of us. He's been on his cell with several law enforcement agencies, trying to get BCI and the local jurisdiction on board. I've got Mona on my cell.

"I ran Rosanna and Vernon Detweiler through LEADS," she tells me. "No warrants. No record. But I have an address from the county auditor tax roll for a property owned by Vernon Detweiler. 8184 White Oak Road, Bracks Hollow."

I type the address into my laptop maps software, watch it fill the screen. It's a rural area a few miles east of Ironton, north of the river. "Do either of them have a driver's license? ID card?"

"Vernon Detweiler has a driver's license."

"Physical description?"

"Six feet, four inches. Two twenty. Brown. Brown."

"What do you have on the property?"

"A hundred and fifty-two acres."

"Can you get me a plat?"

"You got it."

"Look, I'm with Agent Tomasetti. We're in Crooked Creek, twenty minutes from Bracks Hollow. He's working on an affidavit for a warrant. We're going to move as soon as it comes through. None of this is for public consumption."

"Roger that. Anything else, Chief?"

"A prayer for the girl might help."

"Done."

I hit END and turn to Tomasetti, who's frowning at me. He's dressed and restless, his expression grim. "Vernon Detweiler is six-four," I tell him. "Two hundred and twenty pounds. I bet the farm he's a size-thirteen shoe."

"Amish?"

I nod. "We need that warrant yesterday."

"Sheriff Pallant and the judge are golf buddies. He's on his way."

I think about Elsie Helmuth. The violence her abductor is capable of. The number of days she's been missing. All the things that could happen to a little girl in that time frame. "How long?"

He shrugs. "Hard to tell. An hour."

"Do you think it's a good idea to wait? Tomasetti, what this guy did to Mary Yoder . . . that girl has been at his mercy for days now. We may already be too late."

He's still looking at me, cocking his head slightly. "You go in without a warrant and you risk blowing the case if it goes to trial. You know that."

"We've got exigent circumstances. A missing endangered minor child—"

"We need to get this right."

I turn away from him. He's right, of course, but it doesn't allay the sense of urgency or the fear that has crept up the back of my neck. And yet here we are, waiting.

"You believe this couple are the parents of Elsie Helmuth?" Tomasetti asks.

"There's no way those dates are coincidental."

"What's the connection to Miriam and Ivan Helmuth? Or *is* there a link at all?"

"I don't think anything that happened with that baby was random."

He considers that a moment. "Every person who was murdered or targeted was somehow involved in the taking of or the transporting of the infant to Painters Mill. Sadie Stutzman. Bishop Schwartz. Bishop Troyer." He scrubs a hand across his jaw. "How does Mary Yoder play into this?"

"Maybe she was . . . collateral damage." I shrug. "She tried to stop him, tried to protect her granddaughter, and he killed her for it."

"Stabbed twenty-two times." He shakes his head. "That's a lot of violence. A lot of rage if all he intended to do was take the girl."

I stare at him, my mind blinking back to my exchange with Sadie Stutzman when I asked about Byler.

They shamed her to death. That's why she jumped. They shamed her. Shamed her. *Like mother, like daughter. One and the same—both were bad eggs.*

At the time I'd thought the words were the ranting of a woman whose mind had been devastated by a stroke. Now I'm not so sure. Maybe Sadie Stutzman was a hell of a lot more cognizant than anyone gave her credit for. . . .

"A name that has come up repeatedly in the course of this case is Marlene Byler," I say. "She lived in Scioto County."

"Mary Yoder's sister." His eyes narrow. "Miriam's aunt. Elsie's great-aunt."

"It's a familial connection." I tell him about Marlene Byler's suicide. "Rumor has it she took her baby with her when she jumped off the bridge."

"Does Byler have other children?"

"Not that we've found."

"If she does," he says, "they might be worth a look."

"I'll get with Mona, tell her to keep digging."

A sharp rap sounds at the door. Tomasetti and I exchange a look and for the first time I realize Pallant will know we shared a room. Nothing we can do about it now.

Growling beneath his breath, Tomasetti goes to the door, yanks it open. Sheriff Pallant and another deputy are standing in the dark and drizzle, looking in.

"Morning." Pallant's eyes slide from Tomasetti to me and back to Tomasetti.

"Any luck with that warrant?" I ask.

Pallant slaps a rolled-up stack of papers against his palm. "Got it."

Tomasetti steps back, all business. "In that case, come in."

An instant of awkwardness descends when the two men enter the cramped confines of our room. It doesn't last; there's too much focus on the case, on what lies ahead.

"What does the warrant cover?" I ask.

"In light of a missing minor child, the house and property," the sheriff tells me. "The judge was pretty gung-ho and kept it broad."

"Which means we can basically go in and look at whatever we want," Tomasetti says.

Pallant nods. "That's about the size of it."

"Do either of you know Vernon or Rosanna Detweiler?" I ask. "Have you met them? Dealt with them? Do you know anything about them?"

The sheriff shakes his head. "We've never had any dealings with them. Never taken a call that involved them. Never had cause to go out there or talk to them." He grimaces. "How sure are you these people have the kid?"

I recap what I know and explain the significance of the dates. "Add to that the plaster from the size-thirteen work boot and Detweiler's height, and we've got probable cause."

Pallant doesn't seem convinced. "The judge bought it."

"Does anyone know if Detweiler has guns on the property?" Tomasetti asks. "Does he hunt?"

"We don't know," Pallant responds.

"If they're Amish and live on a farm, we have to assume they do," I say. "Most Amish hunt."

"David Troyer was likely shot with a muzzle-loader," Tomasetti says.

"The only thing good about that is a muzzle-loader is slow to load," Pallant adds.

"Anyone know the layout of the property?" I ask.

The two men shake their heads.

"It's a big spread," the sheriff says.

"They run cattle," the deputy adds. "I've seen them when I drive by. A couple dozen head."

I go to the desk, pull up an aerial view on my laptop, and zoom in close. "In addition to the house, there are at least three good-size outbuildings."

"Lots of places to hide," Tomasetti says.

The sheriff leans closer, squints at the screen. "Any other buildings?"

"Not on this aerial, but it's over a year old." I indicate what looks like an excavated area at the rear of the property. "Not sure what that is." Using my mouse, I zoom in, but it doesn't help. "A pond that's gone dry?"

"There's a quarry on the northwest corner of the property," the deputy says. "It's defunct now. There used to be a lot of gravel trucks coming and going through a gate at the back."

The sheriff indicates a greenbelt that bisects the property. "Creek runs through there, too."

"A lot of trees," I murmur.

"So what's the plan?" Tomasetti asks.

The sheriff looks at his watch. "It's six A.M. Let's execute the warrant. Search the house, outbuildings, and the property." He makes eye contact with me. "I've got two more deputies en route. Everyone has been briefed. Once we execute the warrant, my guys will enter the property through that back gate and work their way to the front." He addresses me and Tomasetti. "Before we do anything, might be a good idea to talk to the couple, feel them out, and then search the house and outbuildings."

"I think we're good to go," Tomasetti says.

"Let's do it." The sheriff brings his hands together. "My deputy and I will ride together. You two follow."

I stride to the TV stand, snatch up my shoulder holster and .38, shrug into it. I grab my jacket out of the closet. I gather the file. My laptop.

Tomasetti reaches for the keys and the four of us go through the door.

CHAPTER 25

One hundred eleven hours missing

It's still dark with drizzle and fog as Tomasetti and I follow the sheriff's cruiser to the Detweiler property, which takes twenty minutes. The lane entrance is overgrown, without a mailbox or any indication it's a residence at all, and we drive by twice before realizing we've arrived at our destination.

The brake lights flash as they make the turn. Tomasetti follows, muttering a curse as he wrestles the Explorer over deep ruts and through hip-high grass and weeds. A hundred yards in, he jams the Explorer into four-wheel drive. We pass by a low-slung hog barn that looks abandoned. The ground is muddy and torn up, but there are no hogs in sight. No lights as far as the eye can see. A quarter mile farther in, trees encroach on the driveway. We climb a hill, and a small frame house looms into view. No shutters or landscaping. The downstairs window glows with light. Someone is awake.

Beyond the house, a falling-down bank barn leans precariously. It was once white, but the decades have eaten away most of the paint. A chicken house stands next to the barn. There's a smaller hog barn with an attached pen where several dozen hogs mill about. Two horses stand inside a loafing shed, munching on a round bale of hay, watching us.

Tomasetti parks next to a black buggy, our headlights revealing the lack of a slow-moving-vehicle sign. There's no reflective signage of any kind. But it's the lack of a windshield and the sight of the dual kerosene lanterns that confirm what I already know. The Detweilers are Swartzentruber.

"Interesting that he's got a driver's license and a buggy," I say.

"I guess all those Amish rules are a pain in the ass when you have a kid to abduct and she lives four hours away." Tomasetti jams the Explorer into park and looks at me. "You got a vest?"

"Didn't think I'd need it."

Giving me a dark look, he swings open the door and gets out. "Keep your goddamn eyes open."

The four of us meet next to the sheriff's cruiser. I'm keenly aware of the silence. The whisper-hiss of drizzle. The totality of the darkness pressing down. The sense of abandonment that seems to permeate the place.

The sheriff slaps the rolled warrant against his palm, then addresses his deputy. "Stay here, keep an eye on things. Get on the radio, tell those guys in the back to stand by." He looks at me and Tomasetti. "Let's go serve this bastard."

Cold drizzle floats down from a charcoal sky as we take a stone path around the side of the house to the front. We ascend the steps and cross the wooden porch. There's a single large window that's covered with a dark pull-down shade. Standing slightly to one side, Sheriff Pallant knocks on the door. Tomasetti and I stand behind him and to his right.

Footsteps sound and the door swings open. An elderly Amish woman blinks owlishly at the sight of us. "Oh my. What's this?" She's wearing a gray dress that falls nearly to her ankles. A *kapp* covered with a black bonnet. Black apron. Practical black shoes. A dish towel in her hands, fingers bent with arthritis.

I know immediately this woman isn't Rosanna Detweiler. If Rosanna Detweiler had a child in 2012—even if she had a child late in life—there's no way she could be much over fifty. This woman looks to be around seventy.

"Is something wrong?" she asks in an accent that tells me she speaks more *Deitsch* than English. "Has something happened?"

Pallant has his official ID at the ready. "Are you Rosanna Detweiler?"

"I'm Irene Detweiler." The woman's eyes flick from him to Tomasetti to me and back to the sheriff. "What's this about?"

He identifies himself. "We're looking for Vernon and Rosanna Detweiler. Are either of them here?"

"No."

"Do they live here, ma'am?"

"No. This is my home."

"Are you related to the Detweilers?"

"Vern's my son. Rosanna is my daughter-in-law." Rheumy blue eyes skate from Tomasetti to the sheriff to me and for the first time she looks alarmed. "Has something happened to them?"

Tomasetti and the sheriff exchange a look. "When's the last time you saw them?" Pallant asks.

"I haven't seen my son or his wife for several years. Not since the bishop put them under the *bann*. Said they were backsliders," she tells him, using the Amish term for someone who doesn't follow the rules set forth by the *Ordnung*. "I always hoped they'd change their ways, but they didn't and they never came back."

"Do you know where your son is living now?" I ask.

"Like I said, I haven't seen him in years." Her brows furrow. "Did they do something wrong?"

This isn't what I expected. "Your husband's name was Vernon?" I ask.

"Yes."

It hadn't occurred to me that the property deed might be in her husband's name, not her son's. A rookie mistake. I kick myself for not anticipating it, for not checking.

Stepping back from the door, Pallant frowns at us and lowers his voice. "Someone get their information wrong here?"

"She could be covering for them," Tomasetti says in a hushed tone.

Pallant holds his gaze for a moment, then goes back to the door and passes the warrant to the Amish woman. "I've got a warrant to search your house and your farm, ma'am. I suggest you read it carefully."

"A warrant? But . . ." She takes the paper, and looks down at it as if it's covered with some lethal virus. "What on earth are you looking for?"

"Everything you need to know is in the warrant." Opening the door wider, the sheriff pushes past her.

She steps aside, incredulity flashing in her eyes. "Has my son done something wrong?"

The sheriff ignores her question, his eyes already skimming the darkened room. "Is there anyone else here at the farm this morning, ma'am? Family member? Farmhand?"

"It's just me."

I follow the sheriff into the house. Tomasetti comes in behind me.

"Are there any firearms in the house or on the property?" Pallant asks, his voice amicable.

"Just that old muzzle-loader that belonged to my husband."

The three of us exchange looks.

"Where is it?" I ask.

"The mudroom." The Amish woman starts toward it.

The sheriff reaches out and touches her arm, stopping her. "I'll get it, ma'am. Why don't you just have a seat and relax?" He starts toward the kitchen and the back of the house.

My eyes adjust to the dimly lit interior. We're standing in a living room with battered hardwood floors. Dark blinds hang at the windows. In the flickering light of a single lantern, I see a quilt wall covering above a ragtag sofa. A coffee table. An oval braided rug covers the floor. The house smells of kerosene, coffee, and toast.

I see Tomasetti, taking in the details, looking past me into the kitchen. There are stairs to our right. A darkened stairwell that goes to a second level.

Visibly upset, the Amish woman unrolls the warrant and blinks at it as if it's written in a language she doesn't understand.

The sheriff returns to the living room. He's wrapped the long gun in what looks like a dish towel. "We'll tag it and start a return sheet," he says to no one in particular.

"You can't just walk into someone's home and take things." Irene Detweiler walks to the center of the room and faces the three of us. "What on earth do you want?"

"Everything you need to know is in that warrant, ma'am," the sheriff tells her. "Why don't you take a seat on the sofa over there and read it?"

She holds her ground, hands on her hips, glaring at him.

"That's not a request, ma'am."

He stares at her until she acquiesces; then he speaks into his lapel mike. "Warrant has been executed." He gives the go-ahead for the deputies at the back of the property to enter through the rear gate.

Pallant looks at me. "Chief Burkholder?"

I look at the woman, address her in *Deitsch*. "Mrs. Detweiler, we're looking for a missing child. A seven-year-old little girl. Is it possible she's somewhere here on the property?"

"A little girl?" She fingers the collar of her dress. "Lord no. There's no child here."

"Is it possible she's with your son or daughter-in-law?"

"What on earth would they do with a child? Why would they even *have* a little girl?"

I translate for the sheriff.

"All right." Pallant looks from me to Tomasetti. "I've got a female deputy on the way to look after Mrs. Detweiler while we search the place. If you'd like to go ahead and start, I'll stay with her."

"Sure thing." Tomasetti turns and takes the stairs to the second level.

Doubt whispers in my ear as I start toward the kitchen. Is it possible I'm wrong about this? Not only is the property not owned by the Vernon Detweiler we're looking for, but Irene Detweiler seems credible and genuinely confused by news of the missing girl. Is she telling the truth about her estrangement from them? Is her son living elsewhere? Are the dates coincidental?

The kitchen is a large room and the heart of the house. What looks like a picnic table is covered with a plain tablecloth. A lantern flickering in the center throws off a dim glow. There's a sink to my right. Thin predawn light slants in through the window. A cast-iron skillet on the stove. A roll of paper towels. There's no refrigerator. No pantry. Pulling my mini Maglite from my jacket pocket, I move on to the mudroom.

It's a narrow, cluttered space. Hooks for coats on the wall. A door that leads outside. Through the window I see our vehicles and the deputy with his flashlight beyond. I run the beam of my flashlight along the hanging coats. A barn coat. A woman's slicker. Three of the hooks are unused. There's a pair of dirty, adult-size sneakers on the floor.

Rubber muck boots. None are large enough to be a men's size thirteen. I even check the floor for loose boards that might lead to a crawlspace. But there's nothing there.

I walk back to the living room to find a female deputy standing next to the sofa where Irene Detweiler sits. She's a big woman, tall and substantially muscled, with blue eyes, buzz-cut blond hair, and the tail end of a tattoo peeking out of the uniform cuff at her wrist.

I cross to her, introduce myself, and we exchange a quick shake.

"Sheriff went out to help search the barns," she tells me.

Tomasetti jogs down the stairs, Maglite in hand. "Upstairs is clear," he says.

"Attic?" I say.

"Nothing there." He crosses to me. "You want to take a look around?"

Anxious to get outside, I'm already striding toward the door.

The gray light of dawn hovers atop the tree line to the east as Tomasetti and I make our way to the hog barn. Two more cruisers are parked in the driveway. Rain pours from a low sky and I'm relieved we had the forethought to bring slickers. We find Sheriff Pallant, and two deputies, flashlights in hand, running a dozen or so hogs from the barn. The smell of manure hits me like a sledgehammer when I walk in the door. To my left, one of the deputies wades through muck, arms spread, herding the last of the hogs through the lower half of a Dutch door and into the muddy pen outside. None of the men look too pleased to be here.

Pallant is smoking a cigar and saunters over to me. "You still think this mystery couple has a kidnapped child somewhere on this property?" he asks.

Skepticism rings hard in his voice; I feel that same doubt crowding my own certainty. "I don't think I'm wrong about this." I'm aware of Tomasetti standing a few feet away, watching the exchange. Even the deputy has paused. "It's the best lead we've got," I tell them.

After a moment, the sheriff sighs. "Well, we're here. We got the warrant. Let's do our jobs. If there's a kid here, we'll find her."

While the deputies and sheriff continue their search of the hog barn, Tomasetti and I move on to the bank barn. Rain patters against our slickers as we wade through mud and clumps of grass and weeds. Tomasetti slides open the big door. It's a massive structure. The interior is dark and dusty and jammed full of ancient farming implements—a wooden wagon, a manure spreader, a rusty harrow, and a beat-up galvanized trough.

"We don't have enough manpower to search a farm this size," I say as I step inside.

"We've got our warrant and a sheriff who's bent over backwards to accommodate us." Tomasetti shoves open the sliding door as far as it will go, trying to usher in more light. "Let's give it our best shot."

Sighing, I raise my Maglite. There's a row of horse stalls to my right, the boards covered with cobwebs and dust. Ahead, there's a raised wood floor where a dozen bales of hay have been left to rot. To my right are the stairs to the loft. Beneath the stairs, burlap bags containing some kind of grain have been torn open by rodents.

"I'll take the horse stalls," I say.

"I got the loft."

I go to the stalls, checking the trough as I walk past. I stop at the first door, slide it open. It's a typical twelve-by-twelve horse stall with a wood hayrack. Any manure or straw left on the floor has composted to dirt. At some point a groundhog has dug a hole in the corner. I check all four stalls, even the floor for trapdoors, but it's obvious no one has used this place for years.

A few minutes later, I meet Tomasetti in the aisle. He doesn't say anything as we make our way toward the door, but I can tell by his expression he's thinking the same thing I am: The missing girl isn't here.

"Tomasetti, I don't think that old woman abducted Elsie Helmuth."

"She's not your typical child abductor. Then again, she could be lying about her son."

"What if I'm wrong about this?" I say as we go through the door and into the pouring rain.

"We don't always get it right, Kate. We do our best. That's all we can do." He slants me a look. "It doesn't mean we should pack it up and go home. Let's finish this. Walk out of here with the certainty that we've done our jobs to the best of our ability and the girl isn't here."

Not an easy task when you have a hundred and fifty rugged acres to cover and a handful of people with which to do it. To make matters worse, the temperature is hovering somewhere around forty degrees and the rain shows no sign of abating.

It's eight A.M. by the time Tomasetti and I reach the back of the property. A Scioto County cruiser is parked on the other side of the gate, but the deputies are nowhere in sight. More than likely they followed the fence line due west to the property line and then turned south toward the house and outbuildings.

Tomasetti stands there a moment, shaking water from his slicker, and looks around. "If you were going to stash a kid outside, where would you put her?"

As if on cue the tempo of the rain increases, pounding the canopies and ground. *Shit,* I think, but neither of us complains.

"A cave. A defunct mine." I think about that a moment. "Storm shelter. Root cellar."

"Didn't someone tell us there was an old quarry on the property?"

I nod. "I saw it on the aerial view. It's to the west, past the creek."

"Let's head that way and then cut south toward the house."

We slog through high weeds and grass and mud for twenty minutes. We're standing on a relative high point of the property. Despite the bad weather, the views are pretty. A few yards ahead, the ground drops away steeply. At the base of the hill a muddy creek the color of creamed coffee churns south toward the river. Even though we're fifty yards away, I can hear the rush of water. Beyond are the house and barns. I can see the lights of the sheriff's department cruisers. Disappointment presses into me when I realize we've covered the entire property.

"I hate to point out the obvious," Tomasetti says.

"She's not here," I mutter.

We stand in the rain, soaked and cold, and take in the scene for a moment. "We did our best," he says. "We followed through."

"A seven-year-old little girl is still missing. Tomasetti, after what that son of a bitch did to Mary Yoder . . . she may not even be alive. The statistics are not in her favor."

"Fuck the statistics," he growls. "Let's talk to the old lady again, see if she has anything to add."

Heart heavy, the sense of defeat, of failure, a physical weight on my shoulders, I start down the hill and head toward the house.

CHAPTER 26

One hundred and fourteen hours missing

I find Sheriff Pallant and two deputies standing in the rain next to their cruisers, the engines running, headlights on, emergency lights off. Waiting for us. One of the deputies has already left.

"There's no child on this property," the sheriff says as we approach. "We searched the house, the land. There's nothing there. I've got deputies canvassing, talking to neighbors, and no one has seen either Detweiler in the vicinity. No one recalls seeing a light-colored truck in the area."

"We've run both of them through the system," Tomasetti adds. "No warrants. No criminal record."

Pallant makes a sound of frustration. "We tried locating known associates, but we haven't had any luck. None of the Amish have phones." He sighs. "Part of the problem is these Old Order Amish stay off the grid. No electricity. No phone. No driver's license."

"Did you get anything from Irene Detweiler?" I ask.

"We talked to her at length," he tells me. "She doesn't know anything about a missing child. And she doesn't know where her son and daughter-in-law are. I guess they had some kind of falling-out with the Amish, got them excommunicated or something."

The sheriff tips his hat and water runs off the brim. "Look, we've done our due diligence and there's nothing to be had. We're going to call it a day."

"Do you mind if I speak with her?" I ask.

"Look, I'm sorry this didn't pan out for you, Chief Burkholder. I'm sorry we didn't find the girl." He jabs a thumb at the house and lowers his voice. "I know you two want to find that kid; believe me, we do too. But you can't get blood from a turnip."

"There's a familial connection," I tell him. "I'd like to ask her about it."

Neither of us moves. The sheriff holds his ground, his expression steely and set.

"With Chief Burkholder's roots being Amish," Tomasetti says, "she may have some insights into the culture, into this family in particular, that might help jog this woman's memory or open some doors."

The sheriff sighs. "Well, hell, we're here. You do what you need to do." He looks at his watch. "We're going to take off. All I ask is that you not overstep."

"Of course," I say.

Tomasetti and I watch them pull away, and then we go back to the house. He knocks on the door. Irene Detweiler peers out at us. "I thought you were finished," she says.

"Just a couple of quick questions," I say in *Deitsch*.

Looking put out, she opens the door and ushers us inside. At some point, she's lit another lantern, and the living area glows with golden light.

The woman shuffles to the sofa, lowers herself onto it, and picks up some knitting project—two needles and a ball of yarn. Tomasetti holds his ground near the door. I sit in the chair next to the sofa and spend a few minutes trying to build rapport, gauge her receptivity to my being formerly Amish, hoping it will somehow garner me an added level of trust.

I take her through some of the questions that have already been asked, hoping for more detailed answers or something she'd forgotten to mention before. She remains consistent, giving me nothing.

"Did Rosanna have any children?" I ask.

"The Lord never blessed them with little ones. She was *ime familye weg* once or twice, but . . . no babies." She gives a shrug. "She never spoke of it, but I know it was hard on her. You know how important children are to the Amish. To tell you the truth, I never felt close enough to her to ask. Lord knows the men don't talk about such things. The women used to gossip about poor Rosanna and her not having any little ones. Some said worse."

"Worse like what?"

"Cruel nonsense mostly. Gossipmongers saying she wasn't fit to be a mother." The Amish woman clucks in disgust. "It must have hurt her something awful."

"Why would they say such a thing?" I ask.

"Rosanna was a quiet thing. Serious, you know. Different. She didn't laugh much. Didn't get close to people like most of us do. Some of the Amish thought that was odd. I suppose I did, too."

"Why were they put under the *bann*?"

"Vernon bought a truck." She makes a sound of disapproval. "I didn't have them over anymore after that. You know how it is. I couldn't take meals with them. No one would do business with them. I urged them to mend their ways. To honor their baptismal promises."

"Do you know what kind of truck it was? Color?"

"Never saw it. I wouldn't let him bring it on the property."

I nod, thinking about a woman without children, isolated from her family, and how both of those things could affect someone who is part of a community in which children are so highly valued.

"Did you know Mary Yoder?" I ask.

"I don't know who that is."

"What about Marlene Byler?"

The knitting needles go still. "She's the woman who killed herself all those years ago. Jumped off the bridge."

"Did you know her?"

"I know the name is all. Lots of people around here remember that name. What she did . . . such an awful thing."

Her eyes don't meet mine. She stares at her knitting, realizing she's dropped a stitch.

"Marlene Byler and Mary Yoder were sisters," I tell her.

The woman stares at me, her mouth working. I see the wheels of her mind spinning and I get the impression she's struggling with some internal dilemma.

"Mrs. Detweiler, a little girl's life is at stake," I say quietly. "She's seven years old. *Amisch*. If you know something that might help me find her, I need to hear it."

For the span of a full minute, the only sound comes from the hiss of the lantern, the patter of rain against the window, the splat of water against the sidewalk as it overflows the guttering outside.

"I never got to know my daughter-in-law well." The woman tightens her mouth, looks down at her knitting, picks at the yarn. "Chief Burkholder, Rosanna told me a strange story once. You have to understand, she was . . . a peculiar girl. Always saying odd things no one really understood or knew how to react to. You never knew if it was true or make-believe."

"What did she tell you?"

"She told me that Marlene Byler was her *mamm*."

My pulse jumps at the possibility of yet another familial connection. "So Marlene Byler had more than one child?"

"Oh no. You misunderstand. Marlene only had *one* child."

I stare at her, my mind scrambling to make sense of what I've just been told. "Are you telling me Rosanna is the baby that went off the bridge with Marlene?"

"I'm telling you that's what Rosanna said. I don't know if it's true. Lord knows she told her share of tall tales."

"Did she tell you how she survived the fall?" I ask. "Did she say who raised her?"

"Her grandmother."

I pull the spiral pad from my pocket. "Do you have a name?"

"Rosanna only mentioned her once or twice in all the years I knew her." Closing her eyes, she presses her fingers to her temples. "Ruby something. I remember because it's kind of an unusual name for an Amish woman." She massages her temples. "Mullet." Her eyes open. "Ruby Mullet."

Behind me, I hear Tomasetti move. "Does she live in the area?" he asks.

"Last I heard she owned a farm down south, on the other side of the river. Eads Hollow, I think."

Ten minutes later, Tomasetti and I are back in the Explorer. "If she's right about Rosanna being Marlene Byler's daughter, then Mary Yoder was her aunt," I say.

"There's your connection. Might be why the bishop chose the Helmuths. To keep the child with family."

"What does it mean in terms of the case?" I ask.

"It means we have one more place to look for that girl." Tomasetti puts the Explorer in gear and starts down the lane. "I don't have to tell you we're going to be a couple of light-years out of our jurisdiction."

"I'm aware." I type Eads Hollow into my phone. "We're twenty minutes away."

He sighs as he makes the turn onto the highway.

I call Dispatch. "Lois, can you pull up the tax roll for Boyd County, Kentucky, and do a property search for Ruby Mullet?" I spell the last name. "I'm looking for an address."

"Sure."

Keys clack on the other end. Lois makes a few noises, including a "crap" and "dang it," and then she tells me, "It looks like Ruby Mullet owns a thirty-acre tract in Eads Hollow." She rattles off an address.

I enter it into my GPS. "Any news on David Troyer?"

"No change, Chief. Last time I checked he's still in a coma, but holding his own."

"Let me know if anything changes." I end the call and recite the address to Tomasetti.

"Get the Boyd County Sheriff's Department on the line," he says.

I'm already dialing the number. It takes a few minutes, but I finally get connected with the chief deputy, who agrees to have a deputy meet us at the Mullet address.

CHAPTER 27

One hundred and seventeen hours missing
We cross the Ohio River at the Twelfth Street Bridge and enter Kentucky. From there, Tomasetti takes us south on US 23 through the verdant foothills of the Appalachian Mountains. A few miles before Catlettsburg, the GPS instructs him to make a right on Route 168 and head west. I'm thinking about the things I've learned about Rosanna Detweiler and all the dark possibilities they present. My conversation with her mother-in-law hovers in the backwaters of my mind.

The women used to gossip about poor Rosanna and her not having any little ones.

Gossipmongers saying she wasn't fit to be a mother.

It must have hurt her something awful.

I'm so lost in my thoughts I don't notice when Tomasetti nearly misses his turn. Cursing, he brakes hard, then backs up twenty feet or so to make the turn onto Johnson Fork Road. Another mile and he takes an unnamed dirt track. A half a mile in we reach our destination.

"Home sweet home," he mutters as he parks the Explorer on the barely-there shoulder.

The property owned by Ruby Mullet has the look of a place that's been abandoned for many years. A gray frame house sits fifty yards off the road, nestled in a thicket of trees and nearly hidden from view. There's no sign of the Boyd County sheriff's deputy's cruiser.

We get out. It's so quiet I can hear the breeze hissing through the high grass. The rattle of tree branches against the steel-shingled roof.

"Let's see if Grandma can shed some light on the situation," Tomasetti says.

My boots sink into mud as I walk to what was once a driveway. It's little more than an impression in the weeds that cuts through the trees. It looks driven upon, but any tire tracks have long since been washed away.

"Keep your eyes open," Tomasetti says as we start down the driveway.

There's a dilapidated barn to my left. Farther back, a corn silo squats on the side of a hill. There's a sorrel horse standing in a small pen behind the barn. Beyond, a dozen or so goats graze on grass that's shorn to dirt.

"Someone lives here," I say.

We reach the crumbling sidewalk and take it to the front porch. The wood planks creak beneath our feet, the wood warped. Dark curtains on the windows are closed.

I reach the door and knock. "Hello?" I call out. "Ruby Mullet?"

A diamond-shaped window is set into the door. Cupping my hands, I put my face to the glass and peer inside. I see a small living room, plainly decorated. A coffee table with a lantern in the center. An oval rag rug. A wicker basket loaded with dried flowers and fall gourds.

"Looks occupied," Tomasetti says.

The crunch of tires on gravel alerts us to an approaching vehicle. I glance over my shoulder to see a Boyd County Sheriff's Department vehicle roll up behind the Explorer.

We leave the porch and meet the deputy in the driveway. He's about thirty years old, with the build of a heavyweight boxer, a bald pate, and eyes the color of a bruise. He's wearing a crisp uniform with military-style boots and an expensive-looking pair of sport sunglasses. He's chewing gum so vigorously I can hear his teeth chomp.

Introductions are made.

"I understand you're looking for Ruby Mullet?" he says.

Tomasetti lays out the fundamentals of the case. "Do you know who lives here?" he asks.

The deputy shakes his head. "I've patrolled this area pretty regularly for almost a year now," he tells us. "Used to see Amish people out here every so often. Place is off the beaten path, so I don't get out this way much."

"A couple?" I ask.

"Older lady." He motions toward the house and we start that way. "Haven't seen anyone in a while."

We walk to the porch. I stand aside and the deputy knocks on the door. "Boyd County Sheriff's Office!" he calls out. "Ruby Mullet?"

No one answers. We wait for about a minute, listening, but there's no sound of footsteps. No voices. No sign that there's anyone inside.

The deputy knocks with a little more vigor. "Sheriff's department! Mrs. Mullet? Can you come to the door please?"

He leans closer, peers through the window. "No one's home."

"Can we do a welfare check?" Tomasetti says. "Make sure everyone's okay?"

The deputy tilts his head and speaks into his lapel mike. "This is 392. I'm on scene 2292 Johnson Fork Road. No sign of the home-owner. I'm going to ten-thirty-four-C," he says, using the code for a well-being check.

"Roger that," comes a staticky female voice.

The three of us leave the porch and walk back to the driveway. "We can't do much since this is just a welfare check," the deputy tells us. "I'll take a quick peek in the barn, see if there's a buggy."

I look at Tomasetti. "Maybe we ought to try the back door."

He shrugs. "If she's elderly, she may be hard of hearing."

The deputy heads toward the barn. Tomasetti and I start toward the back of the house. The grass is knee high and looks as if it hasn't been cut in months. There's an old well with a steel hand pump. A massive maple tree trembles in the breeze, leaves catching and flying.

We climb the steps to the small concrete porch. There are no curtains on the window set into the back door. I peer through the glass into small room. There's a wood bench against the wall. A rocking chair in the corner. A pair of boots. Farther, a doorway leads to what looks like a kitchen.

"Hello?" I call out loudly as I rap my knuckles against the glass. "Ruby Mullet? I'm a police officer. Is everything okay in there?"

We wait a couple of minutes, but no one comes.

I look at Tomasetti. He stares back, his expression reflecting the same uneasiness I feel climbing up the back of my neck.

"So if you're on the cops' radar and trying to stay off the grid, where would you go?" he says.

"A relative," I tell him. "Someone with a different last name. Not closely connected. Not easily tracked."

"In the middle of fucking nowhere." He sighs. "Kate, getting a warrant might be tricky. State line is going to complicate things, but I can get it done. Let me get on the horn, see what I can do."

He's already tugging his phone from his pocket as he walks down the steps.

I stand there a moment, looking out over the property. I'm thinking about walking the perimeter of the house when I notice the small fenced area twenty yards away. The picket fence was once white, but the elements have eroded the paint and turned the wood gray. The enclosure is about thirty feet square, with an arbor-type gate covered with winter-dead climbing roses.

I hear Tomasetti talking to someone on the cell as I start that way. I'm midway there when I realize it's a family cemetery plot. They're not uncommon in this part of the country. There are five markers—small wooden crosses—arranged in two neat rows. The hinge screeches with unnatural sound as I let myself in. I pass beneath the arbor, go to the first marker, and kneel. The cross is covered with lichens and mold. A name and dates are burned into the wood. Reaching out, I brush the surface with my fingertips, and read aloud.

"Ruby Marie Mullet. Born May 22, 1938. Died February 2, 2019."

The owner of the property. Rosanna Detweiler's grandmother. If she's been dead since February, who's been living here?

I go to the next marker.

MARTIN ROY MULLET.
BORN APRIL 30, 1932.
DIED NOVEMBER 23, 2012.

The next marker gives me pause.

AMOS WAYNE DETWEILER.
BORN JULY 17, 2008.
DIED AUGUST 19, 2008.

An infant, I realize, and my conversation with Irene Detweiler floats through my mind.

The Lord never blessed them with little ones. She was ime familye weg *once or twice, but . . . no babies.*

Or were there?

I go to the next marker.

BONNIE ANN DETWEILER.

BORN OCTOBER 2, 2010.
DIED JANUARY 3, 2011.

The final marker slants at a severe angle. The grave has been disturbed, the earth freshly turned. Either this small grave has recently been dug or someone has done something unthinkable. Dread rises inside me when I look into the shallow hole. There's nothing there— no casket or remains—just the wet, black soil of a pit that's about three feet deep. I kneel next to the marker and read.

NETTIE MAE DETWEILER.

BORN MARCH 14, 2012.
DIED MARCH 14, 2012.

For the span of a full minute the only sound comes from the tinkle of rain against the treetops, the rumble of thunder in the distance, and the white noise of my brain as I ponder the possibilities.

"Warrant is in the works."

I straighten, turn to see Tomasetti standing at the gate, just outside the cemetery. His eyes moving from me to the markers and back to me.

"I never understood why an Amish bishop, an Amish midwife, would remove a baby from its mother," I say.

He comes through the gate, goes to the nearest marker, and reads.

"According to Irene Detweiler, the Amish community was suspicious of Rosanna. The women gossiped about her. Said she was unfit to be a mother."

Tomasetti says nothing.

"I don't want to be right about this." I look around. "If Sadie Stutzman was concerned about the welfare of the children, if she thought Rosanna was somehow unfit, I can understand her going to the bishop. I can see the bishop stepping in."

He looks away as if digesting the dark undercurrents, his eyes skimming the surrounding land, the fields, the woods beyond. "We don't know what happened here."

"No, but we have a theory." A theory that's so hideous, neither of us says the words aloud . . .

Tomasetti's phone chirps. He looks down at it. "Kentucky Department of Criminal Investigation. Hang tight." Turning away, he sets it to his ear.

I glance toward the barn. The big sliding door stands open. There's no sign of the deputy. I leave the cemetery and walk back to the house. The curtains at the window are parted by a couple of inches, so I go to it and peer inside. The interior is murky. I see light blue cabinets. An old-fashioned porcelain sink. Gas stove. Farther, I can just make out the corner of a kitchen table. I'm about to turn away when I hear a resonant thump from inside the house.

Turning my head, I set my ear against the glass. I hold my breath and listen. The faint sound of pounding reaches me. Cupping my hands, I look, try to see past the grime and dim light. There's no one there, but I've no doubt I heard something.

Muttering a curse, I try the knob, find it unlocked. I push open the door and step inside. There's a row of windows to my right. A bench seat to my left. The room is dirty. There are clumps of dried mud, leaves, and grass on the floor.

"Hello?" I call out loudly. "I'm a police officer. Is someone there?"

The house reeks of mildew and dust and day-old garbage. I continue on, enter the kitchen. It's tidy and a bit cleaner, with a table and four chairs. A dozen or so mason jars sit on the counter next to an old-fashioned bread box. A towel is draped over the edge of a sink.

The sound of pounding startles me. It's muffled; I'm not sure where it's coming from. Rounding the table, I move to the living room. Beyond is a murky hall with two doors. One opens to a bathroom. The other door is closed. There's a padlock, shiny and new and starkly out of place.

The pounding sounds again.

Senses on alert, I go to the door, set my ear against the wood. "Who's there?"

The tempo of the pounding increases. "Let me out!" A little girl's voice, high-pitched and panicked.

"Elsie?"

"Let me out! Let me out! I promise to be good!"

A hundred thoughts tear through my brain. I lift the lock, but it's engaged. I look around for the key, but it's nowhere in sight.

Caution makes me hesitate. I don't know if there's anyone else in the house. I don't know if the girl is alone. If there's someone with her. If they're armed . . .

"Are you alone?" I call out.

"Yes! I'm scared! Pleeeeeeease lemme out! I promise not to run away!"

"I'm a policeman," I tell her. "Stay calm and keep quiet, okay? We'll get you out."

Either the girl doesn't hear me or she's too panicked to comprehend my words. The pounding becomes frenzied. I can hear her crying, little fingernails scratching the door. No time to comfort her.

I spin and dash through the kitchen. I tug out my .38 as I go through the mudroom; then I'm on the porch. Tomasetti stands a few feet away, on the phone. "I got her!" I say to him.

He whirls, a collage of emotions playing in his expression. He's already moving toward me. "Anyone else in the house?"

"I don't know. She said she's alone."

Reaching into his jacket, he pulls his Kimber from his shoulder holster. "Let's go get her."

We burst into the house, run through the kitchen. Tomasetti reaches the door first.

"Can I come out now?" comes a tiny voice. "I want my *mamm*."

"Stand back," he tells her. "I'm going to break down the door."

Silence.

We exchange a look. "Are you away from the door, sweetheart?" I ask.

"Ja!"

Stepping back, Tomasetti raises his right leg and slams his foot against the door, next to the knob. Wood cracks, but holds. He kicks it again. On the third try, the wood jamb splits. The hasp holds. A final kick and the door flies open.

It's a tiny bedroom. Windows covered with plywood. Little Elsie Helmuth stands a few feet away, tears streaming, her hands over her face. It's a heartrending sight. I want to go to her, put my arms around her. Let her know she's safe. But we're not sure what we've stumbled upon, so I hold my ground.

Tomasetti enters the room, goes to her, bends to her. "We're the police," he says gently. "We're here to take you home."

The girl rushes to him. Tomasetti sweeps her into his arms. I see her arms go around his neck, her legs wrap around his waist.

"I want Mamm," she sobs.

For the span of several seconds, he holds her. He presses his cheek to the top of her head. "Let's get you out of here."

The sight of him with the child in his arms moves me so profoundly that for a moment I have to blink back tears.

Still wearing her dress and *kapp,* the little girl clings to Tomasetti, her arms tight around his neck, her legs around his middle, her face pressed against his shoulder. Tomasetti is holding her against him with one arm, the Kimber in his other hand.

"I'm going to take her to the Explorer and call this in." He flashes me a look, his expression a mosaic of relief and trepidation. "Get that deputy. Keep your eyes open."

Taking a final look at them, I turn and jog through the kitchen, go out the back door, and sprint toward the barn. The door stands open, but the interior is dark.

"Deputy!" I call out.

No answer.

I reach the doorway, give my eyes a moment to adjust to the dim light. It's a huge structure with a low ceiling and support beams as thick as a man's waist. To my right are tumbledown stalls with sliding doors in the front, Dutch doors that likely open to the outside pens. Some of the stall front boards are missing and have been piled on the floor. To my left are stairs that lead to the loft. Ahead, an old water trough is filled with wood planks and steel T-posts. Next to it, a tangled roll of rusty barbed wire lies in the dirt.

"Deputy!" Gray light slants in through grimy windows; some of the panes are broken or gone. A large sliding door at the back of the barn stands open. I've just reached the door when I spot the deputy outside, sprawled on the ground, arms and legs splayed. A copious amount of blood covers his jacket.

My .38 at my side, I start toward him. I'm midway there when I spot the pickup truck in the trees twenty yards away. Tan. Short bed. Tailgate down. A man stands on the other side of the truck, looking at me, his rifle leveled right at me.

A gunshot sears the air. I spin, run back to the barn, throw myself against the nearest beam. Another shot rings out. The wood inches from my face explodes. Shards pierce my cheek, my temple, and my scalp. I reel backward, stumble, nearly fall.

Through the open door I see the man round the truck. Rifle at his side.

"Police!" I scream. "Drop your weapon!"

He doesn't obey my command.

I raise the .38 and fire three times.

The man wobbles, goes down on one knee. He looks my way. Face a mask of rage. He raises the rifle. The gunshot sears the air. I turn and run. Thoughts of Tomasetti and the girl flash. But I know he heard the gunfire.

I look wildly for cover, sprint to the nearest stall, throw myself inside and to the floor. I speed-crawl to the front rail, peer between the wood planks. The shooter stands silhouetted at the door, rifle in hand, looking around. He's a large man, tall and heavily built. Black jacket.

Vernon Detweiler.

He doesn't see me, but I'm not well hidden. Slowly, trying to stay quiet, control my breathing, I kneel and shift into position for a shot. The light is bad; the angle is worse. He's forty feet away. This is my only chance. I have two bullets left. I set the .38 between the planks.

If he looks in my direction, he'll spot me. I'm visible between the rails. I take a deep breath, release it slowly. He walks into the barn and stops thirty feet away. He glances at the stairs to the loft, tilts his head, listening.

He looks right at me, brings up the rifle. I pull off two shots. The man goes to his knees. Blood blooms on his shirt, but he doesn't fall.

I watch in horror as he struggles to his feet. Blood streaks down the right leg of his trousers. A red stripe on his hand where he holds the stock. He starts toward me.

"The thief comes only to steal and kill and destroy," he says.

Panic slams down on me. I'm out of ammo and facing an armed killer. No place to hide. My only chance is to run and pray I don't get shot in the back.

I scramble to my feet, fling myself to the Dutch door that will take me to the pens outside. I slap off the hook latch. Hit the door with both hands. It doesn't budge. I ram my shoulder against it. I step back, kick it. The door refuses to open. Something blocking it on the other side. I unfasten the hook latch of the top door, slap my hands against it, shove. The door doesn't move. I glance to the next stall, but there's no way to reach it. Boards go all the way to the ceiling. Nowhere to run. Nowhere to hide.

I hear him at the stall door, just ten feet away. I glance over my shoulder, see him standing in the doorway of the stall, looking at me, the rifle at his shoulder, finger inside the guard.

Dear God he's going to kill me.

A horrific sense of helplessness assails me. I turn to face him, raise my hands, knowing they won't stop a bullet.

"Ich vissa si nemma deim bobli!" I scream the words. I know they took your baby!

A tremor passes through his body. He lowers the rifle, cocks his head, stares at me as if I'm some apparition that can't be explained.

I don't know if it's my use of *Deitsch* or the mention of his daughter that kept him from pulling the trigger. All I know is it worked. I'm alive. I keep talking.

"I know they took Nettie." My voice is breathless and high, my breaths labored. I'm shaking so violently, I can barely stand. I can't believe I'm still alive.

"They shouldn't have taken her," I choke.

Confusion suffuses his expression. "They told us she died. Our sweet

Nettie. But they took her. They left us to mourn the way we'd mourned the others. All this time. Such a wicked thing. They *knew*, and yet they said nothing. They let us suffer."

I stare at him, my mind racing for the right words. "Vernon, I don't blame you for being angry. I would be, too. But this isn't the way to make things right."

"Some things cannot be made right. Too much time has passed. Too much grief." The muscles in his jaw flex. "The cruel things they said about my wife. All the talk. So vicious. I cannot stand for it."

"Put down the gun," I say.

"I won't let you take her."

"I'm not going to take her. I'll help you. Please put down the rifle so we can talk." When he doesn't move, I add, "If you can't do it for yourself, do it for your daughter. Do it for Nettie."

"Too late for talk, Kate Burkholder. You should've stayed in Painters Mill." He raises the rifle, levels it at my chest.

Everything grinds to a horrifying slow-motion clip. His finger curls inside the guard. On the trigger. Tomasetti . . .

"No!"

The scream shatters the air. An Amish woman runs to him from behind. Forty years old. Gray dress. Black winter bonnet. Rosanna Detweiler.

"No more killing," she cries.

Detweiler looks at her over his shoulder. "They are going to take Nettie from us."

A gasp escapes her when she notices the blood on his jacket. "This is not the way," she says breathlessly. "It's not our way. Not this."

When he doesn't lower the rifle, the woman steps around him. Even from ten feet away I see her shaking. Her hands. Legs. Shoulders. Tears streaming, she levers down the nose of the rifle.

"Those who use swords are destroyed by swords," she says.

"We are her parents." He shakes off her touch, raises the rifle. "They cursed our lives. Caused us untold grief."

"What about the grief you've caused?" she cries. "All this killing. When will it stop?"

"I did it for you, Ros. For us. All of it."

"It's too late." The words are the howl of a wounded animal. "That poor child has been crying for her *mamm* since the day she arrived. We're not her family. I'm not the one she needs. We are not the ones she loves."

The Amish man chokes out a sound that's part sob, part gasp. "It was God's will," he whispers. "The way things should have been all along."

"We have to let her go," the woman says.

He sways, sets his hand against the stall door. A collage of emotion infuses his face. Grief. Resignation. All of it overridden by pain, both physical and psychological.

Movement at the door draws my attention.

"Drop the rifle! Do it now! Drop the weapon!" Tomasetti stands at the sliding door, his Kimber leveled on Vernon Detweiler. "Drop your weapon and do not move. Do it or I will shoot you where you stand!"

For an instant, I think the Amish man is going to follow through on the feral light in his eyes; he's going to raise the rifle, kill his wife, finish me—or Tomasetti. For an interminable moment he stands frozen, labored breaths hissing between clenched teeth, eyes wild, rifle steady in his hands.

He looks at the woman. "They shamed you."

"I am not ashamed," she whispers.

Another flash of emotion in his eyes, sharp edges cutting.

The rifle clatters to the ground.

"Get your hands up!" Tomasetti is halfway to us, crouched, moving fast, cautious. "Do not move! Get on your knees! Do it now!"

Never taking his eyes from the woman, Vernon Detweiler raises his hands and drops to his knees. Beaten, he lowers his head as if in prayer.

I get to my feet. My body quakes with such intensity I have to grab on to the rail as I make my way to the stall door.

Weapon trained on Vernon Detweiler, Tomasetti nudges the rifle away with his foot, out of reach. "Get down on your belly," he tells the Amish man. "Spread your hands and legs."

Vernon Detweiler obeys.

Tomasetti casts a look at me. "You okay?"

"Yeah. The deputy is down."

He curses. "County is on the way."

I cross to the woman. "Rosanna Detweiler?"

"Yes." The Amish woman raises shaking hands, like a child reaching out to break a fall, and looks at me. "Where's Nettie?"

A hundred questions boil in my brain. But I'm ever cognizant of my status as a civilian here in Boyd County, Kentucky. I can't Mirandize her. I can't ask the things I so desperately need to know. Conversely, neither can I keep her from speaking if she so wishes to do so.

"Safe," I tell her.

While Tomasetti puts the zip ties on Detweiler, I perform a cursory pat-down on Rosanna. Finding nothing, I motion to the ground directly in front of the stall. "Have a seat and do not move."

She obeys.

Tomasetti walks over to me. "Keep an eye on him. I'm going to stay with the deputy until the paramedics get here."

Turning slightly, I position myself so that both Detweilers are readily visible and accessible if I need to reach them. While Tomasetti attends to the deputy a few yards away, I fish the speed loader from my duty belt, load the rounds into the empty cylinder of my .38, and I place the gun back in its holster.

"You treated the girl well," I say in *Deitsch.*

"Of course we did. We're not monsters."

The irony of the statement burns. I think about Mary Yoder. Noah Schwartz. Sadie Stutzman. Bishop Troyer. Three lives snuffed out, a fourth irrevocably changed. And for what?

The Amish woman looks up at me. "You're *Amisch?*"

"I was," I say, hoping she'll talk to me, *willing* her to talk.

In the distance, sirens wail. Vernon Detweiler lies prone and unmoving just a few yards away. Outside the sliding door, Tomasetti kneels, speaking quietly to the injured deputy.

I look at Rosanna Detweiler and I feel a hundred unasked questions pushing against the floodgate.

"I know what it's like," I say to her. "All those rules. All the expectations."

She stares at me, saying nothing.

"There's a lot of pressure to conform when you're Amish," I say slowly. "A lot of cultural norms. I couldn't do it. Couldn't abide. I couldn't be the girl they expected me to be."

"The Amish and all their morals." Bitterness rings hard in her voice. "How moral were they when they took my baby?"

I wait, hoping she'll continue.

Her gaze settles on her husband. Pain flashes in her eyes at the sight of him facedown in the dirt, the blood on his clothes. Tears squeeze between her lashes. "All he ever wanted was to have a family," she whispers. "Little ones, you know. It was the one thing I couldn't give him. I tried, but . . . He went to them, you know."

"The Helmuths?"

"Vern went to see Mary Yoder. A week ago in Painters Mill. He asked her to return the girl. The child that was rightfully ours." Her mouth tightens. "The old woman refused. She threatened to go to the bishop. The police, even. Such a selfish, stubborn woman." Her lips tremble. Tears stream down her cheeks. "I realize this must sound crazy now, but had things worked out differently, Vern would have been a good *datt.*"

It's an outrageous statement, but I let it go without a response.

"Sadie thought I was hurting the babies." She whispers the words as if she's sharing some secret that's so forbidden it cannot be uttered aloud. "She never said as much, but I knew. I could tell by the way she looked at me. All the questions.

"I didn't hurt them. I would never commit such a terrible sin. Maybe I wasn't as good a *mamm* as I should have been. You know, cooing and kissing and the lot. I think Sadie must have picked up on that."

She's thoughtful for a moment. "They were special, you know. Little Amos and sweet Bonnie. They were slow learners. Like Nettie. The doctor said it was too early to tell, but I knew."

"They had Cohen syndrome?" I ask.

Nodding, she raises her hands, brushes tears from her cheeks. "The doctor said it was SIDS that killed them. That didn't keep people from talking. You know how the Amish are. They may be pious, but they love their gossip—almost as much as they love God." A bitter smile plays at the corners of her mouth. "Vern and I heard every cruel word."

I think about Sadie Stutzman. The minutes I spent with her at her small house on the river. *Those poor babies . . .* The midwife's concern had not been ambivalent. Were her suspicions correct? Or is this woman telling the truth or some version of it? Is it possible Sadie Stutzman and the bishop did something unthinkable?

"And Nettie?" I say.

"I barely remember the birth. It was difficult and long and I was half out of my mind with pain and exhaustion. Afterward, Sadie told me she was gone. We didn't question. We never got to see her. Or hold her. We were so grief-stricken it's all a blur."

"And the grave?" I ask. "The marker?"

She shrugs. "Someone dug the grave the night she was born. They put up the marker. I don't know who."

The sirens are closer now. Two of them, rising and falling in a weird harmonization. I stare at the Amish woman, my heart tapping a hard tattoo against my ribs.

"At some point, you realized the truth," I say.

"Vern was always suspicious. I mean, after Nettie. A couple of months ago he ran into Elmer Moyer. They'd had a falling-out over money before. Elmer had accused Vern of shortchanging him. That night, Elmer was drunk and started taunting Vern, telling him he'd driven a baby up to Painters Mill. Vern came home in a state. Angry, you know. Furious, in fact."

She closes her eyes, tears squeezing between her lashes. "He dug up the grave later that night and, dear God in Heaven, there was nothing there."

"What happened to Elmer Moyer?" I ask.

"He left town. Ran away."

I nod, find myself thinking about Patty Lou and that dumpy little bar in downtown Crooked Creek, and I wonder if Elmer will ever find his way back to her.

"If Vern had found him," Rosanna tells me, "he would have killed Elmer, too. He's the only one who got away."

Putting her face in her hands, she begins to sob.

CHAPTER 28

Four days have passed since Tomasetti and I discovered a frightened and confused Elsie Helmuth locked in a bedroom at the Mullet farm. Over the course of several interviews, the girl revealed that Vernon Detweiler abducted her that day at the Schattenbaum place. After murdering Mary Yoder, he dragged Elsie to his truck and drove her to Crooked Creek.

In the following days, Rosanna Detweiler fed her, washed her clothes, cooked her meals, and took her for long walks in the woods. They'd called the girl Nettie, and they'd told her they were her family now and that she would never be going back to Painters Mill.

According to Elsie, the couple didn't hurt her, not physically. But there are a lot of ways to harm a child. She'd been taken from her family, her loved ones, and everything she'd ever known. When she tried to run away—and find her way home—the Detweilers had locked her in the bedroom for hours on end. All of it had frightened Elsie terribly. Last time I talked to Miriam Helmuth, she told me the girl was having nightmares and couldn't be left alone. I suspect little Elsie Helmuth will be dealing with her fears for some time to come.

Life is slowly returning to normal. Painters Mill is blissfully quiet. The Amish are busy cutting and bundling the last of the season's corn.

SHAMED

The Harvest Festival started this morning. The merchants and shop-keepers along Main Street are reveling in the influx of tourists.

I should be feeling celebratory. A little girl is safe and home with her family. I'm alive and being credited in part for solving one of the most heinous and complex crimes involving the Amish in the history of the state. The Boyd County sheriff's deputy who was on scene that day at the Mullet farm survived a serious stabbing. Bishop Troyer is recovering at home now; he's going to be around a few more years to keep all of us wayward souls in line. I'm thankful for all of it.

But I didn't walk away from this case unscathed. I've spent too much time thinking about Rosanna and Vernon Detweiler, trying to answer the questions that continue to nag. According to the people who knew them, Rosanna Detweiler rarely left the property, venturing into town only to buy groceries and household goods. She spent her days tending her garden and walking in the woods.

Vernon Detweiler was a silent, brooding man. He doted on his wife and was vocal about the prospect of one day having a family. He also had a temper and, despite his being raised Amish, a propensity for violence.

From what little I've been able to piece together, Rosanna was, indeed, the daughter of Marlene Byler—and likely the baby she held in her arms when she jumped from the bridge. No one knows how she survived the fall. An Amish woman who'd been close to Ruby Mullet confirmed that Rosanna was raised by her grandmother and inherited the farm when her grandmother passed away.

Rosanna and Vernon claim they are the biological parents of Elsie Helmuth. They claim Sadie Stutzman and Noah Schwartz convinced them their infant child was stillborn—and then transported that child to Miriam and Ivan Helmuth. At some point, DNA testing will be done to determine parentage. I told the Helmuths it might be wise for them to retain an attorney, but I don't believe they'll do it. The Amish are a nonlitigious group.

There's one unanswered question that continues to haunt. The one that keeps me awake nights. According to Rosanna, she lost two newborns. The death certificates listed SIDS as the cause of death, but no autopsies had been performed. I can't help but wonder: *Did Rosanna Detweiler harm her children? Or was Sadie Stutzman wrong?* They are profound and disturbing questions that may never be answered.

It's late afternoon when I take the Explorer down the lane of the Troyer farm and park next to the bishop's buggy. Around me the day is cold and gray. The smell of woodsmoke drifts on the air as I take the sidewalk to the door.

Freda Troyer answers. Emotion flickers in the depths of her eyes at the sight of me. She says my name softly. "You're here to see David?"

I nod. "How is he?"

"He's a grouchy old goat. I'll be glad when he's up and about so I can put him to work outside." She pushes open the door. *"Kumma inseid."* Come inside.

I enter an overheated kitchen that smells of lavender and lye. Soap-making items—measuring containers and forms lined with plastic sheeting—are spread out on the table.

"He's in the next room, resting." Freda goes to the counter and picks up a dishcloth. I wouldn't have discerned that her surliness was an act if I didn't notice her hands shaking when she dried them.

I'm midway to the door when she whispers my name. I turn to her, shocked to see her frozen in place, tears on her cheeks. Looking annoyed, she swipes at them with the dishcloth, comes to me, takes my hand.

It's the first time in all the years I've known her that Freda Troyer has shown any kind of affection—toward me or anyone else. She grips my hand hard, trembling, her eyes holding mine. For a moment, I think she's going to say something. Instead, she releases me, stiffens her spine, and turns back to the sink.

"Don't keep him long," she says. "He gets tired."

In the living room, a gas lamp hisses, casting yellow light on a brown sofa, two rocking chairs, a rustic coffee table. A cast-iron woodstove squats in the corner. The bishop lies on a cot, his head and shoulders propped on pillows, an afghan thrown over his legs. He's dressed, less his usual jacket and hat. He's always been larger than life to me, especially those piercing eyes that miss nothing. This afternoon, clutching an ancient copy of *Martyr's Mirror* in hands that aren't quite steady, he looks fragile and pale as he takes my measure.

For the span of several heartbeats, we stare at each other, unspeaking. "How are you feeling?" I ask after a moment.

"Stronger," he tells me. "Thankful."

I move closer, trying not to notice the needle marks and scabs on the backs of his hands. "Vernon and Rosanna Detweiler are being extradited to Holmes County," I tell him. "They'll face an array of felonies here, not the least of which is murder. I thought you should know."

"I will pray for them." The old man nods, thoughtful. "The Amish community will support them."

Forgiveness is one of the hallmarks of the Amish faith. I'm well aware that the capacity to forgive is a virtue, but I knew at an early age that it was a tenet I would never be able to put into practice.

"Bishop Troyer, I know what you did. I know Sadie Stutzman and Noah Schwartz took a newborn infant from Rosanna and Vernon Detweiler. I know they brought that baby to you here in Painters Mill. I know you took her to the Helmuths and asked them to raise her as their own. I know that infant is Elsie Helmuth."

The old man stares at me, impassive. "*Es voah Gottes wille.*" It was God's will.

"How much did the Helmuths know?"

"I told them nothing."

"Bishop Troyer, you can't take a baby from someone and just give it to someone else."

"She was taken to a family member. It was up to them to work things out." His expression doesn't alter. "What we did, Katie, it was the only way to save the life of the child."

"You should have gone to the police. There are laws in place to protect children at risk."

"And have the child taken by the social services people?" His voice clangs like steel against steel. "To be raised by strangers who do not understand the Amish way? I think not. It was an Amish matter to be handled by the Amish."

I've heard the sentiment a hundred times over the years. Every time it grates on my sensibilities. This time, it's particularly painful, because this man's rigid adherence to Amish doctrine may have contributed to the deaths of four people.

"Had you gone to the police, Mary Yoder would still be here," I whisper. "Sadie Stutzman. Noah Schwartz. That wasn't God's will."

He stares at me, the steel gone from his eyes, his expression faltering. "It's done, Katie. We can't go back and change it." Wincing, he leans forward and sets the book on the coffee table. "I prayed to God for the wisdom to do the right thing. I did the best I could. We had no way of knowing this would happen. Had we not acted, Elsie Helmuth might have died before she ever had the chance to live."

The exchange drives home the myriad reasons I left my Amish faith behind. While I will always hold close a great deal of love for the people, the culture, and the religion, I'm once again reminded of how far I've strayed, and that I made the only decision I could have.

I hold his gaze for a moment longer, words best left unspoken passing between us. After a moment, I turn and leave the room.

CHAPTER 29

One of the most satisfying aspects of closing an investigation is that golden moment when the facts come together and you finally figure out the how and why. It's not always a pleasant moment, but rewarding nonetheless.

I'm trying hard to believe that as I make the turn into the lane that will take me home. I pull up behind the house to find Tomasetti's Tahoe parked in its usual spot. I sit there a moment, watching the snow fall, drinking in the simple beauty of my surroundings. The barn with its peeling paint. The farmhouse with its drafty windows and a porch that's in dire need of a new railing. A dozen or so Buckeye hens peck around on the ground outside the Victorian chicken house Tomasetti built for me last month.

The snow is coming down hard when I get out and take the sidewalk to the back door. I find Tomasetti sitting at the kitchen table, his laptop open in front of him, a cup of coffee at his side.

His eyes find mine. "How's the bishop?"

"He's going to be all right, I think."

Rising, he crosses to me, relieves me of my laptop case, sets it on the floor next to the coatrack, and eases my coat from my shoulders. "How about you?"

I turn to him. "I'm glad this godforsaken case is over."

He goes to the counter, pours coffee for me, and sets it on the table. "Have a seat."

I take the chair across from him. "The Helmuths didn't know," I say.

"Bodes well for them." He sips coffee, looking at me over the rim.

"The bishop chose them because they're blood relatives," I tell him. "Ostensibly, they could work out any custody issues among themselves. He knew they were a good, solid Amish family. Their home was a place where the baby would be safe, and grow up with traditional Amish values, surrounded by family and community."

I think about the cemetery plot at the Mullet farm. "I don't know what Rosanna did or didn't do. Some of it may come out during trial. But I get the sense that, as an Amish woman, she felt a certain amount of pressure to conform to all those societal roles, to have children, raise a large family."

"That can be a lot of pressure."

"Especially for someone not equipped to handle it. Someone with no support system."

"As twisted as all of that is, it fits." Tomasetti sips coffee. "You've been dwelling in some dark places."

"I knew the truth was in there somewhere."

His gaze meets mine. In their depths I see comprehension and the insights of a man who has experienced the many facets of life, both good and bad. "You and I have been around long enough to know that Lady Justice doesn't always get it exactly right."

"Tomasetti, what they did was incredibly . . . misguided."

Leaning forward, he reaches across the table and takes my hand. "That's true, Kate. But however misguided or wrong or immoral, they may have saved the life of a child. All things considered, I don't think that's such a hard thing to live with."

Rising, I go to him. He gets to his feet. I fall against him. Something settles inside me when his arms wrap around me.

"Do me a favor?" Setting his fingers against my chin, he tilts my face to his. "Stay out of those dark places."

"I'm working on it."

My cell vibrates against my hip, the ring that follows tells me it's Dispatch.

"I've got to take it." Pulling away, I put the cell to my ear. "Hey, Lois."

"Chief, I just took a call from Mr. Shafer with the Buckeye Credit Union on the traffic circle. He says there are a bunch of teenagers parked in his customer parking spots." She sounds frazzled. "He says he asked them to leave and they refused."

"Let Mr. Shafer know I'll be there in a few minutes."

"Copy that."

Tomasetti picks up our cups and sets them in the sink. "Sounds serious."

"You have no idea." I soften the words with a smile. "I have to go."

Behind him, outside the window above the sink, snow swirls down, lending a magical quality to the fading afternoon light.

"Want some company?" he asks. "I hear the Harvest Festival is in full swing. Once you're off we could drink some hard cider and check out the new antique shop on the south end."

"Tomasetti, that's the best idea I've heard all day."

Standing on my tiptoes, I pull his face to mine and press my mouth to his. "Let's go."

Turn the page for a sneak peek at
Linda Castillo's new novel

Outsider

Available July 2020

PROLOGUE

She'd always known they would come for her. She knew when they did that it would be violent and fast and happen in the dead of night. Despite all the training, the mental and physical preparation, she'd also known that when the time came, she wouldn't be ready.

She wasn't sure what woke her. Some barely discernible noise outside the front door. The scuff of a boot against a concrete step. The clunk of a car door as it was quietly closed. The crunch of snow beneath a leather sole. Or maybe it was that change in the air, like the energy of a static charge an instant before a lightning strike.

She rolled from her bed, senses clicking into place. Her feet hit the floor an instant before the front door burst inward. She smacked her hand down on the night table, snatched up the SIG Sauer P320 Nitron, seventeen plus one of lifesaving lead. In the living room, a dozen feet thudded against the hardwood floor.

A cacophony of shouted voices rang out. "Police Department! Get on the floor! Hands above your head! Do it now!"

Two strides and she was across the room. She slammed her bedroom door shut, slapped the lock into place. Spinning, she yanked her jacket off a chair back; she jammed one arm into the sleeve, covered her head and shoulders, and sprinted to the window. Without slowing, she bent low and dove. An instant of resistance as she went through. The sound of snapping wood and shattering glass. The pain of a dozen razor cuts.

The ground rushed up, plowed into her shoulder. Breath knocked from her lungs. Snow on her face, down her collar, in her mouth. Spitting, she barrel-rolled and scrambled to her feet, kept moving. Keeping low, every sense honed on her surroundings. She stuck to The Plan, the one she'd lived a thousand times in the last days, and she sprinted to the hedge that grew along the chain-link fence. Around her, snow floated down from a starless sky. A glance over her shoulder told her there were vehicles parked on the street, no lights. Typical no-knock warrant. Or was it?

She was midway to the alley at the back of her property when she spotted a silhouette in the side yard, thirty feet away, moving toward her fast, equipment jingling. "Halt! Police Department! Stop!"

In an instant she noticed a hundred details. The big man dressed in black. POLICE emblazoned on his jacket. The nine-millimeter Beretta leveled at her, center mass.

"Show me your hands! Get on the ground!" Crouched in a shooter's stance, he motioned with his left hand. "On the ground! Now! Get down!"

She swung toward him, raised the SIG. Simultaneously, recognition kicked. He was a rookie. Young. A good kid. She murmured his name, felt the knowledge of the decision she was about to make cut her and go deep. "Don't," she whispered.

His weapon flashed and the round slammed into her shoulder. Impact like a baseball bat, the momentum spinning her. Pain zinged, a red-hot poker shoved through bone marrow from clavicle to biceps. An animalistic sound tore from her throat as she went down on one knee.

Get up. Get up. Get up.

Out of the corner of her eye she saw him step back, lower his weapon. He went still; looked at her for a too-long beat. "Drop the weapon! Get on the ground! For God's sake, it's over." Then he was shouting into his lapel mike.

She launched herself to her feet, flew across the remaining stretch of yard, her feet not seeming to touch the ground. A volley of shots thundered as she vaulted the chain-link fence, pain snarling through her body. All the while she imagined a bullet slamming into her back.

Then she was in the alley. No police lights. No movement as she darted across the narrow span of asphalt. Heart pumping pure adrenaline, she hurdled the fence, entered her neighbor's backyard, stumbled to the garage door. She twisted the knob, flung the door open, lurched inside, slammed it behind her. Breaths hissing through clenched teeth, she rushed to the truck, yanked open the door, and threw herself onto the seat, trying desperately to ignore the pain screaming in her shoulder, the knowledge that she was badly injured, and the little voice telling her The Plan wasn't going to work.

Her hands shook as she fished out the key, stabbed it into the ignition, turned it. She jammed the vehicle into reverse, stomped the gas pedal. The pickup truck shot backward. A tremendous *crunch!* sounded as the bumper and bed tore the garage door from its track. The metal folded over the tailgate and was pushed into the alley, crushed beneath her rear tires.

She cut the steering wheel hard. Red lights in her rearview mirror. Twisting in the seat, she raised the SIG and fired six rounds through the rear window. A thousand capillaries spread through the glass. The smell of gunpowder in the air. Ears ringing from the blasts. Ramming the truck into drive, she punched the gas. No headlights. Moving fast. Too fast. She sideswiped a garbage can, sent it tumbling, over-corrected. The truck fishtailed and she nearly lost it, regained control in time to make the turn. On the street, she cranked the speedometer to eighty, blew the stop sign at the corner, kept going.

For the span of several seconds, she was an animal, mindless and terrified, hunted by a predator that had scented her blood. The only sound was the hiss of her breath. The pound of a heart racing out of control. The hum of panic in her veins. The knowledge that there was no going back. Her entire body shook violently. Her brain misfiring. Fear shrieking because she didn't know how seriously she was hurt. Because she knew this wasn't over. That this nightmare she'd been anticipating for weeks now was, in fact, just beginning.

At James Road she hit a curb, backed the speedometer down to just above the speed limit, forced herself to calm down, kept her eyes on the rearview mirror. No one knew about the truck. All she had to do was stay calm and get the hell out of the city. For God's sake, it had seemed like a good idea when she'd conceived it.

As the adrenaline ebbed, the pain augmented. Her shoulder throbbed with every beat of her heart. Looking away from the road, she risked a glance at it. Blood had soaked through her shirt, into her coat—which still wasn't on properly—red droplets spattering onto the seat at her hip. The sight of so much blood piled another layer of fear atop a hundred others. Nothing broken—she could still move her arm—but it was bad, potentially life-threatening if she didn't get to a hospital. But she knew emergency-room personnel were required by law to report all gunshot wounds to law enforcement. For now, she had no choice but to keep going.

Eyes on the rearview mirror, she made a right at Broad Street and headed east, praying she didn't run into a cop. Even if they didn't have her plate number or a description of the vehicle, she'd have a tough time explaining the bullet holes in her rear windshield, not to mention the blood.

By the time she hit the outskirts of Columbus, the snow was coming down in earnest. The wind had picked up, driving it sideways, and she could see the whisper of it across the surface of the road in front of her. Soon, it would be sticking. As much as she didn't relish the thought of slick roads, especially with an injured shoulder, she knew it might work to her advantage. If the state highway patrol was busy with accidents, they'd have less time to look for her. The problem was they weren't the only ones looking. The state police were the least of her problems. They weren't the ones who would cuff her, walk her into a cornfield, and put a bullet in her head. She needed help, but who could she trust?

Twice she'd picked up her cell phone to make the call. Twice she'd dropped it back onto the console. The realization that there was no one, that at the age of thirty-five she'd cultivated so few meaningful relationships during her lifetime that there wasn't a soul on this earth that she could call upon, made her unbearably sad.

Against all odds, The Plan had worked; it had gotten her out the door and into her vehicle. How ludicrous was it that she didn't have a destination in mind? Or maybe she simply hadn't believed she was going to survive long enough to need one.

She took Broad Street past Reynoldsburg and the Pataskala area and then turned north onto a lesser county road. The snowfall was heavy enough to obscure visibility by the time she hit the outskirts of Newark. The bleeding showed no sign of abating. As the miles inched past, it formed a sickening pool on the seat at her hip. There was no pulsing or spray, which meant there was no catastrophic vascular damage. Still, the pain and trauma were making her nauseous and light-headed.

By the time she hit Ohio State Route 16 East, her heart was racing and she was shivering beneath her coat. Her hands were shaking and wet on the steering wheel. To make matters worse, visibility had dwindled to just a few feet and she inched along at an excruciatingly slow pace. Three hours had passed since she'd fled her house. Early on, she'd made good time and managed to put more than fifty miles between her and her pursuers. In the last hour, conditions had deteriorated; she'd encountered a total of two motorists and a single snowplow. The pavement was no longer visible and she'd fallen to using mailboxes, the occasional fence line, and the trees and telephone poles on either side just to stay on the road.

It wasn't until she passed the sign for Holmes County that she thought of her old friend. A lot of years had passed since they'd spoken. There was some baggage between them—and probably a little bit of hurt. But if there was anyone in the world she could count on, it was Kate. . . .

As she drove through another band of heavy snow, even the poles disappeared from view. It didn't look like a plow had made it down this particular stretch; the snow was several inches deep now and there wasn't a single tire mark. Slowing to a crawl, she drove blind, squinting into the whiteout, struggling to find the road. If the situation hadn't been so dire, the irony of it would have sent her into hysterical laughter. That was how they would find her—bloodied and clutching the steering wheel and laughing like a hyena.

The truck wasn't equipped with four-wheel drive, but the tires were good and holding their own. The tank had been full, and there was still half a tank left. Enough to get her where she needed to go. All she had to do was stay on the road and not get stuck.

She idled over a small bridge, reached down to turn up the defroster. The tree came out of nowhere, a black beast rushing out of the maelstrom like an apparition. She yanked the wheel right, but she wasn't fast enough. Steel clanged. The impact threw her against her shoulder harness. The front end buckled; the hood flew up. The airbag punched her chest hard enough to daze.

Cursing, she disentangled herself from the airbag, wincing when her shoulder cramped. The truck sat at a severe angle, nose down, bumper against the tree. The engine had died. The headlights illuminated a geyser of steam shooting into the air.

Struggling for calm, she jammed the shifter into park. If she could get the truck started, she might be able to wire the hood shut and be on her way. She twisted the key.

Nothing.

"Come on," she whispered. "Come on. *Come on.*"

She gave it a moment and tried again, pumping the gas this time, but the vehicle refused to start.

Closing her eyes, she set her forehead against the steering wheel. "Fate, you are a son of a bitch."

The raised hood caught wind and rattled, spindly branches scraping against the surface. Pulling out her phone, she checked the battery. Plenty of juice, but no bars . . .

The laugh that tore from her throat sounded manic in the silence of the cab.

She had two choices. She could leave the relative shelter of the vehicle and find help. Some farmer with a tractor who could pull her truck from the ditch so she could be on her way. Or she could stay put and wait for dawn, which was hours away, help that might not come—or the local sheriff, who would likely ask a lot of questions she didn't want to answer.

As far as she was concerned it was a no-brainer.

Unfastening the seat belt, she shoved open the door and stepped into the driving snow.

Pam Lary

Linda Castillo is the *New York Times* bestselling author of the Kate Burkholder novels, including *Sworn to Silence*, which was adapted into a Lifetime Original Movie titled *An Amish Murder* starring Neve Campbell as Kate Burkholder. Castillo is the recipient of numerous industry awards including the Daphne du Maurier Award of Excellence and the HOLT Medallion, and she received a nomination for the RITA. In addition to writing, Castillo's other passion is horses. She lives in Texas with her husband and is currently at work on her next novel.